The Li

The Life Story Of A House

By:

Kendra Doggett

In Memory of:

Anna Amelia Butts

To:

God and Family

The Life Story Of A House

My Grandma told me once that she wrote a story when she was in school about a soldier's knapsack. She told of the places it had been and the things it had seen, the teacher thought it was a great story and made her read it to the class. She said she always wanted to write a story about a house, tell the story of the people that lived there and the things that happened to the house through the years. She never had the time to write the story and I had told her it sounded like a good story to tell, she told me maybe I could write it. It is probably not the way Grandma would have told the story but I hope she would have liked it.

It seems like only yesterday when there were people living here, but I'm getting ahead of myself. The first thing I can remember is the frame of one room. The men building me only did the work when it was getting late in the day, and what the people called, the week-end. Oh yeah, I heard one of them call the other two, men. They were making me tall, they said two-stories. It seemed like forever before there was a roof put on me, but when they did, I could not see the bright little lights overhead, but I was getting tired of being rained on. Anyway, that is what the men called it. Sometimes, the men would bring what they called wives with them. The wives made the men something that they would put in their mouths. I later found out they called it food and drink. It seemed like they were working on me forever. The more they worked on me, the stronger I felt. When the men put up the walls, it was dark. Sometimes they used what they called candles, and it put off light. The men cut holes in my side, and that helped make it light again. The men called what they put in the holes, windows. The men put what they called, shingles, on my roof. It felt like they were putting shingles on my outside walls, too. I noticed the men built a little house away from me, they called it an outhouse. I do not know what goes on in there, but sometimes the men will take something in with them, they say to read. I wonder if the little house feels like I do. The men worked real hard and put what they called a fireplace in the center of me. The fire the men started scared me at first, but it made me feel warm all over. The men dug a deep hole next to me, and then they put a bucket tied on the end of a rope down the hole, and brought up what they called, water. Finally the men said they were done, and I felt solid as a rock, so the men said.

The next thing I know is one of the men and one of the wives is bringing in what they called furniture. At first, it seem like they had much, but as time when by they got more. They had a table and chairs, a bed and dresser, a trunk and a couple of chairs just to sit on. I learned all of these words from the man and wife, but I couldn't seem to make them hear me. I don't know how I heard them, I don't have any ears. Maybe I just feel what they say.

The man must have been strong, because he carried the wife through the door. The man had to chop a lot of wood for the fireplace, too. It seemed they cooked over the fire in the fireplace. Other than the little house, I could not feel any other house close by. I heard the man say he liked the country life. Most days the man came home dirty, he said from work. His wife said he was the only blacksmith in town, I don't know what that means, but he comes home awfully tired every night.

The Life Story Of A House

Only one day the man and wife got dressed in their best clothes and were gone for the morning. He always left in a wagon pulled by a horse. It seems they have a couple of horses, some pigs and chickens, one cow. I do not know what they are for, other than the horses do a lot of work, and the wife goes outside and sits on a stool on the side of the cow and pulls on something until some white stuff comes out, something they call milk. Something called a rooster wakes the man and wife most days.

I thought it was strange, the man and wife were calling each other something. I guess they wanted to be called that. The man is called Ellis, the wife, Anna.

Anna stays home and sews, makes candles, washes clothes, plants a garden and cooks. Ellis goes to work in the morning with a pail and when he comes home at night, Anna has his meal ready. One time Ellis came home from work and Anna had water running from her eyes. Ellis wanted to know what was wrong, and Anna said she was with-child. Ellis gave her a big hug and picked her up and twirled her about. As time went by, Anna's belly got bigger. I didn't know what was going on, but I knew it was something.

As Anna's belly got bigger, Ellis brought strange furniture home with him. There was a small wooden bed that rocked back and forth, a dresser which they filled with little clothes. Anna even had an item that made noise when you shook it.

Later when Anna's belly looked as if it couldn't get any bigger, Anna stayed in bed that day. Ellis brought a woman home with him. I was really confused then. The strange woman went into Anna's room while Ellis paced back and forth downstairs. The woman asked for some hot water, so Ellis had to put a pot of water over the fire. In a little while, something slid out of Anna. The woman cleaned it, the whole time she was doing this, the little thing was crying. It was like a light came on and I realized Anna was carrying a little person in her belly. A sense of

The Life Story Of A House

warmth and happiness came across my whole being. Ellis ran up the stairs when he heard the little person cry. Anna was crying, too. Ellis sat on the bed and held the little person wrapped in a piece of cloth. Anna told Ellis that she wanted to call the little person Benjamin, and that is what they called it. I heard them say a lot of other words later that pertained to Benjamin, like boy and son. Ellis went off with the woman again, and then came home alone.

Anna stayed in bed for a couple of days, but what she was doing was odd. Anna put Benjamin up to her bare chest and it was like Benjamin had his head buried in it. Anna and Benjamin kept up this strange event happening for a while. One time I heard Ellis call it feeding. Benjamin's food must come from Anna's body. Ellis could not give Benjamin any food from his body.

I found out that besides all the other things Anna had to do, Benjamin stayed home with her while Ellis left. Once in a while Anna would change the piece of cloth on Benjamin's privates. I heard Anna call them a diaper one time. Sometimes when Anna changed Benjamin's cloth, it stunk.

Benjamin seemed like he was getting bigger. Anna seemed like she was really happy when Benjamin rolled over by himself, it must have been a big event. Before you knew it, Benjamin was sitting up, and Anna was smashing the food that they were eating, and Benjamin ate it.

Then it got cold out, they kept the fire in the fireplace burning hot. During the night the fire would go out and it was so cold that my rafters shook. Soon, there was something white and fluffy falling from the sky. Ellis said that this would make the trip to work that much harder. I wondered why. I thought something strange because when they went out to the outhouse, they didn't seem to take as long a time as they did when it was warm outside.

One day, Ellis brought a green tree in the house with him. Anna put some shiny things on it and Ellis and Anna stood around it and sung.

The Life Story Of A House

That is what they called it anyway. There were a couple of packages wrapped in paper under the tree. The next morning, Anna unwrapped one of the packages, and it had something wooden with wheels on it for Benjamin to play with. Anna opened another package and it had a new dress in it. She gave Ellis a big hug. Anna handed Ellis a package and it had a shirt in it that Anna had made. Ellis gave Anna a kiss, and they told each other thank you. I heard Ellis say it smelled wonderful in the house.

They always did something they called praying before they ate or went to bed. I heard Anna say that is what they did when they left in the morning on Ellis's day off from work. Sometimes on this day, they would have a strange man over for a meal. Anna called him the minister. One day when the minister was over, Benjamin grabbed Anna's chair and stood up. They were all happy he had done this.

Some night's I would hear Anna giggling. I did not know what was going on then, but a while later; Anna told Ellis she was with-child again. I wondered if the giggling had anything to do with Anna being with-child again. They were happy and told Benjamin that he would have a little brother or a little sister. About this time Benjamin was standing more, as long as he was holding on to something.

Finally, the white fluffy stuff that was outside went away and didn't come back for a while. Anna acted happy working in her garden, Benjamin at her feet. Anna would do something that she called humming.

One of the days that Ellis, Anna and Benjamin went away for the morning, they came back with a lot of people. The men started to build the frame of another structure. I thought that they were going to replace me. The men came back a couple of times until they were done. Ellis called it a barn; it was for keeping the cow and pigs out of the weather. I was relieved I was not going to get replaced. Ellis built what he called a fence around the front of the house.

The Life Story Of A House

Sometimes I would see a man in the back of the house; he was guiding a horse with a metal thing being pulled behind it. Ellis said a farmer was putting in his crops. Pretty soon there were little green things poking out of the ground, until they got really big. The farmer and some other men did something they called picking, all I know was the green stuff turned brown before they knocked it down.

Once in a while a man would walk in front of the house; on something Ellis called the path. Sometimes it was a man on a horse or a man, horse and wagon, sometimes a whole family.

I felt no other buildings around me other than the barn. I wondered how close the nearest house was.

Pretty soon, Anna was picking things out of the ground in her garden. Anna told Ellis she would can some of it, and that maybe next year they could dig a root cellar, whatever that is.

All during the warm weather, Anna's belly was getting big again.

Soon the white, fluffy stuff was falling again, and it was cold again. But I felt all warm because Benjamin started to walk. The feeling of his bare feet on my floor felt incredible.

Ellis brought the green tree in the house again and Anna put shiny things on it again. They stood around the tree singing like they had done the last time. There were three wrapped boxes under the tree, but before they could open them, Anna told Ellis it was time. It was time for what? Anna went and laid down on the bed and Ellis left. When Ellis came back, he had that lady with him that he brought when Benjamin came. Ellis was carrying Benjamin, but he was walking all over the house again. Pretty soon, I heard crying, and Ellis came running into the room. There was another little person there. Anna told Ellis it was a girl and she wanted to call her, Amelia. Ellis said that was a fine name for a daughter. Ellis left with the strange woman and then came back alone, like last time. After a couple of days of rest, Anna was up and about. Luckily, Benjamin was eating the same food as Anna and Ellis, because Anna was holding Amelia up to her bare chest so she could feed her. They finally opened the boxes that were wrapped. Anna got a nice hat, Ellis got a shirt again, and Benjamin had something wooden again. Ellis said it was a toy gun. Anna did not know if she wanted Benjamin playing with a gun or not as it hadn't been that long since the Civil War got over. Ellis finally talked Anna into letting the boy keep it. Ellis said, "It was just a toy".

The white, fluffy stuff, that Ellis called snow, was bad this time around. The snow was so deep, Ellis had a hard time going out to the barn, and he stayed home from work for two days. Ellis said he was about ready to climb the walls, but I don't know what that meant.

Finally, the snow went away, and pretty things started to come out of the ground. Anna said she had planted something called flowers, there. They were pretty.

Anna kept Amelia close by and she did not let Benjamin wonder off to far from the house. Benjamin had started to talk a little, just a few words. It was cute, I was so happy; there was so much love in the house.

I heard Ellis talk about the root cellar he was going to dig. Ellis would dig a hole in the ground, build wooden walls and roof, and then put some of the dirt back on the top. Ellis would put stairs going down and a door on it. Ellis said that the whole family could go down there if the weather turned bad. I do not know what that means, but it does not sound good. While Ellis was working on the root cellar, he had so much water coming out of him, Anna kept bringing him water to drink or something called lemonade or tea. Ellis finally finished and it looked just like a door stuck in the ground.

One day, someone came to the door when Ellis was at home. When the stranger left, Ellis looked sad and Anna started to cry. Ellis told Anna that his Father had died. The next day, Ellis and Anna got all dressed up and took Benjamin and Amelia away in the wagon. It got dark and they still were not home. I started to worry when they did not come home the next day, also. They came home on the third day. I hope they never go away like that again.

One day the sky was all dark and the wind was blowing, hard. Ellis had to go to work, but told Anna if it got too bad to go to the root cellar. By mid-afternoon the sky had turned green and everything went calm. The stranger out in the field came running up to the house. He frantically knocked on the door. Anna came to the door and the stranger said that a twister was coming and you must go to the root cellar. The stranger grabbed Benjamin and Anna had Amelia. The four of them just got the door to the root cellar closed when the wind blew as hard as I had seen. I know why they call it a twister; it looked like the ground was going in a circular motion. I could feel the shingles come off my roof. It only took a minute, but when the cloud went by, the barn was gone. I did not know what happened to it. The stranger came out of the root cellar with Anna, Benjamin and Amelia. Anna was crying because the barn was gone, but where did it go? The stranger tried to tell her it could have been worse, it could have taken the house, taken me where? Anna thanked the stranger and waited for Ellis to come home. Ellis came home early that day. It was like he knew something had happened. Ellis put his arms around Anna and tried to give her words of comfort. Anna told Ellis that the cow was gone, where? Ellis told Anna that they could get another cow. Ellis said that the chickens were still here, but Anna said that they would be too scared to give them any eggs for a week. Anna and Ellis laughed a little at that.

Benjamin had been biting down on a wet cloth for a while. Anna said Benjamin was teething. Sometimes Benjamin would cry for what seemed like no reason.

Ellis brought home another cow, which made Anna happy. Ellis told Anna that they would replace the barn next year. I wondered what a year was.

The Life Story Of A House

After a while it turned cold and started to snow again. Anna said finally Benjamin's baby teeth came in. I did not understand. I was starting to wonder if there were a lot of things I did not understand.

After another cold, snowy winter, Anna said she was with-child again. I knew what that meant. There would be another set of feet walking on my floor. I really loved the feeling on the children crawly or walking around on my floor.

It was a month Anna said was September when Ellis went and got the woman to help Anna. It was pretty soon and there was crying Anna had a boy. Ellis and Anna named him Joshua.

Time seemed to go by so quickly. The seasons changed, first the warm, wet weather, then the cold and snowy weather. Anna and Ellis had more children, Ruby, Paul, Abraham and Mary. Benjamin, Amelia and Joshua were riding into town with their Dad and going to someplace they called a school. If it was nice weather, the three would walk home. The three children sat around the kitchen table and did something called homework. Benjamin said it was not much fun, but Amelia seemed to like it. Joshua never said.

Ellis looked like he was tired every night he came home. Anna would rub his shoulders and he would sit and rest the rest of the night. Anna would read some of the Bible every night before she went to bed. At bedtime, I would hear seven little voices talking to God. God must be really important for everyone to ask him for something, I have never seen him though.

One night Mary was sick and Ellis had to go back to town and get the doctor. The doctor was new to the area and Ellis and Anna had never brought him out to the house. The doctor went upstairs to see Mary and he told Ellis and Anna there was nothing he could do for Mary. The doctor left and Anna was crying. Anna sat on the side of Mary's bed all night, praying.

The Life Story Of A House

The next morning Anna was crying, she said that she could not wake Mary up. Ellis led her out of the room and made her sit in the kitchen. Ellis said he was going to town and getting the doctor again. It was normally the day that they all got dressed up and went to church, but not today. Ellis came back with the doctor and they both went upstairs to look at Mary. The doctor said that she was dead, what does that mean? The doctor said he was sorry and he left. Ellis tried to comfort Anna, but nothing worked. The rest of the children were crying, too. Anna went upstairs and cleaned Mary up, and then they brought her downstairs and laid her across the table. Ellis said he had to go into town for a while, when he came back, he had a wooden box and they laid Mary in it. What does this mean, being dead? The next day a lot of people came to the house. All the women were wearing black dresses, it looked very strange. The people stood around for a while and then someone nailed a lid over the box with Mary in it. Won't Mary be scared in the dark? A few of the men carried the box outside and went to a place not that far from the house. There was a hole in the ground there. What was going on, what happened to Mary? The minister said some words over the box and then Anna and Ellis walked off. Some men lowered the box with Mary in it down in the hole. What's happening, the men are filling the hole in with dirt. When the hole was filled in, the men put a wooden cross in the dirt. I am so sad, dead must mean you no longer exist. I will never forget lovely Mary.

It was sad for a long time around the house. Anna didn't hum when she worked in the garden anymore. Ellis did not say much when he came home at night. The children acted like they did not know what to do. Anna did not read the Bible at night before going to bed. She must be angry with someone, she snapped at the children a lot. Ellis and Anna seemed to be arguing, too. They never did that before Mary left.

The years past like this for a while. Benjamin was going to leave and go to a college. College is somewhere you can do more studying. Benjamin had a suitcase full of clothes, all he had. Ellis took Benjamin into town to catch something called a train. Anna cried and kissed and hugged Benjamin. Ellis and Benjamin rode away, I wonder if I will ever see Benjamin again?

A boy, Andrew, was coming around to see Amelia. They held hands a lot; sometimes Amelia would give Andrew a kiss on the cheek. Anna and Amelia were making a dress on the sewing machine. Anna called it a wedding dress. Anna seemed better than she did when Mary first went away. Ellis stayed in town longer since Mary left. Anna said that he smelled like liquor when Ellis came home. I do not know what liquor is but sometimes it makes Ellis walk funny, sometimes he even falls down. The other children are still going in town to go to school. I hear Joshua whispering to the other children that he couldn't wait to be old enough to be on his own. Own what?

Amelia said she was done with school, so she and Andrew were going to get married. They were going to live with Andrew's mother for a while; it seems Andrew's father is dead, just like Mary.

Benjamin came home for Amelia and Andrew's wedding. The wedding was held outside in the yard, there were lots of strange people there. Amelia and Andrew celebrated a little while and then left. Anna cried the rest of the day. Benjamin stayed just one day and went back to college. Ellis continued to come home late and he and Anna were arguing more and more. Joshua told the rest of the children that he was leaving; he wasn't going to wait another minute.

During the night, Joshua crawled out of the window onto the front porch roof. Joshua jumped to the ground from there. He waved good-by to Ruby, Paul and Abraham and ran over to the barn. Joshua had already made up a knapsack with some food in it. When he got to the barn, he stole his father's horse and road off.

The next morning Ellis went out to the barn to get his horse to leave for work and it was gone. Ellis walked back to the house and took off his belt. Anna asked him what was wrong and he told her. She asked him what he was going to do with the belt. Ellis told her that he was going to find out who took his horse and where. Anna said, "You are not going to use that belt on any of my children". Ellis pushed Anna out of the way to go upstairs. That was the first time Ellis had ever touched Anna in anger. Ruby was scared because she had heard the rough words from downstairs and she heard the footsteps coming up. When Ellis got upstairs, he counted heads. He asked Ruby where Joshua was. Ruby was scared to death. Anna came in and stood between Ellis and Ruby. Paul sat up in bed and screamed, "You ran him off". Ellis walked downstairs, out the door, and started walking into town. Anna hugged her three children and asked them if they knew where Joshua was going. They all three said Joshua wouldn't say. Anna started to cry again. How did her life turn out like this? I was sad, sad to see Joshua go and sad to see Anna so unhappy.

When Ellis came home that night, he had another horse. Anna didn't say a word to him. I couldn't figure out what had happened to Ellis to make him so angry.

Another couple of years went by like this. Benjamin had come home with a piece of paper that said he was a teacher. Anna was so proud of him. Benjamin was going to teach in town and find a room to sleep. There had been no sign of Joshua. Ruby had just finished her schooling and was seeing a boy, Alexander. Paul and Abraham had a few more years of schooling.

Ellis was really looking old and worn out, but he was still drinking. Anna had given up on Ellis, he had quit going to church and she was sleeping upstairs with Ruby.

Ellis had started to drink at work. As he was trying to shoe a horse it got spooked and kicked him, knocking him to the ground and stepped on him. The boy that worked for him ran for help. The Doctor and Preacher came as fast as they could. There is nothing they can do, so Ellis asks to be taken home to Anna, the preacher told Anna later.

The Life Story Of A House

Anna was working out in the garden when she heard the wagon coming up the path. It was the preacher and one of men from the church. As they got closer, I could tell there was a bundle in the back of the wagon followed by a rider less horse. The wagon pulled up short of Anna and the two men got off the wagon and told Anna something. Anna began to cry as she looked in the back of the wagon. The men carried Ellis into the house, putting him in bed. Ellis held his hand out to Anna and asked her to forgive him for the way he had acted since Mary died. Ellis said he was sorry he didn't handle the pain of their loss better. He shouldn't have turned his back on her and God. Ellis asked Anna to tell the children he was sorry and that he loved them all. He told Anna that he loved her, too. Anna tells him she loves him too. Ellis smiles at her and she gives him a kiss, then he closes his eyes for the last time.

The next day the two men brought the wooden box out to the house and placed Ellis in it. Anna had already cleaned and dressed him. Anna was so sad that Ellis was gone, but happy that they had made their peace with each other and he with God. Anna sat up with the body all night, praying.

The next day, the townspeople came out from town like they had for Mary. The minister said some words over Ellis and then Benjamin led the family away. The hole was next to Mary's, the men put the box in the ground just like they did Mary's and covered it with dirt. I wonder what happens when you are dead.

Benjamin told Anna that if it was alright with her, he would move back to the house and then he could take the boys to school. Really, Benjamin was thinking that his mother could not afford to stay in the house with no money coming in. Anna told Benjamin that she would like that, so Benjamin moved back to the house the next day. I thought once you moved away, you couldn't come back home.

The Life Story Of A House

A light, fluffy snow was falling and the trees and bushes looked beautiful. It was late in the evening when Benjamin took everyone outside. Benjamin was lighting something that looked like a small cylinder and throwing it. It made a huge noise and I heard Abraham say it was a new century. I don't know what that means, but they seemed to be laughing and having a good time. They had to come into the house because everyone was getting cold. I heard Paul tell Abraham, "Happy New Year". Anna said, "It is now 1900". I wondered if that was good or bad, but they seemed happy.

Ruby married Alexander when the weather was getting warm. They said they were going to live in a house with Alexander's parents. They must have a big house to hold two families.

Amelia and Andrew were at the wedding and Amelia has a big stomach. Amelia must be going to have a baby. The house where they live will be so happy. I miss the little feet running around on my floors.

Benjamin is still taking Paul and Abraham to school with him. Paul and Abraham are getting big. I guess when you get so big, you move out of the house you grew up in. I wonder if that means the house will be empty eventually.

Joshua still has not made contact with anyone.

When the family sits down for supper, Benjamin tells his Mother Anna things he has heard in town. Benjamin said there was a coal mine explosion in West Virginia and it killed 50 miners. I don't know what a coal mine is, but I know what kills mean, it's another word for dead. 50 miners know longer exist, how sad.

Anna seems to be happy again. I wonder if it has anything to do with Benjamin moving back home. Anna hums in the garden again.

Benjamin comes home and tells Anna about another mine explosion killing at least 200 people in Utah. Working in a coal mine must be very dangerous. I hope being a teacher isn't that dangerous.

Paul and Abraham are home for the warm months again. It is not like when they were young and playing outside all of the time. Benjamin and Abraham read a lot. Paul walks down the path almost every day. Paul goes the opposite way they do when they go to town. Abraham says Paul has a girlfriend. I wonder if that is like having a wife, but you live in the same house as you grew up.

The warm months seem to go by so quickly. Benjamin, Paul and Abraham leave almost every morning to go to town again. Paul says this is his last year for school. Abraham calls him a lucky duck. I don't know what that means, but the two boys laugh.

One night Benjamin tells Anna that someplace named Galveston, Texas had a hurricane. I don't know what that is, but Benjamin said it killed between 6,000 and 12,000 people. Hurricanes must be worse than mine explosions.

Anna, Benjamin, Paul and Abraham still go to church. Abraham teases Benjamin about having a girlfriend. Anna tells Benjamin to invite the girl for supper so she can meet her properly. The next time they go to church a young woman comes home with them. She is pretty. Benjamin calls her Mary. Can this be the Mary that was put in a box and covered with dirt? I didn't see anyone dig the box up out of the ground. I am really confused; can more than one person have the same name? Mary is polite, and after dinner her, Benjamin and Anna sit around and talk. Anna does not hug Mary like she did before. This must be a different Mary. After a while Benjamin and Mary leave. Anna says it is nice to meet you, to Mary. Maybe Anna doesn't recognize Mary because she is not small anymore. Benjamin and Mary ride off in the wagon.

When Benjamin comes home, Anna asks him if he is serious about Mary. Is he serious about what? Benjamin says yes. Anna says she is glad.

The cold weather comes again. One time it snowed so much that Benjamin, Paul and Abraham did not go into town for a long time. When Benjamin went out to feed the animals, the snow was up past his knees. I heard Anna say that they had plenty of food for a while and that they still had firewood. They did not even go to church at that snowy time. Anna read some words out loud out of the Bible. They sounded like good words.

The snow finally melted enough for the three boys to go to town. Anna tells Benjamin to bring back some things; she hands him a piece of paper.

Once in a while Ruby and Alexander visit and Ruby has a big stomach. The last time Amelia and Andrew came for a visit there was baby with them and Amelia had lost her big stomach. The baby must be a boy because they called it William.

There is still no sign of Joshua.

One night at the supper table, Benjamin told Anna about someone striking something called oil in Texas. I wonder if the hurricane had anything to do with it.

Spring finally comes and Anna is planning another wedding. Benjamin and Mary are going to get married. Anna says they can stay at the house after they are married. Benjamin says thank you, they will.

Paul says that today is the day of the wedding and asks Benjamin if he is nervous. Benjamin says no. Paul seems disappointed about it. Mary looks lovely standing next to Benjamin. This must be a different Mary because Amelia and Ruby don't seem to recognize her. Anna cries, she says it is because she is happy. Anna tells Benjamin that she wanted the

The Life Story Of A House

house to stay in the family. I don't know what that means, but I am glad Benjamin and Mary are going to live here with Anna and the two boys.

Benjamin says he is going to stay teaching in town. Mary is going to stay home and help Anna with the chores. Paul says he is almost done with school, Abraham is jealous. Benjamin tries to tell Abraham that someone has got to be the youngest.

Benjamin comes home and tells Mary and Anna that there was a huge fire in Jacksonville, Florida. Benjamin says he does not know how many are dead. Anna says you hear so much bad news nowadays. I know what fire is, but I don't understand a whole town burning.

Paul wakes up one morning, and says, "Today is the day". I wonder what it is a day for. Abraham mumbles something that I cannot hear. Anna makes a special breakfast for everyone. Benjamin asks Paul what he is going to do without school. Paul says, "Be happy". Benjamin asks Paul what kind of work he is going to do. Paul gives Benjamin a funny look but doesn't say anything.

When Benjamin, Paul and Abraham come home that night, Paul is very quiet. Anna says, "I thought you would be happy when you got out of school". Paul said he hadn't thought about work. Anna tells Paul that he can go into town next week and look to see if anyone needs a helper. Abraham says he is glad the summer is finally here. Anna rubs Abraham's head and says that he still has two years of school left so he better enjoy his summers off.

I find it awfully quiet when it gets dark. They all go to bed and go to sleep when it gets dark. It must be something about the dark.

After church, on the day no one works, Amelia, Andrew, William, Ruby and Alexander come home for dinner. Ruby looks as if her stomach is ready to bust apart. Ruby starts to hold her stomach and cry. Anna tells Alexander, "It is time". Anna, Ruby and Amelia go into a bedroom. Anna tells Amelia to bring her a warm, wet cloth. Ruby lies on the bed and it looks like she is trying to push something. Pretty soon something slides out of her and it starts to cry. Anna wipes it off and hands it to Ruby. Ruby says, "It is a girl". Anna goes out of the room and gets Alexander. Alexander sits on the bed next to Ruby. Ruby tells Alexander, "It is a girl, what should we call her?" Alexander says, "How about, Alva?" Ruby cries and says that would be nice. Anna comes back into the room, and Amelia tells Anna that they are going to call the girl Alva. Anna says that is her middle name. I did not know people had more than one name. Ruby, Alexander and Alva have to stay for a couple of days. Amelia, Andrew and William leave.

The summer goes by to quickly for Abraham. Abraham says out loud, two more years. Abraham has really gotten taller this year. Abraham is even taller than Benjamin and Paul. Benjamin and Paul tease Abraham about his height.

Paul goes into town three days in a row and comes home not having found work. On the fourth day, Paul comes home and says he has been hired as a baker's apprentice. Anna tells him that is wonderful. Paul asks Anna if it would be alright to stay here at nights. Anna tells Paul, "You can stay as long as you want to". When Benjamin and Abraham get home from school, Paul tells them everything about the job. It is what Anna does sometimes, and the rest of the people say how wonderful it smells.

Benjamin and Abraham come home from school and tell Anna and Mary that the President has been shot. They tell them that the President is still alive, though. The President must be someone important, Anna cries a little. Paul comes home and tells the same story about the President.

While Anna was at church, she came home and told Paul they all prayed for the health of the President.

The Life Story Of A House

Benjamin and Abraham come home one night and tell Anna and Mary that William McKinley is dead, and that Theodore Roosevelt is the new President. Anna says a prayer for both men.

Mary tells Benjamin that she is with-child. They are both happy and can't wait to tell Anna. Anna is happy, also. Anna says that the more grandchildren she has, the better. I don't know what that means, but I think Anna is happy.

The man that works out back in the dirt has not been around lately. There has been a different man. I wonder what happened to the other man.

It is time for the cold and fluffy snow. Benjamin says it seems to come earlier every year. Anna laughs at him and says the older you get, the faster time goes by. I wonder what that means.

It is time to bring in the green tree again. This time they all seem happy and sing loudly about someone called Jesus. Anna says he is the Savior. I have never heard of him being mentioned. Anna says the Bible has some stories about him. I wonder why I have never heard of him, or why he has never came by. A couple of days later, Benjamin say it is 1902, a new year. Anna says, "She hopes it is a good year for everyone. Mary's belly is getting bigger.

Anna cries at night, wondering if Joshua is alive and well.

It is almost time for the grass to turn green and the flowers to open up. I dislike this time, now that there are no little footsteps on my floor. When Amelia or Ruby visits, I get that feeling again, but it is sad when they leave again.

I wonder what happened to the first man, the second man is out working in the dirt. Sometimes he uses the outhouse. Sometimes Anna takes him out something to drink.

The Life Story Of A House

One day, after Benjamin and Abraham are done with, what they call the school year, Mary starts holding her stomach like it hurts. Anna sends Abraham to town, and Abraham rides away on the horse faster than I have ever seen the horse go.

When Abraham comes back there is a man riding in a wagon with him. They call the man, doctor, but he looks older than the doctor who came when Mary was sick. The doctor asks Anna for a warm cloth and some water. After Anna brings the doctor the things that he asked for, he asked Anna and Benjamin to leave the room. After a while, Benjamin gets worried, he has not heard a baby cry yet. The doctor comes out of the room, and says, "He is sorry". Sorry for what? Benjamin goes into the room and sits on the edge of Mary's bed. Mary tells Benjamin that she is sorry. Sorry for what? The doctor tells Anna that the baby was still-born. Anna starts to cry and the doctor puts his arm around her shoulder. The doctor goes back in the bedroom and gets the baby. The baby still isn't crying. Isn't the baby supposed to cry? Anna says, "It was a little boy". Was? Anna takes the baby into her room, cleans him and puts a little gown on him. He still does not move. Benjamin comes out of the room and says," Mary is sleeping now". Anna tells Benjamin that she is sorry the baby was born dead. Dead? How can a baby be born dead? Benjamin tells Anna that he hopes Mary is alright. Why wouldn't Mary be alright?

Benjamin helps Mary walk out to where Mary and Ellis are in the dirt. The whole family is there. The minister says some words and then they lower the small box into the ground. The people leave and two men throw dirt in the hole. The families sit around the house and cry. Andrew tries to tell Benjamin that they can try for more. Benjamin just nods his head. Mary went back to bed and cries.

It has been a while, and Mary is back to working in the garden, but she seems weaker. Abraham walks off somewhere almost every day. Paul has moved out and says he is staying in town. Anna sits on the porch now more than ever. Benjamin rides in to town once in a while to get supplies. One day Benjamin comes home and tells Mary about another coal mine disaster. 112 miners were killed in someplace called Johnstown, Pennsylvania. Anna doesn't act like she cares; she usually says a prayer for the dead.

Abraham is getting ready for the first day of his last year in school. It just seems like yesterday he was crawling on the floor. It still makes me feel warm and happy whenever I think about it. Anna kisses Abraham on the cheek for good-luck and Abraham gives Anna a big hug. Mary tells Benjamin and Abraham good-by.

Benjamin and Abraham come home from the first day of school and say it was alright. The boys say they saw Paul at the bakery. Abraham has homework to do before he can go for a walk down the path in front of the house. Abraham always goes the opposite way from town and then comes home from the way he left. Anna says Abraham must have a girlfriend.

Weeks later Abraham seems to be in a hurry to get home. He runs in the house to tell Anna that someone named "Kid Curry" Logan had been sentenced to twenty years of hard labor and he had been the second-in-command of Butch Cassidy's Wild Bunch. I don't know what twenty years of hard labor is, but Abraham seems excited about it. Benjamin finds it funny that Abraham still gets excited by things that happen in the old west. I wonder what the old west is?

Soon the man is picking the things that are growing out of the ground, Anna calls it corn.

It is time for the green tree again, but no one seems happy but Abraham and Paul. Paul comes in the day of the big feast and brings a cake. Paul says he made it himself. Amelia and Ruby's family do not come this time. I wonder why.

The Life Story Of A House

Soon, Abraham says it is 1903, and he only has a half of a year to go to school. Benjamin asks Abraham what he is going to do when he gets out of school. Abraham just shrugs his shoulders.

Abraham keeps going on his walks and usually doesn't come home until it is almost dark. Finally, Anna asks Abraham who he is seeing on the walks that he takes every night. Abraham says it is Mary Ann Miller. Anna said Mr. Miller had a big farm. Benjamin says Mr. Miller must like playing in the dirt to have such a big place. Abraham says he has cattle, also. I don't know what cattle are.

It is warm again and Abraham says this is the last day he has to go to school. Benjamin tells Abraham, unless he flunks. Abraham says don't even sat that, even in jest. I wonder what flunks mean.

Benjamin and Abraham come home mid-afternoon, Paul is right behind them. The whole family comes over for supper, except for Joshua. I haven't seen Amelia and Ruby for a while. William and Alva are getting bigger. Paul asks Abraham what he is going to do. Abraham says that he is going to work on the Miller farm. They all seem happy that Abraham will be staying around here, whatever that means.

The party gets over and everyone leaves except for Benjamin, Abraham, Mary and Anna. Anna says that she is happy to have seen all of her children graduate high school. Anna says Ellis would be proud, too. Proud must mean happy.

Abraham starts work the next day. Benjamin says he is home for three months. Abraham comes home right before it gets dark out and says that his job is to help watch the cattle, and it is hard work. Anna tells him he had better find an easier job if that one is too much for him. Abraham says maybe it will get easier. Mary says she is with-child again. Maybe there will be the love and warmth that you get from a baby.

The Life Story Of A House

It is about time for it to get cold again. Benjamin has gone back to work at the school. It seemed weird not having Abraham lay around this year. Abraham says farming is not getting any easier.

The man is picking his crops again. Sometimes Anna goes out to talk to him. Mary is starting to get a big belly. This time she spends most of her day in bed, though.

They bring in the green tree and everyone gets together for the day. Anna says she wonders where Joshua is.

Benjamin says it is almost 1904, and then he tells Anna about a fire at someplace called the Iroquois Theater in Chicago, Illinois, and it kills 600 people. That is a lot.

Paul comes to visit in a wagon and he has a woman with him. He tells Anna the woman's name is Wanda Avery and they are going to get married. Anna hugs them both and says that makes her happy. Benjamin and Mary are happy, too. Abraham is too tired to care. Paul tells Abraham that the general store in town is getting bigger and that they might need some help. Abraham says thank you but he will have to think about it. Abraham tells them that he makes pretty good money at Miller's farm.

One day before Benjamin leaves for work, Mary tells him it is time. Benjamin rides into town to get the doctor. They get back and Mary is sweating and puffing. I wonder if this helps. Anna brings the doctor a clean cloth and hot water and the doctor doesn't even have to ask her. The doctor tells Benjamin to stay in the other room. The doctor tells Mary to push, and something comes out and starts to cry. Anna cleans it off and says it is a boy. The doctor says we are not done, he tells Mary to push again. Pretty soon something else slides out of her. The doctor said it is twins. Anna gives Mary the boy so she can clean the other. Anna says this one is a girl. Anna hands the other baby to Mary. The doctor goes out of the room and shakes Benjamin's hand and says he has twins. Benjamin looks as if he was going to pass out, but the doctor holds him up. The doctor pats Benjamin on the back and tells him to go in and see his babies. Benjamin goes in and Anna comes out of the room. Anna and the doctor go downstairs and have a cup of coffee.

Benjamin gently sits on the bed and Mary hands him a baby. Benjamin acts like he is afraid he will break the baby. Mary asks Benjamin what he wants to name them. Benjamin says Caroline for the girl, and Mary agrees. Then Benjamin says Charles for the boy, and Mary nods her head.

Abraham comes home and the doctor is getting ready to leave. Abraham asks the doctor if it is good news or bad. The doctor says you are an uncle, twice. Abraham gets a big smile on his face and he goes in the house to see the babies.

It is the time for the warm weather when Mary has her and Benjamin's two babies. The man is out putting seeds into the ground. Benjamin comes home and tells Mary and Anna about a fire aboard the steamboat General Slocum in New York's East River that killed 1,021. I can't believe so many people can die at the same time. Just thinking of all the holes they have to dig makes me dizzy.

Paul and Wanda get married at home. Everyone looks so happy, except for Abraham. William and Alva are running around the yard and Amelia tells Anna that she is with-child again. Anna laughs because Ruby had just told her she too was with-child again. They all have a big laugh over that. Benjamin walks over to Abraham and asks him what is bothering him. Abraham says he thinks he loves Mary Ann but he does not know if he wants to farm the rest of his life. Benjamin tells Abraham that he should think about going to a trade school. Abraham says he really doesn't want to go back to school. Benjamin tries to tell Abraham that it is different than a regular school. Benjamin tells Abraham that he is young enough to do whatever he wants to do. Abraham says he is afraid if he doesn't keep farming for the Miller's that Mary Ann won't care to see him anymore. Benjamin says if that is the case she doesn't love you anyway. Benjamin tells Abraham that the fall semester is only a ways away and if he wants, he will help him enroll. Abraham says he will think about it and thanks Benjamin for his advice.

Abraham comes home tired and dirty every day. He tells Benjamin he is seriously thinking about going to trade school. Benjamin tells Abraham that one is supposed to open in town.

Anna spends most of her time working out in her vegetable garden or with her flowers. Mary has started taking care of the chores in the house. They do split up the cooking though.

Paul and Wanda come to visit often. Paul always brings a cake with him. Paul says he likes being a baker.

Benjamin comes home one night and tells Mary and Anna that Theodore Roosevelt has won the election for President of the United States.

It is time for the cold and snowy weather again. It seems to be coming more often now Abraham says, or maybe as Benjamin says, faster. The men bring the green tree in the house and they sing around it again. A couple of days later everyone comes home, except for Joshua. There is a lot of warmth and love when the family all get together. I wonder if all houses feel these feelings.

Benjamin says it is 1904 now. I wonder why the numbers keep changing.

It is still cold and snowy. It seems like it is taking a longer time to warm up this time. Abraham still comes home complaining, which is what Anna calls it. Abraham swears that next fall he is going to take a class to learn something. I wonder why Abraham does not like farming.

Benjamin comes home one day and tells Mary and Anna that a shoe factory's boiler exploded and killed 58. The shoe factory was in someplace Benjamin called Brockton, Massachusetts.

The Life Story Of A House

Anna tells Benjamin and Mary that Amelia and Andrew had a baby girl, Anna. Now I'm really confused, more than one person can have the same name.

I have noticed that when Mary does what is called the washing, she hangs it on a line outside that are held up over the ground by to wooden poles. When she does the washing when it is cold weather, she puts lines up in the house. I wonder why she does that.

Abraham comes home with his hand wrapped in white cloth. He says he got his hand caught in, what he called a wire fence. Abraham says he is going to take a couple days off to recuperate. The next time it is daylight Abraham is still at home. Recuperate must mean to stay at home.

Anna tells Benjamin and Mary that Ruby and Alexander had a baby boy. They called him Ellis. I don't understand how you know who is talking to who when people have the same names.

Benjamin comes home one day and tells Mary and Anna that there was a tornado in Snyder, Oklahoma, and it killed at least 97. Benjamin said that wasn't that far from them. I wonder if we are in Oklahoma. Benjamin also tells Mary that he will be glad when the school year ends in another month. There must be a certain time of the year when you have to go to school.

Abraham goes into town and says he is not coming home until he finds a new job.

Benjamin says there was something called the Chicago Teamster's strike that lasted three months with 21 killed and 416 injured in the violence. Benjamin says he doesn't understand when people kill other people. I don't understand either.

The Life Story Of A House

After three dark periods, Abraham comes home and says that he is doomed to a life of servitude in farming. I don't know what that means but Abraham does not look to happy.

Benjamin says that the summers are getting shorter. Is that possible?

Abraham comes home and says that Mary Ann Miller has been leading him on and wasn't really serious about him. Anna tries to comfort the boy. Abraham tells Anna that he no longer wants to work at the Miller farm but there are no jobs.

Benjamin comes home from work and tells the two women about a train derailment in Manhattan on an elevated train. It killed 19 and 48 were seriously injured.

Abraham comes home one night and tells the others that he quit his job and is taking the horse to town tomorrow to find a job. Anna cries herself to sleep. I wonder why.

The next morning Abraham rides off at day-break, even before Benjamin. Abraham has his clothes with him. I wonder what that means.

When Benjamin comes home that night Anna asks him if he has seen Abraham. Benjamin says that he hasn't. Anna cries herself to sleep again when Abraham does not come home.

The next morning Anna tells Benjamin that she has lost two sons. Benjamin tries to reassure her that Abraham is probably looking for a job until he finds one. After a week, Benjamin doesn't even believe that.

It is cold and snowy again. Anna cries herself to sleep every night. Anna hopes that her boys are not out in this weather.

When the green tree is brought into the house everyone seems excited, except for Anna.

The Life Story Of A House

Benjamin says that it is 1906 now. They don't celebrate the changing of the years like they used too.

Benjamin comes home from town on a cold, snowy day and tells Mary that there was a landslide in Haverstraw, New York, killing 21 people. Anna does not seem interested in the stories anymore. I am beginning to think that there are a lot of people killed accidently.

Anna has quit going to church, although, she still reads the Bible. Benjamin's family still goes.

Amelia and Ruby tell their Mother that they are with-child again. Anna tells the girls that she hopes their boys don't break their hearts like Joshua and Abraham did hers.

It has warmed up some and the flowers are beginning to bloom. Benjamin talks Anna into going to church, so he hooks the horses up to the wagon. He, Anna, Mary and the twins take the wagon to church.

I see two men riding up the path as Benjamin and the family head the other way. The two men stop at the house and walk in. It is Paul and Abraham. Abraham looks different; he has hair on his face. Paul says that the family must have gone to church. Wanda is not with them. The two boys sit at the table and talk. Paul asks Abraham if he remembers sitting by the fireplace and reading. Abraham says that he does. Abraham asks Paul if he can remember the great smells that hung in the room when their Mother was cooking. Paul nods his head yes. Paul asked Abraham if he had heard about the earthquake in San Francisco, California. Abraham said, yes, wasn't that terrible. From what Paul says, an earthquake is bad. Most of the town was destroyed, killing at least 3,000 people, leaving 225,000-300,000 homeless. Abraham doesn't understand why they built the city on the San Andreas Fault. I don't know what a fault is but I hope we are not built on one.

Paul and Abraham continue to talk to each other until Benjamin and the family comes home. Benjamin is puzzled because there are two horses tied up outside the house. Benjamin tells everyone to stay outside until he goes in the house to see who the horses belong to. Benjamin sticks his head in the door, looks back and says that it is safe to come in. Benjamin is hugging his brothers when Anna comes in and sees Abraham. Anna starts to cry and goes over to give her boys a hug and kiss. Mary starts making dinner while Abraham tells everyone what he has been doing. Abraham says he went into town where Paul works, but there were no jobs. Abraham says he went on to the next town and he got a job in a glass factory. I don't know what a glass factory is, but it seems to have made Abraham happy again. Abraham says he has rented a small place but they can visit anytime they wish. Anna is smiling again, she seems happy. They all sit around the table to eat and Anna even says a prayer. They all sit around talking until it starts getting dark, then Abraham says he had better go so he doesn't have to be on the path at night. Abraham tells Anna that he will come more often now that he is settled. Anna cries as Paul and Abraham leave. I cannot tell if she is crying from being sad or happy. That night Anna says a prayer to God, thanking him for taking care of her boys. I wonder if that has anything to do with the family leaving for a half a day once in a while.

Anna is humming again while she is working in the dirt.

Benjamin comes home from town one night and says school is closed for the summer. I wonder why the school closes for the summer. When Amelia and Ruby come home, Anna tells them where Abraham is. Both girls are happy, and both girls look like their bellies are getting bigger, too. The girls and their children stay for the day. It seems to me that Amelia and Ruby go the other way down the path than Benjamin, Paul and Abraham do.

Mary tells Benjamin she is with-child again. Benjamin grabs her and twirls her around and then they go outside to tell Anna. Anna is happy to have so many grandchildren on the way. On the way to where, what does that mean.

The Life Story Of A House

Something must be wrong with the man that works out back in the dirt. I haven't seen him this summer.

One day when it was raining, little balls of ice started to come out of the sky. Benjamin said it was hail, whatever it was it pounded on my roof.

Summer must be over; Benjamin says he has to go back to school. He seems disappointed. Working at the school must be hard.

Amelia comes to visit and her big belly is gone. Amelia is carrying a new little person. She tells Anna that it is a boy and Andrew wanted to name him after his Father, Robert.

Ruby comes home a couple of nights later and says that she has a new baby girl, Doris. Anna tells Ruby that Mary is with-child again. Anna says that she has eight grandchildren, soon to be nine.

Benjamin comes home from town one evening and told Mary that there was something called a race riot in Atlanta, Georgia. Twenty-seven people were killed and the black-owned business district was severely damaged. I wonder what a race riot is.

This day that the family calls Thanksgiving, everyone comes home except for Joshua. Anna is happy that everyone else is there. They say it smells so good in the house but I still like the smell of spring. There are babies everywhere, Anna takes turns holding one and then another. Anna seems like she is really enjoying herself. Someone is riding up the path and the turns in the path toward the house. He gets off of his horse and knocks on the door; he has his hat tipped down. Benjamin opens the door and just stands there and stares for a moment. Benjamin tells Anna it is for her. Anna goes to the door and starts to cry as she hugs the man. They both come in the house and the man takes off his hat. It is JOSHUA. Joshua sees all of the babies and asks if he is in the right house. Everybody laughs and take their turn hugging the man.

When they all sit down to eat, Anna says a special prayer and starts to cry again. Anna says they are happy tears. Joshua says that when he left, he went northeast and joined the merchant marines. I do not know what that is until Joshua tells everyone what he has done for the last few years.

After the meal, everyone sits around the small dining room talking. Joshua asks Anna if it is alright for him to spend a week there. Anna says of course. Everyone stays later than they were going too because they don't know when they will see Joshua again.

The next day, Anna and Joshua walk out to where Ellis and Mary are buried. Anna tells Joshua what happened to Ellis, Joshua hugs Anna. Anna spends most of the next week with Joshua. The day Joshua is to leave, Anna cries. Joshua tells her he will return again but Anna tells him that she will probably be gone by then. Where is Anna going? Anna cries the rest of the day.

The time for the green tree comes and goes. Benjamin gets a week off of work, just like all the previous years. Teaching must be hard work but they sure get a lot of days off.

Benjamin says it is 1907.

One evening Benjamin comes home from work and tells Anna and Mary that two ships have collided in a place called Long Island Sound. Anna asks if it is a ship Joshua is on. Benjamin says no, it is the steamship Larchment and a ship called Harry Hamilton, he also tells them that 183 people were killed. Anna is relieved it is not Joshua's ship but sad for the lives that were lost. It sounds like there are many ways to get killed and die.

Luckily Mary has her baby when Benjamin is home so he can go get help. Mary has a boy, Gordon. The house has the feeling of love and warmth again.

The Life Story Of A House

The spring comes with all of its wonderful smells. Benjamin should be about finished with this school year. It is strange that the man is not working out in the dirt again.

One day Benjamin comes home with that look on his face, the look that he is done with school for the summer.

Paul and Wanda come to visit and tell Anna that Wanda is with-child. Anna says that is wonderful news.

Another strong storm hits. It is not as windy as the one that took the barn, but this one rains so hard I can't even see the outhouse in the backyard.

Benjamin comes home from town where he has been shopping. Benjamin tells Anna and Mary about the lumber schooner San Pedro colliding with the SS Columbia off the coast of a place called Shelter Grove, California. The Columbia sinks, killing 88 people. I wonder what a lumber schooner is and why didn't it sink?

Ruby, Alexander, Alva, Ellis and Doris visit. Ruby tells Anna that Alva had been in bed sick for a week. Anna picks up Alva and says, "Poor baby". Ruby says that Alva had a fever, diarrhea and throwing-up. That doesn't sound nice to me, poor Alva.

Summer must be over because Benjamin is complaining about having to back to work next Monday. Benjamin suggests that the family go on a picnic, whatever that is. Anna and Mary put some food in a basket and Benjamin gets the wagon out. Benjamin tells the women of a nice pond they will go to. What's a pond? I don't like it when they leave me alone, I'm afraid they will never come back.

It is starting to get dark out before the family comes home. I wonder why Anna and Mary are crying and Benjamin is just hanging his head. I only see two children, I wonder where one is? As soon as Benjamin gets the family in the house he gets something small out of the wagon that is wrapped in a blanket. Benjamin brings the item in the house and that makes the women cry harder. What's going on? Benjamin puts the item on a bed and uncovers it. IT IS CHARLES.

Amelia and family, Ruby and family and Paul and Wanda come to the house the next day, along with the minister and a lot of people. Benjamin is talking to Andrew and Alexander, and he says they were finished with their picnic and were just sitting on the ground enjoying the nice day. The next thing they knew there were only two children there. Benjamin ran to the pond and little Charles was lying face down in the water. Benjamin said that he dove into the water to get Charles, but he was already dead. Paul is holding Anna up as they walk over to where Ellis, Mary and the dead boy were in the dirt. Everyone was crying as the minister talked about Charles having a short life and we would never know what he could have accomplished. The minister said some other words but I tried not to hear them. The people walked away and when they were gone, four men lowered the box with Charles in it in the hole and covered it up with dirt. What is the purpose for one so young to die? They have not had a chance to grow-up, get married and have a family of their own. How sad.

Benjamin stays home during the first week of school; he stays in bed a lot. Mary tries to keep her other two children occupied. Anna spends most of her time standing over the graves of Ellis and the rest, sometimes sitting on the ground pulling weeds growing on top of their graves. When Anna does come in the house she doesn't talk very often, neither does Mary or Benjamin. Benjamin tells Mary that he is going back to work on Monday. The three of them do not say another word the rest of the night.

When Benjamin comes home from the first day he has worked, the three of them are still not talking.

Amelia and Ruby try to visit more often, as does Paul and Wanda. Wanda's belly is getting bigger.

The cold, snowy weather comes again and still the three are not talking to each other much.

The only reason that they celebrate Thanksgiving is for the children. There are eight children playing together in the house, unaware that Charles is not there. Paul tries to start a conversation over the turkey dinner by bringing up that the Indian Territory and the Oklahoma Territory were combined to make the 46th U.S. state, named Oklahoma. Everyone acts interested but Benjamin, Mary and Anna. After the meal the women clean up the dishes then they all go home with their families.

The time for bringing in the green tree comes and Benjamin doesn't act like he wants to. Mary tries to tell him that they have two other children that need attention. Benjamin reluctantly goes out and gets a tree. Mary tells Benjamin to stop at a store after work and pick up presents for Caroline and Gordon.

The family all come together for Christmas dinner. The adults are trying to be cheery for the sake of the children; Paul even tries to get the adults to sing Christmas carols to no avail. Paul, Andrew and Alexander are talking amongst themselves as the women do the dishes; Paul asks the two men if they had heard the news of the two disasters? Paul tells them that in a place called West Virginia, a coal mine explosion kills 362 workers. In a place called Jacobs Creek, Pennsylvania, a coal mine exploded, killing 239 people. It is hard for me to comprehend the deaths of so many and the families left behind to make a living on their own. I know without Benjamin moving in, Anna would have lost the house, and I would be alone right now.

Benjamin says it is 1908, and he has to go back to work in a couple of days.

The first day Benjamin is supposed to go back to work the area gets hit by a mid-winter snowstorm. The weather was so bad that Benjamin did not go to work for three days. Benjamin could hardly go outside to feed

The Life Story Of A House

the animals. Benjamin says the storm had dumped eight inches of snow and the snow drifts are over two feet deep. Benjamin says he will try to go to work on the fourth day.

Benjamin must have gotten to work because he did not come home until that evening. Benjamin told Mary that because of the snowstorm he was ready to move to town. Mary asked what they would do about Anna. Benjamin said that she could go too. Mary says she doesn't think she will go. Benjamin says he will wait until summer break to look for a house.

When it is getting close to spring but still cool at night, Paul and Wanda had their child, a girl, and they named her Elizabeth. Paul and Wanda bring Elizabeth out to the house to show her off, and Mary and Anna say she is a beautiful baby. Paul talks to Benjamin a little. Benjamin tells Paul not to say anything to Anna, but he is planning on moving to town in the summer. Paul doesn't know what to say other than he doesn't think their Mother would move. Benjamin says she may have no choice in the matter. Benjamin says he is sick and tired of having to ride into town in all sorts of weather.

Benjamin comes home from work one evening and tells Mary that someplace called Boyertown, Pennsylvania had a fire at Rhoads Opera House and the fire killed 170 people. Mary says it seems like one disaster after another is happening. I agree.

It was end of the month that they call February that Anna did not get out of bed like usual. Mary went into Anna's room but she was cold as ice. Anna was dead. I can't believe it. Benjamin had not left for work yet. Benjamin told Mary that he would go into town and tell the minister to come out to the house in four days. Maybe the ground would be thawed out enough to bury Mother. I will tell Paul and Abraham today and Amelia and Ruby tomorrow.

Benjamin told Mary that evening that Paul and Abraham had been told. There was no way to let Joshua know. Mary has already cleaned

Anna's body and put her church dress on her. What Benjamin and Mary didn't know was Anna had cried herself to sleep; she had overheard Benjamin tell Paul that the family was moving to town and that she would have no choice in the matter. I thought that Anna wants to stay with Ellis, Mary and me. I am so sad that Anna was so upset on her last day on earth.

In rained for three days, and Benjamin said all of that rain should make the ground soft enough to dig in. What is it about some men; Benjamin never shed a tear for his Mother, Anna. Anna was such a sweet woman, I will miss her.

On the fourth day the whole family was here but Joshua. It was still kind of cool so the service was cut short. I thought that there should be more words spoken over Anna. The family mulled around the house for a while until the townspeople and the minister went home. Abraham rode home with Paul and his family, but he too thinks there should have been more words spoken over his Mother.

Benjamin tells Mary that he will start looking for houses before school gets out for the summer.

Benjamin comes home from work and tells Mary that Collinwood School near Cleveland, Ohio had a fire and it killed 174 people. If that wasn't bad enough, Benjamin told Mary that in the towns of Amite, Louisiana, Pine, Louisiana and Purvis, Mississippi the seventh deadliest tornado in U.S. history struck, killing 143 people and injuring 770. It is hard for me to comprehend so many people dying all at once.

One night Benjamin came home and tells Mary that he has found a house in town for sale, one that they can afford. They will put a for sale sign in the front yard of this house when summer break comes. Does this mean I am going to be all alone?

The Life Story Of A House

I know it is spring weather because of the smells, so it won't be long before Benjamin and his family move. I am so sad. I will miss Anna forever, Ellis, too. It seemed like they wanted to take care of me.

It must be summer break; Benjamin has brought Abraham and Paul to help him with filling the wagons full of furniture. I can remember when the three boys crawled on the floor of the house. I was so full of warmth, love and happiness. Once all of the furniture is loaded on the wagons and the house is empty, the three boys walk around the house one last time and then walk out to where Anna, Ellis, Mary and Charles are buried. I watch them ride down the road until they are just a dot. I am so sad.

I don't like being alone, it's kind of creepy. The sun comes up and goes down just like it always did, but now there are no people around. I don't know how long I have been like this, alone. Nobody even visits the graves out in the side yard. I see people going back and forth in front of the house on the path, but no one stops.

It seems like it has been an eternity, but I see a wagon coming up the path to the house. It is a man and woman, they look older. They have a key to open the door that is a good sign. As they walk around the house, it is wonderful to hear voices again. The woman says the house is kind of big for their needs, but the man says the price is right. The man asks the woman if she would give living here a chance, just over the winter. If she doesn't like it they can move again in the spring. The woman agrees. As they walk outside, the man says, "You wait and see, you will love it here in the country". The two get into their wagon and ride off. I watch them until they are just a little dot. I am excited now. I wonder how long it will be before they come back.

It is starting to get cool out and it is cool in here since there is no fire in the fireplace. Every time I see a wagon coming from the direction of town, I get my hopes up. I am thinking the man and woman have

The Life Story Of A House

changed their minds on moving here when I see more than one wagon turning onto the path coming up to the house. The wagons have furniture in them. I wonder if the man and woman have any children. I can't wait until they start a fire in the fireplace that will mean they are going to stay. Goody, that is the first thing they do. It looks to be four men and women moving the furniture in the house. The old man and old woman are not moving as fast as the others. I hear the old man call a couple of the men, son. The old woman calls one of the women, daughter. One of the men calls the old man and old woman Mr. and Mrs. Taylor. As they carry the furniture in, the older children are calling each other their names, but they are saying them so fast, I can't tell who is who. I hear the old man call the old woman, Elsa. After a while the old woman calls the old man, Ronald. As soon as the furniture is brought in the house and put in place, the people stop for supper. Elsa makes a stew and biscuits, which all say are wonderful. They smell terrific, filling the house with the wonderful smell of cooking food. As soon as the meal is done the women clean the dishes while the men talk about spending the winter out here in the country. Ronald said this is all he could afford. One of the men said that he would come back in a couple of days and cut some firewood for them. Ronald tells the man, who he calls Michael, thank you. As the men and women are leaving, Ronald and Elsa tell the others thank you and come anytime you like. They leave one wagon and put two horses in the corral.

Ronald and Elsa are quieter than Ellis and Anna were. Maybe it's because they are older. Elsa reads the Bible by the fire just like Anna did. Ronald pulls something out of his pocket, stuffs it full of something out of a small pouch and puts it in his mouth and lights it on fire. It gives off smoke and a smell I have not experienced before. I can't decide if I like it or not but Elsa doesn't act like she likes it. Ronald tells Elsa that it is too cold to go outside to smoke. That must be what it is called, to smoke. After Ronald finishes his smoke, he and Elsa get ready for bed. Elsa says it might take her a couple of nights to get used to being in a strange place. It is nice to have that warm, lived in feeling again.

The next day, Ronald and Elsa walk around on the outside of the house. They stop to look at Ellis and Anna's graves. Ronald tells Elsa that Benjamin told him that his Mother and Father built the house themselves with help from some members of their church. They finally go in the house because it is getting colder out.

A couple of days later, one man and woman come back to the house to chop firewood. It is the man called Michael, and he calls the woman Nancy. Michael chops wood all day except for stopping to eat. Michael tells Ronald that should be enough firewood for a couple of months. Michael says he will come out and check on Ronald and Elsa every couple of weeks. Elsa says next time maybe you can bring my grandchildren. I know what grandchildren mean, I love grandchildren. I also love any children when they are young. Michael and Nancy leave and Ronald and Elsa spend the evening the same way they spend all of their evenings. Elsa reading the Bible and Ronald smoking, what Elsa calls Ronald's smelly old disgusting pipe. Ronald gets a grin on his face when Elsa complains about Ronald's pipe.

It is cold and snowy again so Ronald and Elsa stay in the house except for Ronald going outside to check on the horses. Elsa put a line hooked to the walls to hang wet clothes on after she washes them. Ronald and Elsa do not have any visitors, unless one of their children comes out to see them. It was a long time before Michael and Nancy came to visit. They brought two children with them. Elsa called them Randy and James. Randy and James are not very big, but big enough to walk and talk. Elsa seems very happy to see them. Ronald and Michael talk about Thanksgiving. Michael wants Ronald and Elsa to come into town for dinner, Michael says all of Ronald's children will be there. Ronald finally agrees to go if it is not snowing or there is not six inches of snow already on the ground. I don't understand Ronald's hesitation; the smells on Thanksgiving are wonderful.

The Life Story Of A House

That night Elsa tells Ronald that she really wants to go to Michael's for Thanksgiving dinner. Elsa says one of these days; they will be too old to go anywhere. Ronald says they would go if the weather permits it.

Thanksgiving morning arrives and it has not snowed or is it going to snow, much to the dismay of Ronald. If it were up to Ronald, they would stay home most of the time. Ronald gets the wagon ready and Elsa wraps herself up to ward off the cold. As they ride down the path and their wagon becomes a tiny speck, I try to remember the smells of cooking on Thanksgiving.

The wagon comes back into sight and Elsa looks like she is really happy, once Ronald puts the horses away, Elsa talks and talks about the day's events. Elsa says that it was good to see all the children in one place, their children, Michael, Lee, Ryan and Norma, and all the grandchildren.

Usually after Thanksgiving someone brings a green tree in the house and puts things on it, shiny things. Elsa asks Ronald if he is going to get a Christmas tree this year. Ronald said that if we were going in town to eat at Michael's, what is the use. Elsa says that she likes the smell of the tree and it wouldn't seem like Christmas if they didn't have a tree. Ronald puts on his coat, he is mumbling something all of the way out of the door. I can't hear him, but I thought I heard, "Darn old lady".

Ronald hooks the horse to the wagon and goes down the path and turns the opposite way from town. Ronald comes home close to dark and brings in a tree that is not that big. Elsa is satisfied and tries to give the old man a kiss. Ronald pretends he is angry but he finally lets her kiss him on the cheek. Elsa spends the rest of the evening putting shiny things on the tree. It is hard to smell the tree over Ronald's pipe though.

Ronald tells Elsa that maybe in the spring; they will get some chickens and a milk cow. Elsa says that it would be nice to have fresh eggs and milk. That must be why someone comes to the house every so often, they are bringing supplies to Ronald and Elsa.

The Life Story Of A House

Christmas morning comes and there still isn't any snow. Ronald complains the whole time they are getting ready to leave. Ronald is still complaining as the two walk out of the door. They ride off toward town and are finally out of site.

Later, when it is starting to get dark, the two finally come home. I was worried. Ronald lets Elsa off at the door and says he is going to put the horse and wagon away. Elsa comes in the house humming to herself, Elsa seems quite happy; she must have had a good visit.

It seems like it is taking Ronald an especially long time to put the horse and wagon away. After a while, Elsa puts on her coat, lights a candle and goes outside to look for Ronald. Walking out the door I notice the worried look on Elsa's face. Elsa goes out to the corral, spends a couple of minutes and comes back to the house. Elsa is crying. Elsa goes and gets a blanket and goes back outside. When Elsa comes back in she does not have the blanket. Elsa is still crying as she does the rest of the night. I wonder where Ronald is.

The next morning Elsa is still crying as she goes outside. Elsa is on a horse and she rides towards town. After what seems like an eternity, a wagon comes back with Elsa, Michael and Lee. Elsa comes in the house while Michael and Lee go out to the corral. Elsa is shaking, I guess from the cold. Elsa makes a pot of coffee. Michael and Lee ride up to the house with what looks to be a big wrapped up thing in the wagon. The two men come into the house and put their arms around Elsa. I can hardly understand them because they are talking so low. It sounds like Michael is telling Elsa that she can stay with him at his house now that Father is dead. DEAD!! Michael tells Elsa to get some clothes for Father and anything she will need until spring. SPRING!! The boys drink a cup of coffee while they are waiting. Finally, Elsa comes out with a bundle of clothes, she is still crying. The boys pour her a cup of coffee and wait until she drinks it. Lee makes sure the fire in the fireplace is put out. They tell Elsa it is time to go and she rubs the door with her hand as she is leaving. Elsa climbs in the wagon that is carrying Ronald and they go down the path towards town until I can't see them anymore.

With no fire in the fireplace it doesn't take long for the house to reach freezing temperatures. I am all alone, again. Once in a while I see a horse and rider or wagon load of people go by. I am very sad.

Spring finally comes and there are a couple of wagons coming down the path. It is Michael, Lee and Ryan. I wonder where Elsa is. As the boys are loading the furniture into the wagon they are talking. Michael says it has been a bad winter with Father and Mother dying. Elsa died too. It was probably from a broken heart. Lee looks at the withered Christmas tree in the corner of the living room, he leaves it there. Lee asks Michael if he remembered to bring the for sale sign. Michael says that he has and was just getting ready to put it out in the yard. Michael takes something out to the front yard and pounds it into the ground. When the three have loaded all of the furniture into the wagons, Michael says that Mom and Dad didn't get to live here very long. They ride off until I can't see them anymore.

I am empty and alone again.

Every time I see a rider or a wagon I hope they are coming here, but they never do. It is warm again so it must be summer. The warmth of the sun feels good.

Here comes another rider to go by like I don't even exist. The rider pulls his horse onto the path coming up to the house. As the rider gets down I get a good look at his face. It is JOSHUA. Joshua gets off of his horse and tries the door, but it is locked. Joshua looks in a window and sees that the house is empty. Joshua then walks around the side of the house where the graves are. Joshua kneels down by his Mother's grave. I cannot hear if Joshua is saying anything or not. Joshua stays there on the ground for a while, then gets up and stares at the ground some more. Joshua finally walks away from the graves and as he is passing by the house, he gives me a pat and said, "Good-bye old friend". Joshua mounts his horse and rides away towards town. After a while Joshua is just a speck.

It is getting to be cold again. I was hoping someone would move in and make it warm and happy again. It seems like it is a longer cold season than usual. Maybe it is because I am so lonely. One day it starts to snow and it does not stop for three days. The snow is piled up past my windows. It is windy also, I feel as cold as I ever have.

The sun comes out from behind the clouds for a week. Some of the snow finally melts and I see a flower trying to pop out from under the snow. It is getting warmer during the day but it is still cold at night.

I see some riders coming up the path towards the house. Two of the men are Michael and Lee, but I do not recognize the other man. The three men get off of their horses and come into the house. Michael is explaining where things are to the stranger. They look all around the house and then they go outside and walk all around the house. As they are walking back to the house, Michael is talking and the stranger is nodding his head. When they get closer to the back door I can hear them. Michael says, "Then we have a deal Mr. White". Mr. White says, "Yes, I'll take it". I wonder if that means he is going to move in. Michael says, "Fine, I will have the papers drawn up". I wonder if a new family is going to move in. All of a sudden, I feel excited for some reason, happy that there might be a chance for a new family to move in.

One morning I see a couple of wagons loaded as full as could be turn onto the path to the house. There is Mr. White, a woman and what looks like six children. Oh it will be so nice to have children laughing and playing again.

As they started to unload the wagons, Mr. White was telling the rest of the family where to put everything. If the children didn't move fast enough, Mr. White raised his voice to them, one time he even kicked one of the boys in the back of the pants. Mom finally told Jack not to be so hard on the children. Jack said that they were his children and he would talk to them anyway he saw fit. Mr. White is acting like Ellis did at the end of his life. I wonder if Jack White is going to die.

When they were done bringing everything into the house, Mr. White told his two oldest boys, Ralph and Edward to put the wagons and horses away. They had brought a cow with them and some chickens and Mr. White told the two boys to see to them too. Ralph and Edward must not have been doing it fast enough because Mr. White yelled out of the back door and told the boys that they had better not be goofing off.

Mr. White called to his wife, Carol, and told her she could put their things away later; it was time to make supper now. Mr. White went to the back door again, but the boys were already hurrying towards the house. Ralph came through the door and Mr. White kicked him on the back of the pants again. Edward got through the door before he could get kicked. Mr. White told the two boys to make sure they put their things away properly, he would check later.

Suppertime comes and Mr. White made sure all of the children had washed their hands. They could sit down to eat then. Mrs. White tried to say a prayer before they ate but Mr. White did not wait until she was done. It seemed like, Mr. White didn't let the children talk at the table and they did not say a word unless they were talked to first.

After supper Mr. White told the oldest girl, Amanda, to help her Mother with the dishes. Amanda only looked to be around 13 years old. Mr. White asked the boys if they had their things put away. Ralph said that they were almost done. Mr. White told them to hurry up and get it done.

The children were talking amongst themselves, but not loud enough for their Father to hear. From what I could tell the youngest was Calvin, a boy who was seven, then Rachel, a girl who was nine, then Frank, a boy who was eleven. The other three are Amanda, 13, Edward 15 and Ralph, 16. The children were talking about how strict their Father was and that Ralph tried to take the abuse aimed at the other children. Jack had never got as physically abusive as kicking Ralph in the back-end. Jack raised his voice quite often and sometimes he raised his arm as if he was going to hit you, but he never did. Jack even raised his hand against Mrs. White, but she always told him that if he touched her it would be the last thing he did. The children hushed up when Mr. White came upstairs to see if they were done putting their things away. They had put their things away properly so Mr. White had nothing to complain about even if he did tell Ralph that something was out of place. It seemed like Mr. White picked on Ralph because he was the oldest.

I got mixed feelings for the first couple of days. There wasn't the total love and warmth that I had felt with Ellis and Anna, not even Ronald and Elsa. It seemed like the younger children were afraid of their Father and their Mother gave them all the love and support that they got.

Mr. White road off toward town every day, so his work must be there. Mrs. White stayed at home and did what Elsa and Anna did, plant a garden, wash the clothes and there was something different. Mr. White expected the children to be clean and well-dressed by the time he got home. He would complain to Mrs. White if things weren't exactly like he thought they should be. I heard Mrs. White tell the children more than once to hurry and get cleaned up before their Father got home.

It must be summer because the children are not going to school. There is more of a chance for them to get dirty now. Mrs. White knew that is what children did, but she could not make Mr. White understand that. Mr. White, on the other hand, came home dirty, and barely washed his hands before supper. I heard one of the children say that their Father worked as a blacksmith.

Some days Mr. Smith was late coming home, but he still expected his family to wait supper for him and for supper to be hot. When Mr. White came home late he always smelled like Ellis did right before he

The Life Story Of A House

died. I wonder if Mr. White is going to die. Mrs. White doesn't say anything, she tells her children it would do no good and it would start a fight. I could tell Mrs. White held her tongue a lot around her husband. Mrs. White seemed to be a kind person who was just trying to avoid confrontation.

Summer seemed to go by quicker than usual. Ralph drove the wagon to school with Edward, Amanda, Frank and Rachel. Mrs. White decided to keep Calvin at home one more year. Ralph carried a heavy load of responsibility getting the other children to school safely, even in bad weather.

The children were well mannered, but they said they could relax a little while they were at school without their Father being around.

One evening towards the time it was getting cool out, right before it got cold, Mr. White saw some animals behind the house, out where the other man worked in the dirt. Mr. White got something hanging over the fireplace, quietly went outside, pointed this thing at the animals, and then there was a loud noise and one of the animals fell. Mr. White told Mrs. White that he had gotten a deer that they could butcher and let the weather freeze it. Mr. White made Ralph go out to get the deer even though Ralph had no desire in what he called hunting. Mr. White took a knife and cut it right down the middle of it, on the bottom of the animal. All sorts of things came out and fell on the ground. When they seemed to have cleaned the inside of the animal, they brought it into the house and cut it up. Mr. White said, "It would be good eating".

Mr. White was happy for a while after he had shot the deer, but that didn't last long. It wasn't very long before Mr. White was giving Ralph a hard time for any little reason. Ralph didn't say anything back to his Father, but he didn't seem to be afraid of him either. Mrs. White tried to tell Mr. White that one of these days; Ralph would just not come home. Mr. White thought that was quite funny as he didn't think Ralph could do anything. Mr. White didn't know Ralph was talking with

The Life Story Of A House

Edward and Amanda about that very thing, not coming back from school. The only thing keeping him there was his fear that his Father would take it out on Edward or his Mother. Ralph had told Edward that if their Father ever touched their Mother, he would kill him. I know what kill and dead means and I hope Ralph doesn't have to kill Mr. White.

It was the morning of a huge snowstorm and Mrs. White asked Mr. White if the children shouldn't stay home from school that day. Mr. White said if he could get to work, then they should be able to get to school. Mrs. White bundled the children as much as she could and sent them on their way. Ralph would say later that it was snowing so hard he was having trouble keeping on the path. When the children arrived home that night, Rachel was cold and white as a sheet. Mrs. White put her to bed and put an extra cover on her. Mrs. White was mad because Mr. White had made the children go to school on such a day that was so bad. Mr. White was late that night and wanted to know why Rachel wasn't at her spot at the table. Mrs. White really let Mr. White have it, I bet she yelled at him a good hour. Mr. White sat at the table and did not say one word. When supper was done Mr. White went upstairs to check on Rachel, she was still shivering. This one time Mr. White knew that he had been wrong.

The next day Rachel was still white as a sheet, so Mrs. White said that she wasn't sending her to school that day and glared at Mr. White, waiting for him to say one word. Mr. White rode off to town without saying one word.

Mrs. White had hoped sharing a bed with Amanda would have warmed up Rachel some, but her skin was just as cold and clammy as it had been yesterday. Mrs. White put a cold, damp cloth on Rachel's forehead. Mrs. White told Calvin that she thought Rachel needed to see a doctor. When the children got home that evening she would send Ralph back to town to bring the doctor. Rachel tried to cough, but seemed like it was too much of a chore for her even to do that. I am worried for Rachel now.

When the children came home that night, Mrs. White asked Ralph to unhook the wagon and ride one of the horses into town and bring the doctor. Ralph knew it would be dark, but hopefully he could see the wagon tracks that he had just made in the snow. Ralph made it to town and told the doctor about Rachel. The doctor got his bag and hooked up his horse to his wagon and followed the young boy out in the country. Ralph didn't even stop to tell his Father that Rachel had gotten worse.

The doctor examined Rachel and said that she was very sick. The doctor asked how it was that she was so sick. Mrs. White told the doctor about Mr. White making the children go to school on that terrible weather day. The doctor just shook his head; he said he had heard of people being so bull-headed. I don't know what that means, but I can guess. The doctor gave Rachel some medicine and said that he would come back tomorrow afternoon. Mrs. White thanked the doctor for coming out on such a cold night. The doctor told her, "It was his job".

Mr. White would say later that he had met the doctor on the path to town and the doctor told him just how sick Rachel was.

The next morning Mrs. White couldn't wake Rachel up. Mrs. White was crying when she stopped her husband and told him to send the doctor once he got to town. Mr. White asked about Rachel and Mrs. White said that the girl was still breathing but she could not wake her.

When the doctor arrived and examined Rachel, he told Mrs. White that Rachel was in a coma. I don't know what coma is, but it must be bad. The doctor told Mrs. White to wrap Rachel as warmly as she could; he was going to take Rachel home with him. The doctor told Mrs. White that she could have Ralph look in on Rachel's condition before he came home from school. Mrs. White was crying as the doctor left with her baby girl. Although Rachel was 9, Mrs. White considered Rachel her baby girl.

After a week Rachel was still in a coma and Mrs. White had started giving Mr. White the silent treatment. It seemed odd that Mrs. White was not talking to Mr. White. Mr. White had even started sleeping on the couch.

One day during the second week the doctor rode out to the house. Mrs. White started to cry. The doctor told her that he did all he could do for Rachel but she had not made it. Made what? Mrs. White started to cry hysterically and the doctor tried to calm her. The doctor gave Mrs. White some powder that he told her to mix with water and that would make her feel a little better. The doctor said that he would go to Mr. White's place of employment once he got back to town. Mrs. White said that the doctor could send Rachel's body home with the children as they had the wagon in town anyway. The doctor asked Mrs. White if she was sure that she was alright and she said yes.

Mrs. White worked around the house to keep herself busy, every once in a while, she would cry. When the children came home, Ralph and Edward carried Rachel's body into the house. I know what it means to be wrapped in blankets and your body is not moving. Mrs. White laid Rachel's body out on her bed and started to clean her. When Mr. White came home, he already heard the bad news from the doctor. Mr. White just kept saying that he was sorry.

Before he had left Mrs. White had asked the doctor to send out the minister on the following day. The ground was too hard to dig so the doctor would take Rachel home with him. The doctor had a special room right out of his back door where he kept bodies in the winter.

They had Rachel's service in the house and then the doctor took Rachel home with him. Mrs. White cried the rest of the day but she also had to console her other children. Mrs. White did not say anything to Mr. White for the rest of the winter.

The Life Story Of A House

When the ground was melted enough to dig, they buried Rachel out by Ellis and Anna. Mrs. White told the children they could stay home for a couple of days. They were confused, but when talking among themselves they decided their Mother just didn't want to be alone. As soon as Mr. White left for work Mrs. White told Ralph to get the wagon hooked up. Ralph gave her a weird look and Mrs. White said, "We are moving". Ralph asked, "What about Father?" Mrs. White said that he wasn't coming. So the family spent half of the day putting as much as they could into one wagon. I was confused by Mrs. White's actions, she was moving without her husband. The wagon was packed and Mrs. White went out back to tell Rachel good-bye one last time. The wagon went done the path until I could not see it anymore.

That night when Mr. White got home he found a half empty house. Mr. White hung his head and sat down. Mr. White wondered out loud how he had managed to run his family off. Mr. White got on his horse and rode off. I figured I was alone again but then Mr. White road back up the path. Mr. White put his horse away and came into the house. Mr. White had a couple of large bottles with him. Mr. White set on the couch and started to drink out of one of the bottles. After a while Mr. White began talking to himself, he was acting like Ellis had done before he died. Was Mr. White going to die? When Mr. White finished the first bottle he threw it in the fireplace. Whatever was in the bottle made the flames of the fire get brighter. Mr. White fell asleep on the couch; he had managed to sit the bottle upright on the floor without spilling any.

The next morning Mr. White held his head and sat on the couch looking down. I wonder what he is looking at. Mr. White finally got up and went outside to get his horse. Mr. White rode off down the lane and again, I felt alone.

I was surprised when Mr. White came back that night. Mr. White had a couple of bottles with him again. Mr. White did the same thing as the night before, drank until he threw a bottle in the fireplace, then drink until he fell asleep.

Mr. White had the same routine for months. Nobody planted a garden; Mr. White hardly bathed and very rarely washed his clothes. Mr. White was losing a lot of weight; too, he was not eating right.

This went on until it was winter again. Mr. White came home the same as he did every night, but this time he took the bottles out with his horse and did not come inside. I wonder what he is doing.

The next morning Mr. White did not come out with his horse to leave for the day. Maybe Mr. White had slipped off while I was not paying attention. I told myself that was it; he would come home in the evening like he always did. But he did not. It was a week before I saw someone coming up the path. They came in the house calling Mr. White's name, it was the doctor. The doctor went out to where Mr. White kept his horse and came out by himself, shaking his head. The doctor rode into town and came back with three other men, one with a wagon. They went over to where the horse was kept and loaded something wrapped in a blanket into the wagon. I guess that is Mr. White. The men took the thing that was wrapped up with them as they rode a way. I watched until all they were was a tiny speck.

I was alone again. Mr. White did not even get buried next to Rachel. I was left to watch people go on the path in front of the house, always going by, never stopping.

The house still had some of the White's furniture in it. The doors were not locked and after a while, animals started coming into the house. Some of them chewed on the walls and floors. I hoped the animals would not eat me, getting chewed on gave me a strange sensation.

I do not know how many snow, cold and warm periods went by. The inside of the house was covered in dust and cobwebs.

The Life Story Of A House

One day in the warm season someone turned in to the path coming up to the house. I am very excited. It is a man, and he stops, gets off of his horse and comes into the house. The man looks around, knocking cobwebs down as he is walking around the house. This fellow looks to be younger. The man goes outside and gets on his horse and rides away. I wonder if this means he is going to move in.

After the cold and snowy weather comes again, I give up on the man and horse coming back. Maybe I will spend the rest of my time having to watch people go back and forth on the path in front of the house.

There are a group of people riding in a wagon that comes up the path to the house. It is two men and two women, and they are coming into the house. I hear the women say, "It will take a lot of cleaning to make the house livable". I get excited thinking that someone might move in and make me a home again. The two men start to take what furniture left in the house outside. They put all of the furniture in a pile and light it on fire. The women start to clean while the men try and get the little animals out. The men get the animals out, there were more living in here than I thought. They must be going to take the house if they are cleaning it from top to bottom. The men go out in front of the house by the front path and put a box on a round piece of wood that comes up to the waist of one of the men. The four people work on the house until it is getting dark. One of the women says that it will take one more day to make it habitable for humans. I do not know what that means, but I hope someone is going to move in. The four get in the wagon and ride off. For the first time in a while, I believe they will come back.

The next morning I can see the wagon coming up the path and it has the same four persons in it. The four talk to each other while they are cleaning. One of the women say it has been five years since Mr. White killed himself. It has been five warm and cold times. I thought Mr. White must have been dead when the other men hauled him off in the wagon, five years ago.

The Life Story Of A House

There is just a little coolness in the air. I think the snowy time is over. The women act happy to be about done with the cleaning. They say they will bring out their furniture tomorrow. Someone is finally going to move in again.

The next morning two wagons come up the path. The wagons are full of furniture, which it does not take the four of them long to bring in the house. From their talking to one another, I figure out that the women are sisters and the two men are their husband's. They are all four going to live here for a while. The two men say they have jobs in town which they are supposed to start on Monday. The two women are going to stay at home for a while; maybe they will get jobs later. I have heard them call each other names since they have arrived. I think I have finally put the names and faces together. The younger sister is Rebecca, and the other one is Ruth. Rebecca is married to Edward, and Ruth is married to Adam. Edward and Rebecca's last name is Todd. Adam and Ruth's last name is Wilson.

The four have the furniture arranged and their bedrooms pick out. Adam says they have put a postal box up out front. I wonder what that is for. Edward starts a fire in the fireplace and they cook their supper over the flames. It smells wonderful and to have the warmth again is wonderful, also. Edward says he and Adam will bring a cook stove home next week-end. I wonder what that is.

The next morning the four of them get all dressed up and head out in the wagon. I heard Ruth ask Rebecca if she was ready to go to church. After the four come home, they eat a small meal and just sit around and rest for the remainder of the day.

The next morning, Adam and Edward ride off on their horses towards town after they have had their breakfast. Ruth and Rebecca say they hope their husbands like their new jobs. Adam is going to be a banker and Edward is going to work at the glass factory. I wonder if it is the same glass factory that Abraham worked at.

The Life Story Of A House

Ruth and Rebecca spend most of the day planting their garden, but first they had to clean up the yard mess, there had not been a garden there for some time. Adam and Edward come home before it gets dark and the women are excited to hear how their day has gone. Both of the men say that they like their new jobs. Adam says he is only a teller now, but the boss said there is room for advancement. That must be a good thing because Ruth seems pleased when she hears Adam say it. Edward says that working in the glass factory is hard, hot work, but he thinks he can handle it. This pleases Rebecca. After the meal, the men share reading a newspaper that they have brought from town. Adam says that it is something that tells them the news of the day before. The women knit some and read the Bible by candlelight.

After the four go to bed, it is nice to hear people talk to each other before they go to sleep. It gives me a comfortable feeling.

It must be the following week-end, because Adam and Edward take the wagon into town. When they return there is a huge crate in the wagon, and there is another man riding in a wagon hauling what looks like black rocks. The three men carry the crate into the house, mentioning that is very heavy. The other man asks the women if they are excited to be getting a new cook stove. Both women say that they are. After the men uncrate the stove, it looks huge. The men are cutting a hole in the wall of the house and it goes to the outside. The men put the stove in place and hook something that looks like a cylinder from the stove to the outside of the house. On the outside of the house, the cylinder goes up towards the sky. The other man unloads his black rocks by the side of the house. Adam brings some of the black rocks into the house and puts them in the stove. Adam gets part of the newspaper he had and puts it with what Adam calls coal. Adam lights the paper on fire and the coal catches on fire. Adam tells the women that the "pipes" are used so that the smoke from the fire goes from the stove to the outside of the house. I see the smoke and feel the heat from the new stove and the old fireplace. The other man leaves and the women start to cook on the new stove. When the women are done and the four of them sit at the

The Life Story Of A House

table to eat, they all comment on how well the food tastes. It still smells good.

I see men working on the path to town. They are putting in the ground huge poles, they are very tall. They seem to be attaching what looks like some kind of wires to them. When the workers get in front of the house, they run a wire and attach it to the house. The workers come in the house and attach the wire to a metal box. The workers leave the house and go on down the path, doing the same thing. When Adam and Edward get home, they are excited to see that the wire has been hooked onto the house. Adam tells Edward that they will start wiring the house this week-end, whatever that means.

It must be the weekend because Adam and Edward do not go to work. After breakfast they start to put holes in the walls and sticking little metal boxes in them. They also put what Adam calls a switch about midway up the wall by the door. The men string wires from the boxes to the switches, then from the boxes to the metal box that the others workers put in the house. It took all day for Adam and Edward to wire the downstairs. Adam stuck something in the little box in the wall. It became bright and Adam called it a lamp. When it got dark outside, Adam had a lamp for each downstairs room and it lit up the room better than a candle did. After they left the room, they would move what they called a switch to the down position and the lamp would go off and the room would get dark again. Now they could light up the whole room with what Adam called electricity. It is amazing to me how you can move a little switch and the room gets almost as bright as during the day. Adam tells the others that they would wire the upstairs later. No more use of candles downstairs.

The women are happy; first they received a new cook stove, now electricity and lamps.

During supper a couple of nights later, Adam tells the woman that a German U-boat sank another ship called the RMS Lusitania, killing 1,198 people. The two women say how awful the news is. After supper the two men share the newspaper and say there are pictures of the Lusitania before it sank.

One day, Adam and Edward go into town with the wagon. The women ask why but the men won't tell them. The women spend the rest of the day talking about what they are going to bring home in the wagon. It is hard for the women to do their work thinking about this. Finally, when the men come home for the evening they carry in a box. When the box is opened the women are surprised to see what Adam calls a radio. Adam plugs the radio into one of the little boxes in the wall and it makes sound. Adam turns a knob on the radio and different sounds come out of the box. Adam calls it changing the station. They play with the box the rest of the night, first listening to music and then some man talking. I wonder how the voices are in the box.

Now after supper the four listen to the radio while they are reading or sewing. It seems strange just by turning a knob you can change from talking to music.

One night when the four are listening to the radio, the man talking says that in Chicago, a steamer called the Eastland capsized and killed 844 people. I wonder what a steamer is and capsized means.

The music is soothing, but I am not sure about the man talking on the radio.

The four seem to be getting along great, but Ruth tells Rebecca something that will change the household. Ruth is with-child; Ruth is going to have a baby. Ruth says she hasn't even told Adam yet. Ruth hopes Adam will be happy as she plans on telling Adam tonight after supper. After supper, when the four are settled into listening to the radio and the other things, Ruth tells Adam she has something to tell him. Ruth goes over and squats by Adam and tells him she is with-child. Adam is very happy. It will be nice to have tiny footsteps running around the house again.

The Life Story Of A House

A few days later the four are listening to the radio, and the man says that there has been a hurricane in Galveston, Texas and New Orleans, Louisiana, killing 275. The man says the hurricane happened over a period of time. A few days after that the man on the radio tells about a 13 year old girl in Atlanta, Georgia being murdered by Jewish American Leo Frank. Some of the people in Atlanta lynched Leo Frank even though they had not proved that he had done it. There seems to be a lot of killing and in different places and for different reasons. Adam says it is nice getting the news on the radio.

It is getting close to the cold and snowy time. The women have brought in all of the things from the garden. They put a lot of what they bring in the house in jars. They say that they will store some in the house in the pantry and some outside in the storm cellar.

The women are excited about Thanksgiving, it will be the first time they get to use the cook stove on a huge meal. There are some other people coming up the path towards the house. Adam and Edward go out to greet them. When they come into the house Ruth and Rebecca hug the two women and the two men. The four strangers are impressed that Adam and Edward have a new cook stove, radio and electricity. Adam had brought home four extra chairs the other day, so all the people could sit around the table. The four strangers have brought dishes filled with food, also. After they sit down for the feast, Ruth says a prayer to God. All of the people seem to be having a great time and the house smells wonderful. About half-way through the meal, Ruth announces to the strangers that she is with-child. The people are all happy about that and kid Adam about it.

As the people are getting ready to leave, they all hug each other, and the strangers tell Adam, Edward, Ruth and Rebecca that they expect them at their house at Christmas.

Adam puts up the green tree but they seem to have different decorations than the other people that lived here had. Christmas morning arrives and each of the four has presents to open, new shirts for the men and perfume and handkerchiefs for the women. The four get bundled up, Edward goes outside and gets the wagon and they head down the path towards town.

It is almost dark when the four get home. As they sit and relax, Ruth tells Adam it is about time to get the baby's room ready.

Over the next several days Adam and Edward take the wagon to work. Every evening they bring home a piece of furniture for the baby's room, Ruth calls it a nursery. It is nice to see the transformation from an empty room to one that gets painted, a tiny bed, dresser and a rocking chair for Ruth to rock the baby to sleep. They start to bring in tiny clothes and the two women start to make, what they call diapers.

The year changes to 1916 and Ruth's stomach is getting really big. Ruth says it won't be long now.

The man on the radio talks about the weather in Browning, Montana. The temperature dropped from 44 degrees to -56 degrees in one day. The man on the radio says that it is the greatest change in temperature for a 24-hour period. I don't know where all of these places are, but by the reaction of Adam and Edward I do not think I would like -56 below zero.

It is close to the end of January when Ruth says she is ready. The women are glad that the men are home. Edward rides into town to get the doctor and bring him back to the house. The baby almost does not wait for the doctor before he arrives; the doctor says he can see the crown of its head. I don't know what that means but it doesn't sound good. The doctor has Ruth push, I don't know what, and then the baby slides out of Ruth and starts to cry. The doctor says that it is a girl and congratulates the couple. The doctor cuts a cord running from the baby to Ruth, cleans the baby some and gives her to Ruth. The doctor asks Ruth and Adam what they are going to name her. Ruth says that she and Adam have discussed the name and she is to be called, Kendra Jean

The Life Story Of A House

Wilson. The doctor says that is a fine name. The doctor examines
Kendra and says that she is fit as a fiddle. I wonder if that is alright.
Ruth and Adam thank the doctor and Edward takes him back to town.
Ruth and Adam hold Kendra a while and then hand her to Rebecca.
Ruth says that she and Rebecca will have fun raising little Kendra.
Rebecca starts to cry knowing that her sister is going to allow her to
help with the baby.

It is almost spring again; I have heard people over time say there were
four seasons, winter, spring, summer and fall.

Adam says it is the middle of March and he and Edward are talking
about Pancho Villa taking 500 Mexican soldiers and attacking a place
named Columbus, New Mexico. Adam says that the U.S. 13th Cavalry
Regiment fights back and drives the Mexicans away, although the 12
U.S. soldiers are killed. Edward tells Adam that President Wilson sent
12,000 U.S. troops into Mexico to try and catch Pancho Villa. Then the
U.S. 7th and 10th Cavalry join the 13th Cavalry across the border on the
hunt for Villa. I don't know where these places are, but that seems like
a lot of men.

The women are working in the garden the first of April, they have little
Kendra in a basket so they can watch her. The man working out back in
the dirt comes and talks to the women. I can't hear what they are
saying, but they are laughing.

The middle of the year Kendra seems to be crying a lot. Ruth says
Kendra is cutting teeth. I don't know what that means, but it seems to
be hurting the little girl. Ruth keeps putting a wet rag in Kendra's
mouth. I wonder if that eases Kendra's pain. After a while, Kendra
returns to normal.

Every night after supper Adam and Edward listen to the radio and talk
about what they have heard. Once in a while one of the women will say
something, but mostly they continue what they are doing.

The Life Story Of A House

It is the middle of summer when the two men are supposed to be home for supper, but are late. It seems it stays lighter longer in the summertime. There is something coming up the path. It looks like a wagon, but there are no horses in front of it, the horses are behind it. The wagon makes a different noise and when it turns in the path to the house it makes an ooga sound. When the wagon finally stops, Adam and Edward climb out of it. The two men were actually inside the wagon and the wagon moved without horses. The women come outside and see what the men have brought home. Ruth is holding Kendra when all five of them climb into this contraption and go back out of the path. Before they turn to the path towards town, it makes the ooga sound again.

It is a while before the horse less wagon comes back up the path to the house. The two men and two women are laughing as they exited the wagon. When they come in the house, all four of them are talking about the new car. Edward says it cost him one thousand dollars. That sounds like a lot. Edward keeps talking about the car to the women. Edward says that car even has a small heater in the cab of the car so it won't be so cold in the winter. Edward has to put something called fuel in something called the gas tank. A thing called the horn makes the ooga sound. Edward says he has to crank something to make the car start, to turn the engine over. What is an engine? Edward says he makes enough money working at the glass factory to afford the car. The men talk about the car the rest of the night.

In the morning, Edward and Adam get in the car and head down the path towards town, after Edward cranks the engine. The women talk about the car before they go out to weed the garden.

The men take the car everywhere they go now even to church. Edward said the people of the church were impressed by the car.

Edward and Adam are listening to the radio after supper when the man said that a bomb had exploded during a parade in a place called San

Francisco, California. The bomb killed ten people and injured 40 others. It seems to me that some people are different than others, crueler. Eight days later the man on the radio is talking about an explosion in Jersey City, New Jersey, killing at least seven people. The man on the radio said German agents sabotaged an ammunition depot. Edward and Adam talk about the Germans for a while. I wonder what the difference between Edward, Adam and Germans are.

The women bring in all of the crops, putting some in the storm cellar. The man out in back of the house that works in the dirt brings his crops out of the ground, too.

The women are talking about making Thanksgiving dinner already, it doesn't seem like it has been that long since they had the four people for supper. Ruth says that the four friends are coming again. Adam and Edward say they are ready for an extra day off. Off from what?

Thanksgiving Day comes and the smells are just as wonderful as ever. The four friends come down the path and Edward meets them to show them his car. They are impressed but do not spend too much time looking at it since they are all cold from the ride.

While the eight of them are eating dinner, the conversation turns to politics. Ruth tells Adam that he isn't going to talk politics today, is he. Adam talks about the Presidential election, anyway. Adam wants to talk to the four friends about Woodrow Wilson defeating Republican Charles E. Hughes. They talk about that for a while, and then one of the friends brings up the German offer of ten thousand pounds for every American lost in the accidental sinking of the Lusitania and the U.S. rejecting the offer.

The subject finally changes to something else. The four women are playing with Kendra after dinner and the men are talking. The four friends are finally ready to leave and remind Adam, Edward, Ruth and Rebecca to come to town for Christmas dinner.

As the four relax, Edward mentions that he is pleased that he and Adam does not have to freeze everyday going and coming from work.

It is soon Christmas day and before the five leave for town, Kendra gets a present to open. Ruth has to help Kendra open it. It is a doll, something for Kendra to hold onto. The five get in the car to leave, Kendra holding her new friend.

When the five get home and get in the house, Adam says that it is a good thing they do not eat like that every day or they would be fat as pigs. A person can get that fat?

It is New Year's Evening, Kendra is in bed and the four are listening to the radio. The man on the radio says that a hotel in North Augusta, South Carolina, one of the most luxurious in the country burned down. The men talk about that for a while, it didn't say if anyone got killed or not. After the clock turned twelve p.m., the four go to bed.

The four are sitting around the fire one night in January listening to the radio when the man says something about German saboteurs setting off an explosion at Kingsland, New Jersey. Adam explains what a saboteur is. I can't believe there are so many people who hate one another. It seems like the man on the radio never has any good news to report. Eleven days later the man on the radio says that President Woodrow Wilson asks for "Peace without victory" in Europe. Adam and Edward talk about this for some time. They talk about what will happen if the United States enters the war. Ruth says that she is afraid Adam and Edward will have to go to war if the U.S. join the war.

The women try and keep their minds on what they are doing, but it is hard because they are afraid that Adam and Edward will have to go to war. That night in February as the four listen to the radio, the man on the radio says that diplomatic relations with Germany have been broken off. On March 1st the man on the radio says that the U.S. ambassador to the United Kingdom, Walter Page, is shown an intercepted telegram in which Germany offers to give the American Southwest back to

The Life Story Of A House

Mexico if Mexico declares war on the United States. The women are getting worried to the point that it is hard to keep their minds from thinking about U.S. and Germany. They talk constantly about the subject. Ruth has something she wants to tell Adam, but he always seems too occupied with the talk about the problem with Germany. Ruth sometimes talks to herself as if she is trying to find just the right words.

It is the 2nd of April and the women start putting their garden in, Kendra is chasing a butterfly. I can't hear the women but they are constantly talking. When the men come home that night, Ruth tells Adam that she has something to tell him after supper. After supper the first thing the men do is turn the radio on. The man on the radio is already talking about U.S. President Woodrow Wilson asking the U.S. Congress for a declaration of war on Germany. Ruth decides to tell Adam her secret when they go to bed.

After the four go to bed, Adam asks Ruth what she wanted to talk to him about. Ruth says that she is with-child again. Adam sits up in bed and says, "That is good news isn't it". Ruth says that she is afraid he will have to go to war. Adam tells Ruth not to worry until it happens. The two cuddle up together, but Adam can't sleep.

Things are normal for a couple of days, but the men come home from work on April the 6th and tell the women that the United States had declared war on Germany. Both women start to cry. The men try to comfort them but it doesn't help. Kendra sees her Mother crying and starts crying herself. The four are quiet through supper that night and don't even turn the radio on.

The four goes days without saying much to each other. Adam turns on the radio after supper on the night of April 10th. The man on the radio is talking about an explosion at an ammunition factory in Chester, Pennsylvania which kills 133 people. Adam and Edward talk about whether the explosion could have been on purpose. Why would anyone do something like that on purpose?

On May 18th Ruth tells Rebecca that she is with-child again. Before Rebecca can say anything, Ruth tells her that she is so afraid Adam will have to go off to war. Rebecca hugs Ruth and tells her that everything will be alright. That night after supper the man on the radio said the Selective Service Act passed the U.S. Congress, giving the President the power to draft men. The two women start to cry again and the men just look at each other. Adam told Edward that he didn't think the U.S. would get into a war overseas. I don't know where the fighting is going on, but it seems like it is a long way from home. Three days later over 300 acres are destroyed in a fire in Atlanta, Georgia. The man on the radio says that it burned 73 blocks. I wonder what a block is. Five days after the fire the man on the radio talks about a tornado that hit Mattoon, Illinois causing destruction and killing 101 people. Ruth says it is like the world is going crazy. What is crazy and what is the world?

Adam and Edward come home on June 5th looking upset. The women ask what the problem is. Adam said that the government started the draft today. The two women start to cry. The two men try to comfort them but nothing seems to work. Kendra starts to cry too. Ruth asks Adam when he will find out if he has to go, Adam just shakes his head and says, "I don't know".

There is no news from the government by the end of July and the four hope that Adam and Edward have been missed. The man on the radio talks about the war every night before he gets to the other news of the day. A labor dispute in East St. Louis, Illinois leads to a riot that killed 250 people. Several hundred farmers against the U.S. involvement in the war took place in central Oklahoma in August; it is called The Green Corn Rebellion.

One day the mailman stops in front of the house and puts the mail in the box like he has done a hundred times. Ruth goes out to get the mail after she hears the mailman leave. When she got the mail out of the box, Ruth drops some letters on the ground and starts to cry. Rebecca and Kendra come out to see what bad news Ruth has gotten, although, Rebecca tells Kendra she knows what it is.

When Adam and Edward come home for the evening, they can tell Ruth and Rebecca have been crying all day. Adam says, "Where are the letters?" Ruth was thinking of burning the letters, but she thought better of it. Ruth pointed towards the fireplace mantel.

There is a letter for both men. They are to report to Biloxi, Mississippi by the end of September. The men try to comfort the women to no avail. They don't listen to the radio that night. The men are trying to explain why they have to go, and they try to explain why there is a war, but the women don't want to hear it, all they know it is going to put their husbands in harm's way. Poor little Kendra doesn't know what is going on. After the men are done trying to explain the war to the two women, I don't get it. Why does man have to kill man over land?

During their remaining time together, Adam and Edward are trying to make sure that the women will be taken care of. Adam asked the mailman to check on the women and he agreed. Edward was trying to teach Rebecca how to drive the car, but he didn't seem to be having too much luck by the way he talked to Adam. Adam and Edward told the two women that there was money in the bank in town. Adam told them they should go into town once a week for supplies.

One morning Adam and Edward didn't get ready for work; instead they had a bag of clothes with them. Ruth made a big breakfast and then the five of them piled into the car and headed down the path and turned towards town. Adam had told Ruth that they would need a ride into town to catch the train to Biloxi. Catch a train?

It was getting dark when I saw the car come up the road and turn into the path to the house. Where five left, three returned. Ruth and Rebecca were quiet for days. They listened to the radio every night, trying to hear any information on the war that they could, it is all they talk about. One night in November they heard about a bomb going off in Milwaukee, Wisconsin at the Police Department killing nine men.

Ruth's stomach has gotten much bigger and she told Rebecca it should be any time now.

There was no celebration for Thanksgiving this year; Ruth said that the two men friends had been drafted too.

At the end of November the mailman came up the path. I thought that was unusual. Ruth and Rebecca met him outside of the house. He said that he wanted to deliver this letter in person. The women thanked him and he drove away. The women came into the house and sit down. Ruth opened the letter and read it out loud. Ruth told Rebecca the letter is to the both of us. Ruth started to read the letter:

Dearest Ruth and Rebecca,

We just wanted to let you know how much we love you and we hope everything is fine there. Ruth should be about ready to have the baby. I hope you and the baby are safe. Give Kendra a hug and a kiss for me. We are leaving by ship tomorrow to Europe. We are not sure how long we will be there. They tell us a year. We have been training every day, so we should be ready. Try not to worry about us too much, it might hurt the baby. You can try to write to us, but we are not sure that it will reach us or not. Send the letter to the return address on this envelope. They say that there is a lot of trench fighting going on over there. I will try to write you when we get over there. I've got to go now, don't forget to kiss Kendra for me, and kiss the new baby for me. Name the baby what you wish. We both love you two very much.

Adam and Edward

Ruth and Rebecca were crying before Ruth was finished with the letter. Ruth set Kendra on her lap and snuggled her, kissing her on the forehead. I feel so sad for the two women and I hope the two men will be safe.

It is the middle of December when Ruth tells Rebecca that it is time for the baby to come. There is a blizzard outside and Rebecca says that she will have to deliver the baby. Rebecca gets a cloth and heats some water. Ruth says that her water has broken and that it won't be long now. Kendra is just walking around, Rebecca tries to get her to play with her doll and she finally does. Rebecca stands in front of Ruth and tells her to push. It takes about twenty minutes but finally the baby slides out of Ruth's belly. Rebecca cleans the baby after she cuts the cord between Ruth and the new baby. Rebecca holds the baby by the ankles and spanks her. Did she do something wrong already? The baby starts to cry and Rebecca hands the baby to Ruth after she has wrapped it in a warm blanket. Ruth says the baby is a boy and she is going to name him Adam junior.

The women have a small Christmas, mainly just for Kendra. Ruth got Kendra another doll as a present. The women made a small meal like any other day. The women had the man that checks on them bring a small green tree into the house. Ruth told Rebecca that it just didn't feel like Christmas without the men there, Rebecca agreed.

1917 turned to 1918 with no hoopla, Ruth and Rebecca didn't even stay up till mid-night. The women wrote their husbands a letter, but they would have no way to know if the men received it.

When winter turns to spring and still no word has come from the men, Ruth and Rebecca starts to worry, so am I.

The man is out back working the dirt, Ruth and Rebecca are trying to keep their minds on something other than the war. They work in their vegetable and flower garden more than usual. Kendra runs and plays in the yard. Little Adam is put in a basket when the women go outside.

The Life Story Of A House

The women listen to the radio after supper trying to hear any bit of information about the war. On May 20th the man on the radio talks about Codell, Kansas, a small town being hit by a tornado for the third year in a row. What is really weird all three tornadoes hit on May 20th.

The man on the radio talked about a train wreck in Nashville, Tennessee, on July 9th. An inbound train collided with an outbound express, killing 101 people. I guess trains are dangerous too.

A strange car came up the path to the house at the last of July. Both Ruth and Rebecca saw the car and began to cry. Two men all dressed up got out of the car and told the women something. Rebecca fell to the ground crying while Ruth tried talking to her. The two men left in the car. Ruth helped Rebecca into the house and to bed. Rebecca was sobbing that she didn't know what she was going to do without Edward. Why does Rebecca have to do without Edward? Rebecca said that the two men said that they wouldn't be able to send the body home for burial. Edward must be dead, poor Rebecca. Ruth tries to tell her sister that she can stay in the house with her and her family. That night they don't say much to each other, the radio is not even turned on.

The women load the two children into the car and take off down the path. It must be the day to go to church. Maybe going to church will help Rebecca. I hear the women talking to God, asking for strength.

The women came home from church later than usual. When the women came into the house, I heard Ruth tell Rebecca that we would have our own service since Edward's body is not coming home. Rebecca just cries.

The next day the women go out to where the other graves are and say a few words. I can't hear them, but they are probably praying to God. God must be someone special since everyone that has lived in the house talked to him.

The Life Story Of A House

Two months go by and still no word from Adam. Ruth is nervous at the thought of being a widow. Ruth has asked God to give her strength in case she becomes one.

The two women have started to listen to the radio again. The man on the radio talks about U.S. Corporal Alvin C. York almost single-handedly killing 25 Germans and capturing another 132. This was October 8th in France. The women are impressed by this. Four days later the man on the radio talks about a fire in Minnesota and some nearby areas, killing 453 people. The man on the radio must be busy. A ship called the Princess Sophia crashes into a reef near Juneau, Alaska killing 353 people. I wonder what a reef is and where is Alaska? On November 1st there was a rapid transit train wreck under two roads in Brooklyn, New York killing 93. How do you get a train under the roads?

Thanksgiving goes by and there is still no word from Adam. Ruth is talking about the worst, if Ruth and Rebecca become widows they will have to move. I wonder why they would have to move if there were no men living here.

In the middle of December a car comes up the path towards the house. Ruth starts to cry telling Rebecca it must be bad news. The door of the car opens and out walks Adam. Ruth goes running out of the house and runs to Adams open arms. Ruth is still crying, I wonder why. Adam has a limp; Ruth helps him into the house. Before Adam can sit down, Kendra runs up and hugs and kisses her Father. Ruth holds out the baby, Adam Jr. for Adam to hold for the first time. After the initial commotion is over, Ruth notices that Rebecca is not in the room. Ruth finds Rebecca lying on her bed crying. Ruth pleads with Rebecca to come to the kitchen to join them. When the two women come into the kitchen, Rebecca hugs Adam. Adam starts telling Rebecca a story of how Edward got killed. Their platoon was fighting the enemy in hand to hand combat. The Americans were holding their own, waiting for re-enforcements. Some of the Americans were fighting in the trenches and some were not. Edward and Adam had been trying to stick together, and had so far. This battle however, was huge, and they had somehow got separated. I was trying to work myself forward, killing the enemy as I went. I was in the trenches and I looked up briefly and saw Edward going forward like I was. As I was running, I noticed the trench curved up ahead. I knew it was probably a trap, but I kept running. There were men behind me and above me. Before I could get to the corner of the trench, Edward jumped in the trench in front of me. I yelled at Edward to wait for me, but he went around the corner and was shot numerous times. The men in the trench stopped but the Americans up above the trench opened fire on the enemy, wiping them out. We only had time to bury our dead before we were supposed to move forward. Edward was buried next to five other Americans. Edward saved my life; it is something I will think about every day for the rest of my life. Rebecca was still crying but she felt pride that Edward had died saving someone else.

They had a green tree this year but they stayed home. Both of their male friends from town were killed. Their wife's had to move back home with their parents. Adam kept telling Rebecca she could stay there but she said she would think about it over the winter.

Soon it turned to 1919, the war was over and Adam hopes for a better year. Adam went back to the bank in town and where they were holding his job for him. Adam seemed to be more thankful for everything he had, Ruth, Kendra, Adam, a house and a job. Adam told Ruth that he felt blessed.

Ruth talked Rebecca in to staying with them for a while, as Rebecca did not have anywhere else to go.

One night when the radio was on the man was talking about a molasses disaster. The man on the radio said that a storage tank exploded sending a wave of molasses through Boston, Massachusetts, killing 21 people and injuring 150. I wonder what molasses is. The man also talks about Prohibition going into effect in something called the

Constitution. The man said it was the 18th Amendment and said people were no longer supposed to drink alcohol. I know what alcohol is but how can someone tell you not to drink it.

Adam was taking Edward's car to work; he said he would pay a little each month to Rebecca for it.

The five of them leave in the car on Sunday going to church when the weather permits.

Spring finally arrives and the snow has melted. Kendra plays outside while the women work in the garden or hang wet clothes outside on a piece of rope tied between two poles. The day after the family goes to church they do what they call laundry. They have two metal tubs, they scratch the clothes on something they call a washboard. One tub has soapy water in it and one tub has clean water in it. They only hang the clothes outside when they weather lets them, the other times they hang a rope in the house.

The summers seem to be going by faster as it is September already. The man on the radio talks about a hurricane hitting the Florida Keys and Texas. The hurricane killed 600 people over a five day period, wow, that's a lot. At the end of the month the man on the radio talks about a lynch mob in Omaha, Nebraska overpowering the police station and courthouse. The mob lynches alleged rapist Will Brown. I wonder what lynches mean, and also rapist.

Ruth tells Adam that she is pregnant again. This seems to please Adam. Ruth tells Adam the baby will come in the summer. I wonder how people figure out when the baby is going to come.

Right before Christmas the man on the radio talks about the Red Scare. The United States deported 249 people back to Russia. I do not know what any of this means.

Christmas comes and they have a big meal this year. The smells are terrific. Kendra gets another doll; Adam Jr. gets a toy truck. Adam Jr. plays with the truck, rolling it back and forth on the floor.

The Wilson's and Rebecca go to church this year on New Year's Evening. When they come home, they have a small party to bring in the New Year, 1920. Adam prays to God that this year is better than the last. If everyone talks to God, I wonder how God hears everyone.

The winter is not too harsh so the family can leave the house more. Adam seems to be taking the family to town more often. I wonder what they are doing; I have not heard them talking about anything in particular.

In March the man on the radio talks about the tornado outbreak that struck from the Great Lakes area all the way down to the Deep South. All of this happened on Palm Sunday. I do not know where those places are, but it did storm here. Adam was talking about the wind when they came back from church.

Summer finally arrives; Rebecca is putting in the garden since Ruth's belly is so big. Adam comes home from work and tells Rebecca that they didn't know what they would do without her. I don't know why, but Rebecca cries. After supper Adam is listening to the radio and starts to laugh. Adam asks the women if they had heard the last story on the radio. They said that they did not. Adam says that the man on the radio said that the United States Postal Service ruled that children may not be sent via parcel post. The women and Adam laugh hysterically. I don't get it.

Ruth tells Rebecca it is time. Rebecca says that she will deliver the baby and then ride into town on a horse and get the doctor. Rebecca boils some water and gathers plenty of clean towels. It seemed like the baby slid out faster than the last time. Rebecca cut the cord that runs from the baby to inside Ruth. Rebecca wipes off the baby, which is crying. Rebecca tells Ruth that the baby is a girl. Ruth seems happy by this news. Rebecca asks Ruth if she will be alright while she rides into town. Ruth tells Rebecca to go ahead; Kendra is there to keep her company. While Rebecca is gone Ruth asks Kendra what they should name the new baby. Kendra does not know she is only four.

The doctor arrives right after Rebecca comes home. The doctor examines the baby and then Ruth. The doctor says they are both healthy. The doctor asks Ruth what she and Adam are going to name the new little girl. Ruth says that she does not know. The women thank the doctor and then he goes back toward town. When Adam gets home from work, he is happy. The doctor already stopped at the bank and told him. Ruth asks Adam what he wants to name the little girl. Adam leans down to whisper to Ruth. Ruth says that is a wonderful idea. Rebecca is about done making supper, when Adam and Ruth call her into the room. Ruth says that we decided to name the new baby, Rebecca. Rebecca does not know what to say, so she cries. Adam goes over to Rebecca to hold her, and then he gently sits her on the bed next to Ruth who hands Rebecca the baby to hold. Rebecca is so happy that she cannot stop crying. When Kendra comes over to the bed and tells her Mother that she is hungry, Rebecca goes and gets supper.

Until Ruth gets her strength back, Rebecca does all of the cooking, cleaning and washing of clothes. Rebecca does not seem to mind, but Ruth wants to be strong enough to help Rebecca bring the crops out of the garden.

One night after supper the man on the radio talked about someone putting a bomb in a horse drawn wagon. It explodes in front of a building in New York City, killing 38 and injuring 400. I wonder what happened to the horse.

There was an early snow this winter, Adam says it is only the first part of November and it is not supposed to snow this early. Adam says that he is glad to have a car to help him stay warm. I wonder who decides when it is supposed to snow. That night when Adam gets home from work, Ruth has made him his favorite kind of pie. Ruth says it would help Adam warm up. How can pie help you warm up. After having pie, Adam brings his coffee to his chair and sits down to listen to the radio. The man on the radio still talks, but they are playing what they call music more. Music is nice and comforting. Before Adam turns the radio off and goes to bed, the man on the radio said that Warren G. Harding has defeated James M. Cox in the U.S. presidential election. I wonder what the president does.

Rebecca and the Wilson's celebrate Thanksgiving, Christmas and it is already New Year's Evening. It is not snowing so they all get in the car and go to church. When they come home they just sit by the fire and talk about all of the things they are thankful for. Junior is sitting on his Father's lap, Kendra on Rebecca's and Ruth is holding the baby, Rebecca. I can feel the love radiating from this one room, it is wonderful.

On the 2nd day of the New Year, in addition to the news the man on the radio tells us, Ruth says they are playing gospel music. It is nice. I wonder if this is part of the reason the family goes to church every week.

It seems like time is flying by, it is spring already. The women are putting in the garden, the flowers are opening up and the man in back is working in the dirt. Ruth is back to helping Rebecca with the chores, they just have one more child to watch.

Adam has to take a week off of work. The doctor said that Adam has some kind of virus. Ruth nurses Adam back to health. Adam manages to go back to work on the second week. Adam is as good as new in a couple of weeks.

It is May already, and the man on the radio says that in Blackstone, Virginia, a 20-ton meteorite lands. I wonder what a ton is and a meteorite.

The Life Story Of A House

In June, the U.S. President, Warren G. Harding, makes his first speech on the radio. The President just sounds like any other man to me.

The family goes to church every Sunday, and Rebecca has been acting extremely happy to go to church lately. Rebecca and Ruth talk about someone named Charles Johnson, and they seem to be quite excited when they talk about him.

A couple of weeks later, Rebecca is wearing her Sunday dress, but it is not Sunday. Ruth and her talk about the special supper they are making for Charles. Adam walks into the house from work and says that it smells good in here. Adam tells Ruth that she did not have to go to all that trouble for him. Rebecca hits Adam in the arm and says, "You know Charles Johnson is coming over for supper tonight". Adam says that he forgot. Adam hugs Rebecca, and says, "I hope he feels for you like you feel for him". Rebecca asks Adam if he doesn't think it's too soon after Edward died. Adam says, "No, it has been five years. You deserve to be happy".

Mr. Johnson comes down the path in a car just like Adam's. Mr. Johnson knocks on the door and Rebecca answers it. Mr. Johnson tells Rebecca how good she looks and that supper smells really good. Rebecca seems pleased. They all talk during supper. The children try to join in on the conversation, but the adults ignore them. From the conversation, I can tell Mr. Johnson owns the grocery store in town and has been a widower for seven years. They all sit around the table having their pie and coffee and Mr. Johnson asks Adam how it is going at the bank. Adam says that he hopes to be head teller soon. Mr. Johnson says that the store is as busy as ever, he might even have to hire another person to help. From what I get from the conversation, Mr. Johnson already has a young man helping him. When Mr. Johnson is ready to leave, Rebecca walks him to the door. Mr. Johnson tells Rebecca that he had a wonderful time and he hoped they could do it again. Rebecca says that she would like that.

The Life Story Of A House

Adam teases Rebecca about having to make plans for a wedding. Rebecca says that she hoped so. I have figured out when Adam is teasing someone.

In July, Mr. Johnson asks Rebecca to go to a dance with him. Rebecca says that she does not know how to dance, Ruth tells her to let Charles hold her and follow his lead. I do not know what this dancing is but the women act like it will be fun. The day of the dance, Mr. Johnson rides up the path in his car. Rebecca is ready, but she is surprised Ruth and Adam are not going. Ruth tells Rebecca that just the two of them would have more fun than if an old married couple was with them. Rebecca reminds her sister that Ruth is only two years older than Rebecca. Both women laugh. Ruth says we don't have a babysitter, anyway. Mr. Johnson knocks on the door and Rebecca answers it and Mr. Johnson says how lovely Rebecca looks. The two of them say good-by and they go up the path toward town. Ruth tells Adam how much fun Rebecca will have. Adam promises to take Ruth dancing soon; they would just have to find someone to watch the children.

Later that evening, a car comes up the path and Rebecca and Mr. Johnson get out. Mr. Johnson walks Rebecca to the door. I don't understand considering it is not very far to the door and it is not that dark out. When the two get to the door, Mr. Johnson kisses Rebecca for a long time. After a while, Rebecca tells Mr. Johnson that she should go in the house. Mr. Johnson says, "Just one more kiss". They kiss slowly and Mr. Johnson says that he wants to see Rebecca tomorrow after church. Rebecca invites him to come there for dinner, but Mr. Johnson suggests that they go in town for dinner. Rebecca agrees, and they kiss one more time before Mr. Johnson leaves. Rebecca goes into the house and Ruth is sitting up with the baby. The baby is teething. Rebecca sits down with Ruth and tells her how her evening went. Ruth says that she is so happy for her. Rebecca tells Ruth that Charles wants to take her in to town for dinner after church tomorrow. Ruth says that maybe Charles is going to ask Rebecca to marry him. Rebecca says, "I hope so".

The Life Story Of A House

Sunday comes and the family goes to church like usual but Rebecca is not with them when they come home. Over dinner Ruth tells Adam that she hopes that Charles asks Rebecca to marry him. Adam says that Rebecca should have some happiness in her life. After a couple hours, a car comes up the path and Rebecca and Mr. Johnson get out of the car and walk toward the door, and they are holding hands.

Rebecca and Mr. Johnson come in the house and tell Adam and Ruth that they have good news. Rebecca says that they are going to marry in the fall. Rebecca and Ruth hug and Mr. Johnson and Adam shake hands. Rebecca says after the marriage they are going to live in town. Ruth says it won't be the same living without you. Ruth doesn't tell the newly engaged couple their secret. After Rebecca left for the day with Mr. Johnson, Ruth told Adam that she was pregnant again. Ruth tells Adam that she is two months along and has seven months to go. Ruth tells Adam that she will tell Rebecca in a couple of days, to let her have her happiness for a couple of days.

That night they listen to the radio and it is playing a different kind of music, not slow. Adam says that he doesn't know if he likes the new-fangled music and then picks up little Kendra and starts to dance around the room. Kendra is squealing because she is happy. Ruth gets into the act, and she starts dancing with Adam Jr. They seem to be having a good time. Rebecca is smiling as she watches the four having a good time, little Rebecca is already in bed. They all go to bed smiling that night; it seems that the music has made everyone happy.

A couple of days later Ruth tells Rebecca that she is pregnant again. Rebecca hugs Ruth and says that she is so happy for her and Adam. Rebecca says that even if she is married, she will come out and spend a couple of days with Ruth until she has her baby. Ruth thanks her and they hug again.

I guess Mr. Johnson's name is Charles that is what everyone calls him. Charles comes out to the house on the week-end and on Wednesday night. Usually Rebecca and Charles go somewhere on the week-end and stay here on Wednesday.

It comes the day of the wedding and both ladies look pretty in their best dresses. Adam is going to take the two ladies and the three children to the church and meet Charles there. Rebecca has already told Ruth that she and Charles are going to live in town at his house. It will be different not having Rebecca around anymore. As they drive down the path, I can't help but feel a little bit sad.

It is late that night when I see headlights coming up the path. It is the family and they all look tired. Ruth and Adam are carrying the children in, Adam carrying the two youngest and they put them directly to bed. Adam and Ruth sit a while and discuss the wedding. They both agree that Rebecca looked wonderful and that she looked happier than she has for a long time.

It is March 1923, and Rebecca has been staying out at the house for a couple of days. They are waiting for Ruth to have her baby. After a couple of more days, Ruth has her baby, a girl. After Rebecca cleans the baby she says she is going in town to get the doctor. As Rebecca rides away on a horse, you can tell it is still cold because you can see her breath. The doctor comes out and checks Ruth and the baby, and says that they are fine. The doctor asks Ruth what she is going to name the baby. Ruth tells him that Adam and she will have to discuss it. The doctor says he can take Rebecca back into town if Ruth is done with her. Ruth knows that she could use the help for a couple of more days, but she tells Rebecca to go ahead and ride back to town with the doctor. Ruth knows that Rebecca and Charles have been apart long enough. Rebecca asks if Ruth is sure she can handle things around the house with a newborn to watch. Ruth says that she can and thanks the doctor and Rebecca for all that they have done for her.

When Adam comes home that night, he sees that Ruth is still in bed. Adam comes over to the bed to see his new daughter; he asks Ruth what she wants to name the baby girl. Adam and Ruth discuss it a while and decide to name her Eva. Ruth asks Adam if he will make the children something to eat. Adam says that he will and tells Ruth that he has taken a couple of days off of work so he can help around the house. Ruth is so happy to hear this that she begins to cry. I wonder what Adam said to make Ruth cry.

Ruth must be feeling better, she is out planting the garden and it has only been a month since she had the baby. Kendra and Adam Jr are running around the house and young Rebecca is trying to keep up with them, but can't. Ruth has baby Eva lying on the ground on a blanket. The man that works in the dirt out back comes into the yard to talk to Ruth; he says that he just wants to see the new baby. He looks at her, says that she is beautiful and then goes back to his dirt. For some reason, Adam doesn't like that the man came over to see the new baby while he wasn't at home. Ruth says that she doesn't understand why Adam is so upset. Adam says it is because we don't know that man. Ruth tries to tell Adam that the man has never come over before, not to worry. Adam says that it is his job to worry. I wonder what this word worry means. Ruth and Adam do not talk to each other the rest of the night. I don't understand. It takes a couple of days, but everything goes back to normal.

Adam and Ruth are listening to the radio and the man says that in Southeastern Michigan they had six inches of snow and what was worse; the temperature fell from 62 degrees to 34 degrees in a five hour period, which was a record for that date. Adam says that he is glad it did not do that here and Ruth agrees.

The older children play outside when the weather allows, and Ruth has told the children to stay in the yard. A lady has started coming up the path to visit Ruth and she has a daughter Kendra's age. Whenever the lady called, Norah comes, her daughter, Janet and Kendra like to play with each other; they try to hide from Adam Jr. Usually while the women talk about current events, the children play. Janet asks Ruth if she has heard that President Warring G. Harding has died in office and the V.P. takes over, and he is Calvin Coolidge.

It is about harvest time and the children are playing in back, even farther back than the outhouse. Kendra, Janet and Adam Jr. are playing hide and seek. Janet has closed her eyes and is counting while Kendra and Adam hide. Kendra runs back toward the house, Adam goes to hide in the corn field out beyond the outhouse. Adam knows he is not supposed to go past the property line. Janet finishes her counting and runs toward the house looking for the other two children. Pretty soon the two girls hear a blood curdling scream. Ruth and Norah run out of the house as the horse raises its legs again and comes down on the little boy. The horse reared its legs up four times, until the man could get it under control. The women run to where Adam's body lay motionless, and Ruth begins to cry as she holds her limp son. The children are crying now. Norah tells Ruth to pile everyone into her car and they will go into town to see the doctor. The man on the horse just keeps apologizing as Ruth holds the limp body of her son. I see the car as it speeds down the path toward town.

When the family comes home later that day, Adam Sr. is with Ruth and they only have three children with them and Ruth and Kendra are crying. Once they get into the house I can hear them talking about having Adam Junior's service. Adam says the service will be at the church and the boy will be buried in the cemetery by the church. Ruth tries to put Kendra to bed, but they are both crying to hard. How sad it is when a little child dies, it is almost like I can feel their pain.

The day of the service arrives and the family head to the church. When they come home Ruth tries to comfort Kendra but she is not having any luck. Adam is just sitting in his chair, looking into the empty fireplace.

Adam doesn't have too much to say when he comes home from work and it stays this way until the end of the year when he starts to open up a little. Having Adam act like that has not helped Ruth heal from the loss of her son, Kendra is still quiet, but she is starting to come out of her shell. Lucky for her Norah still brings Janet over to play.

Christmas just doesn't seem the same without little Adam. Ruth and Adam try to hide their emotions for Kendra's sake, but the little girl can sense the unhappiness and just goes through the motions, too.

It turns 1924 and things are not any better, Ruth does not know if Adam blames her for the little boy's death. At least they have gotten back into the habit of turning the radio on; maybe they are both tired of the silence. Woodrow Wilson, the 28th President of the United States died on February 3, he was 68. Also the man on the radio says that on February 7th in the United States, Nevada has put to death a man in the first state execution by using gas. They actually killed someone; I wonder what he did to deserve to die. In March the man on the radio talks about a mine disaster in Utah. 172 miners were killed. There is so much death on the radio, sometimes I wish that they wouldn't even turn the radio on.

Rebecca has started coming out to visit Ruth, although most of the time they talk about Adam Juniors death or the fact that Adam hasn't said much since the accident. Rebecca says that it helps Ruth to talk about things instead of keeping them all bottled up inside.

Ruth puts in a garden like usual, she reminds Kendra not to go beyond the outhouse. The man that was riding the horse that killed little Adam has come over to the house more than once to say he was sorry and to please forgive him. Ruth told him it was an accident, but Adam doesn't say a word to the man. Ruth tells Adam that it would help him heal if he forgave the man. I wonder how forgiving the man would heal Adam.

Adam tells Ruth that he would like to try for another boy. Ruth tells Adam that nothing would replace Adam Junior. They discuss the matter some more and Ruth finally gives in. Ruth says she will try and get pregnant again. I still don't know how one gets pregnant.

Adam acts a little happier now that they are trying for a boy. I wonder who chooses between having a baby boy or a girl.

Rebecca comes out to visit Ruth more now, I guess because of the accident with Junior. Rebecca still doesn't have any children. Sometimes they don't talk for minutes, but it seems like hours. Finally Ruth tells Rebecca about Adams request and how she doesn't want any more children. Rebecca tells Ruth that maybe she will get lucky the first time and have a boy. Ruth says that she can only hope and pray. I wonder if praying helps to decide if the baby is a boy or a girl.

The man on the radio says that two students murdered a 14-year old Bobby Franks in a thrill killing. The two boys are found out to be University of Chicago students Richard Loeb and Nathan Leopold JR. Why would anybody kill a child?

November comes and there is still no baby. The man on the radio says that Calvin Coolidge has won the presidential election against John W. Davis and Robert M. LaFollette, SR.

There is a Thanksgiving dinner with Rebecca and her husband, Charles. Ruth says there is no news on the baby front. Ruth thinks Adam is getting anxious, like she is trying not to have a baby. I wonder if you can keep from having a baby.

The man on the radio says that U.S. bootleggers are using Thompson submachine guns due to prohibition. Adam talks about this for a while with Ruth. I guess prohibition is that you cannot sell alcohol. Adam says that it will be hard to catch the moonshiners if they have such guns as those. I wonder what bootleggers and moonshiners are and why can't you buy alcohol.

December turns into New Years, it is 1925 and still no baby.

A tornado rages through Missouri, Illinois and Indiana on March 18th, killing 695 people and injuring 2,027. Adam tells Ruth that they had been lucky so far. I remember one going through before Ruth and Adam lived here.

Adam comes home like usual on April 7th. Ruth tells him after supper that she has something to tell him in private. The two go into their bedroom and Ruth tells Adam that she thinks that she is pregnant. Adam is so happy; he hugs Ruth and said he was beginning to wonder if she was ever going to get pregnant. Adam now has the spring back in his step. He even plays with the three girls. I wonder why Ruth doesn't seem too happy by the news.

Rebecca comes out to the house for a visit and Ruth tells her the news. Rebecca is happy for her, but she can tell Ruth is not happy. Rebecca asks her sister why she isn't happy. Ruth says," Adam wants a boy so much that I am afraid if the baby is another girl that he will want to keep trying and I don't feel right this time". Rebecca asks her what is wrong but Ruth says that she does not know. Rebecca tells Ruth that when the time is about to come, she will come out and care for her. Ruth hugs her sister and tells her she doesn't think the baby will be due until the first of January. Rebecca goes home and Ruth starts crying. Kendra comes to her Mother and wants to know what is wrong. Kendra is nine now and curious about everything. Ruth tells her daughter that she is going to have another baby. Kendra hugs her Mother and Ruth tells the girl that everything will be alright.

Adam seems to have a purpose once again for coming home, he seems happier. I don't understand why he wasn't happy before. Adam has a wife and three daughters. Junior has been dead for a year and a half. I wonder how long people think of the people they have lost in their lives.

Adam is listening to the radio on the night of June 29th when the man says that downtown Santa Barbara, California has been destroyed by a 6.3 earthquake. Ruth is starting to show signs of the baby growing inside of her. From listening to Ruth and Rebecca talk, I think I

The Life Story Of A House

understand most of the process of having a baby. I just don't know how a woman gets pregnant.

Thanksgiving turns to Christmas and then to New Years. It is 1926 now and Ruth looks like her stomach is about to explode. Rebecca has been staying at the house since before Christmas.

It is the 10th of January when Ruth starts to have her baby. Rebecca is getting hot water and warm towels. I can't wait to see if it is a boy or a girl. Ruth seems to be having a hard time this time. Rebecca tells Kendra to take the girls upstairs and keep them busy. Rebecca says that the baby is a breach baby. I don't know what that means. Rebecca tells Ruth that as soon as she has the baby, she will go and fetch the doctor. Rebecca seems to have a worried look on her face. Ruth is screaming and Rebecca is trying to hold her up a little. Rebecca tells Ruth to push which it looks like she is doing with all her might. Finally the baby comes out, but Ruth has passed out. Rebecca is worried about this. Rebecca is talking to herself, wondering what she should do now; Ruth had never passed out with any of the other children. Rebecca cleans off the baby, it is a boy. Rebecca calls Kendra down and tells her to sit and watch the baby; she has put the baby in Ruth's arms even though she is passed out. Rebecca tells Kendra that she is going into town and getting the doctor. As Rebecca walks out the door she is crying and says that Ruth is bleeding too much.

The doctor and Rebecca come back and ask Kendra if her Mommy has woke up yet. Kendra says that she hasn't. Rebecca thanks the little girl for being so brave, but now she needs her to go upstairs and check on her sisters again. As Kendra is leaving, Rebecca tells Kendra the baby is a boy. The doctor examines Ruth and says she is barely breathing and that she has lost a lot of blood. Rebecca told Adam before she left town, she says out loud. Rebecca is hysterical; she says all Adam said was, "Is the baby a boy." He didn't even ask how Ruth was. Adam finally shows up at home and finds Rebecca crying and the doctor just pulling the sheet over Ruth's face. Adam said, "What about the baby".

Rebecca lets him have it now. She says, "You bastard, you don't even care if Ruth died or not as long as you got your precious son. Ruth was always a little leery of this pregnancy and she was right. I just hope you are happy now". Before Adam can say anything Rebecca is walking out of the door, getting on her horse and riding off to tell Charles. Adam asked the doctor what had happened to Ruth. The doctor said that she had an aneurism that burst and made her bleed profusely. The doctor told Adam, "Good-luck" as he was leaving. Adam didn't know what to do; he had a dead wife, a newborn baby and three little girls to watch over. Kendra came down and asked if Mommy was going to make supper? Adam just started to cry.

Pretty soon a car came up the path and it was Rebecca, Charles and a strange man. Rebecca came into the house and asked Kendra if she would like to help her make supper. Kendra was excited and forgot all of the things that were bothering her. Charles and the other man cleaned up Ruth, preparing for the burial service. Adam doesn't know what to do, he just holds his baby boy.

After supper and when Charles and the other man had finished with Ruth, Rebecca went upstairs to get the girls some clothes. When they came downstairs, Rebecca told the girls to go and get in the car. Charles comes over to Adam and takes the baby from his arms and Rebecca says, "You cannot watch the children by yourself. If you chose to, you can visit them at my house. Adam tries to argue that he can watch the children, but it is no use, Rebecca is taking the children for their own welfare. As the car pulls out of the driveway and onto the path, Adam talks to himself and asks what just happened.

Adam goes into the house and just stares at the body of Ruth wrapped in cloth. Adam sits on the side of the bed and tells her that he is sorry.

The next day some of the men from town come out to the house and get Ruth's body. Rebecca is with them, she tells Adam that the service will be in town tomorrow. Adam asks how his children are. Rebecca says that they are fine.

Adam dresses in his good clothes and goes into town for Ruth's service. As Adam drives down the path, I wonder what happened, why did Ruth have to die and are the girls going to come back home.

Adam's car comes up the path, but when he gets out he is by himself. Adam just sits in the house, in the dark by himself. Adam goes into town every day, I guess to go to work and comes home by himself every evening. This goes on for what seems like weeks until one day Adam rides the horse into town and comes back with two wagons. I wondered what the wagons were for until Adam started to load all of the furniture and clothes on it. I am so sad; I will never get to see Kendra and the others again. When Adam gets both wagons full, he hooks them together, gets on his horse and rides off.

Before Adam left he nailed something to the front door. I wonder what it is.

I feel lonely already and it has only been one day.

The days go by and turn into weeks, then into months. The man is out working in the dirt. He comes up to the house and walks around it. He stops at the front door and reads what is nailed there, "For Sale". I wonder if that means they are looking for another family to live here.

Before long it is cold and snowing. With no fire in the fireplace it doesn't feel as warm as it did with a family. I am so lonely.

Winter finally turns to spring and the flowers are starting to bloom. It turns warm in the summer and when the man harvests his crops I know it is about to turn cold again.

I miss the people talking, even the man on the radio.

The Life Story Of A House

There is so much dust and cobwebs around the house. I am starting to see little creatures living in the house again. Pretty soon since they are going to the bathroom on the floor instead of the outhouse, it smells awful.

I wonder how long it has been since I have had people inside me. Even the man that works in the dirt doesn't come up to the house anymore, he just uses the outhouse.

There is a huge storm that blows so hard that some of my shingles fly off of the siding and the roof. The weird thing was that there wasn't any rain, just dirt blowing.

This is weird, the man that works in the dirt has planted the field but he hasn't gotten anything to harvest for years.

There is a car pulling in the path, I am so excited, someone may actually look me over. I can't believe it; the car is just turning around. I feel so helpless.

It has been cold but very little snow this winter. The animal population seems to be getting larger. One of the doors blew open, so now there are birds in the house. The birds are very dirty.

Spring again and it is dry and blowing again. With the door flopping open, the dust is even worse. I think the animals are coming in the house to seek shelter from the dust. All of the women of the house kept me so clean, and now I'm dirtier than I have ever been, even when I was first built. The man that works in the dirt doesn't even plant the crops this year.

Another winter, another summer, it seems like no one will ever move back in to the house. People drive back and forth in front of the house, never stopping in.

The years fly by and I have given up hope of ever getting another family to move in. Sometimes I wish this suffering would go away.

The Life Story Of A House

One day in the spring after a good rain which finally made the dust settle, a car pulled into the path, and it is not turning around. There are two men and a woman getting out of the car. The men are talking about something outside, but I cannot hear them. The woman comes in the house and says, "What a mess". Finally the two men come into the house. The woman tells the men that with a little work and a lot of cleaning it could be made a house again. One man tells the other that there is a well in back, unless it is froze up. I thought it was too warm for anything to be frozen up. The woman goes upstairs and yells out, the men run up the stairs only to see a family of animals living in one of the bedrooms. One of the men calls the animals raccoons. The woman says that the house would have to be checked for varmints, whatever a varmint is. One man asks the woman if she thinks it can be cleaned. The woman says if you get all of the critters out; open the windows to let some air in and some of the stink out and a lot of dusting and cleaning. The woman tells the men to go outside and make sure the pump works. The woman is opening windows while the men go outside and find the well handle creaks as it goes up and down. Finally water comes out of the opening, first it is very dirty and then it clears up. One man tells the other that the well can be oiled, whatever that is. Oh please, I hope the man and woman want me. The woman walks outside and walks around the property until she comes upon the graves that are in the backyard. She kneels down to look at each stone. I remember Anna and Ellis and the others. The woman tells the men about them and one of the men asks her if they matter that they are there, she says no. One of the men tells the other man and woman that they will go back to his office and talk price, if they wish. The man looks at the woman, and she nods her head yes. They get in the car and drive down the path and head towards town.

Maybe, oh maybe they will come back.

The next day I hope to see the car come up the path, but none ever does, they only pass in front of the house. Maybe tomorrow I hope.

The Life Story Of A House

The next day a car comes up the path, I am excited because it stops at the backdoor. The man and woman from the other day and two boys and a girl get out of the car. The woman tells the three children and the man what she wants done and in what order. They are going to clean the place. The girl holds her nose and says, "Can you get the stink out, Momma". The woman says that she hopes to with some scrubbing. The man and the boys go upstairs to try and run the animals out of the house. They are using brooms to try and get them to leave. The animals are reluctant to leave but finally the man gets them to leave. The man calls the other men sons, and the woman calls the girl, daughter. It is a family, the children aren't small, but with a little cleaning, I hope they will move in.

It takes a week of hard work to get the place livable again. The man's name is Henry and the first thing he did was make sure there wasn't anything living in the outhouse, just some birds that had made a nest. The man fixed the door and the woman has been burning candles to try and cover the smell. If it were cool, they could light the fireplace, but they only light it once because they wanted to make sure there wasn't an obstruction in the chimney which could fill the house with smoke. The man says, "Good, the chimney is all clear and ready for winter, after I cut some wood". The man called one of his sons, Jacob and the other William. The woman calls the young girl, Lorna. They leave every day when they are finished working and cleaning.

One day there is a whole row of cars coming up the path, but they aren't cars. They look like cars in the front and wagons in the rear. There is furniture on all of the wagons/cars; I wonder what they are called. One man tells another to back the truck up, it is called a truck.

Jacob, William and Lorna are arguing who gets what room. The woman is giving the men directions to where every piece of furniture goes. How exciting to be clean and have people living in me again. The woman is called Amelia. Hey, that's the same name as another girl that lived here. Before they are done unloading, someone calls Henry and

Amelia the Johnson's. When they are done unloading the women have made dinner for everyone. Finally, the smell of food is back and oh how I have missed it.

After everyone has had their fill of food, Amelia thanks all of her friends for helping with the move. Henry and Amelia wave good-bye to their friends as they drive down the path, leaving one car which must be Henry's.

That night Henry lit up what he called a cigar. Amelia says, "We just got one smell out and now you want to replace it with another". Henry just smiles and blows out some smoke and says, "This will cover up the other smells". He is right, the cigar smells a lot better than the way it had smelled. Amelia asks Henry if he is going to turn the radio on tonight. Henry reaches over and turns a knob on a box and it lights up, but there is a different man talking. I wonder what happened to the first man. The new man on the radio is talking about a war. I wonder if the war has started up again. Amelia says, "I hope this whole mess gets over before Jacob and William are old enough to join". Henry puffs on his cigar and nods. The children go downstairs to tell their parents goodnight. Henry teases Lorna, "If you wake up with a visitor in bed with you, don't scream, just roll over and go back to sleep, we'll get it in the morning". Lorna says, "Thanks a lot Dad, now I'll never go to sleep". Henry and the boys laugh, but Amelia takes her daughter up to her bedroom, so she can show her there is nothing up there. When Amelia comes back downstairs, she says, "You shouldn't pick on the girl, she is only eleven". Henry just laughs and asks Amelia if the boys were sharing a room. Amelia says that they were, and Henry says, "Good, good".

When Henry and Amelia go to bed she is still talking about the war. Henry says, "Jacob is 15 and William is 13, if the war is going on that long, we will all be in trouble".

The Life Story Of A House

I feel warm and loved again. No patter of little feet on the floor, but there are people in the house once more.

The next day must be Sunday because Amelia is trying to get the three children to get ready for church. Amelia says that she doesn't know why Henry can't go. I thought everyone went to church unless the weather was too bad. Amelia and the three children get into the car, but something is different. Amelia is driving. They head down the path and towards town. Henry sits in his chair and turns on the radio. The man on the radio says that it is June the 2nd, 1939. 1939, when Ruth died and the house emptied it was 1926.

When Amelia and the three children come home, Amelia fixes lunch. Henry tells the boys that he still has a week off of work and tomorrow they would start on repairing the roof. Amelia reminds Henry to get in touch with the telephone company. Henry says while he is in town getting shingles for the roof he will stop in at the phone office. I wonder what a telephone is. Amelia says that she wishes Henry would just pay someone to fix the roof because he was getting too old to play on roofs. Henry says that he is only 40 and reminds Amelia that she is a year older than he is. Amelia says, "Yes, but I'm smart enough not to go up on the roof". The children laugh, and say, "She got you there, Dad".

Henry and the two boys get in the car and drive down the path and head toward town. Amelia goes outside and tries to clean up the garden space; it is full of weeds which she is trying to pull. Lorna is walking around the yard, looking for nothing in particular. Amelia tells her to stay away from the field in the back.

When Henry and the boys come back, they have a truck. Henry tells Amelia he borrowed the truck from Howard and the ladder, too. Henry puts the ladder up against the house and it extends high enough to reach the roof. Henry asks Jacob if he is afraid of heights. The boy says no. Henry tells William to carry the bundle of shingles over to the ladder and Jacob will carry them up to the roof for me. Henry backs the truck as close as he can get to the house so William doesn't have far to carry the bundles. Henry says, "We might as well have lunch before we get started". At the table, Henry tells Amelia that he had stopped at the Phone Company and they will be out by the end of the week to hook us up. I wonder if hooking up is like when they attached the power cord to the house.

After lunch, Henry and the two boys go to work. William has the easiest job; I think Jacob has the hardest. Jacob has to carry the bundle of shingles up the ladder two stories to the roof. Jacob has to take a lot of breaks because he is soaked with sweat, and so is Henry.

It is not hard for the three to fall asleep that night.

It takes all week, but they get the roof completely covered and without any one getting hurt, which is what Amelia was afraid of. I have a new roof and it feels as good as when I was first built. Henry had enough shingles left to even roof the outhouse. Henry says that he is going to take the truck back to Howard's and get the car and wondered if anyone wanted to come with him. The boys declined so Lorna said that she would go.

When Henry and Lorna get home with the car, Lorna runs in to tell her brothers that Dad had bought her an ice cream cone. Henry told Lorna, "I thought that was supposed to be our little secret". Amelia just wagged her finger at Henry who just shrugged his shoulders.

There are men hooking a wire to the pole outside by the path in front and running it to the house. The men drill a hole in the side of the house and run more wire inside. The men hook the wire up to a box and pick up something that is long enough to go from the mouth to the ear of a person. One man sticks his finger in the box and turns a dial several times. Then to my amazement, the man starts to talk into the hand held device. He talks for a while and then puts it back down on the box. One of the men has Henry sign for his new telephone.

The Life Story Of A House

Henry says that he is going to do nothing for two days before he has to go back to work at the coalmine. Everybody says that coal mines are dangerous.

Sunday comes and Amelia takes the three children to church while Henry just sits in his chair. When the four get home, Henry says that he will start on the sides of the house next week-end.

Henry comes home dirty every night; Amelia heats some water on the stove and puts it into a tub where Henry takes a bath. When he is done, he throws the dirty water outside. Amelia does laundry on Saturday's unless she has to go somewhere. During the summer, Amelia washes the clothes outside. She has one tub of water to scrub them, and one to rinse them and then hangs the cloths on the line.

Saturday comes and Henry and the two boys start to rip off the siding to the house. They get the job done in two days. Henry says he will start to cover the house next weekend.

During the week, Lorna plays with her dolls or goes outside to explore. Jacob and William go fishing a lot. I don't know where they go, but they are usually gone all day. Amelia cleans the house and sometimes when the children are not around, she sits and rests, sometimes even turning on the radio.

On Friday after work, Henry is a little late. He comes up the path with Howard's truck and it is full of wooden slats. On Saturday morning Henry has the boys unload the wood while he makes sure there are no nails left in the side of the house. Henry tells the boys that this will probably take a month doing it on weekends, weather permitting. Sunday it rains and they cannot work on the house, but just by what they did Saturday it made me feel refreshed, wood siding instead of shingles.

The Life Story Of A House

Siding the house takes four weekends, but it looks like a new house when they are done and I feel like a new house. It has been a long time since I have felt this wonderful.

Henry says that since the boys have been working so hard this summer and Lorna staying out of the way, Amelia working just as hard all of the time and because school is close to starting, he is going to take them into town and see a movie. I don't know what a movie is, but the children and Amelia are quite excited by the news. They all get in the car and head down the path and turn towards town.

It had been so long since I was happy, I didn't think I would get to experience that joy again, but I am more than pleased with this family. They all work together and I can feel the warmth and love that I haven't felt for a while.

The car comes up the path and turns in front of the house. As soon as the children get out of the car they are talking about how great the movie was. They keep thanking their Dad. Amelia seems just as pleased and Henry just smiles. After they get inside the three children are discussing the movie, "The Wizard of Oz". Lorna just couldn't stop talking about how the movie turned from black and white to color and then back to black and white. The brothers didn't even care if it was a musical, whatever that is. The children had a hard time going to sleep that night they were so excited.

As Henry and Amelia lie in bed, Amelia told Henry that was a wonderful thing, him thinking to take them to a movie. Henry said, "You and the children have worked so hard this summer that I thought you deserved a little fun". Amelia snuggled up to Henry more than usual.

It was a couple of more weeks before the children had to start school. A woman from down the road was going to stop and pick up the children on her way by. Amelia yelled out the door and thanked Grace for giving the children a ride. It seems Grace only had one girl, Teresa to take to school and then she worked in town part-time, until the children got out of school.

When the children got home that afternoon, Lorna was very excited and the boys were not. Amelia tried to ask the boys what the matter was, but all they would say was that school was getting old. Amelia tried to tell Jacob that he only had two years to go and William only had five. Amelia told them that once you grow up, there is no turning back and to enjoy being young while you still can. That made sense to me.

After supper, Henry lit his cigar and turned on the radio. The man on the radio said that the United States had declared neutrality in the war. There is that talk about war again. Amelia acts most disturbed by this news although Henry tells her that it would be alright.

It is time for the man out back to bring in his crops, which means it is almost the cold and snowy season. This year it will be warm though, Henry has already chopped the wood and had some coal delivered for the cook stove.

Thanksgiving comes with all of the wonderful smells that used to fill the air. Howard and his family come to dinner. Howard's wife's name is Nancy and they have four children. The families all have a good time and turn on the radio for some music, but the adults are talking and the children have gone upstairs. As Howard and family are leaving, Amella says that we should do this more often, Nancy agrees. They all say good-bye and the car goes down the path towards town.

Henry doesn't tell Amelia what the man on the radio means, but Henry is starting to get a little worried. One of the smartest men in the world, Albert Einstein, writes a letter to the President urging him to develop the atomic bomb. An atomic bomb doesn't sound too safe to me.

Before Christmas Henry has a surprise for the family, he is taking them to the movie again. They all dress up on a Saturday night and head into town. When they arrive home, they are just as excited as they were to see "The Wizard of Oz". Lorna is talking about how long the movie was and the boys were talking about what the movie was about. Amelia finally said what the movie was, "Gone with the Wind". Lorna said that the movie was nearly four hours long and she about peed herself, but other than that it was a great movie. Just like the other movie, the children talked about it until they fell to sleep.

Henry and Amelia were invited to Howard and Nancy's for Christmas dinner. They did not leave until the presents were open though. They all got clothes, but they also got one toy a piece, Lorna a doll.

It was New Year's Eve and Henry let the children stay up until midnight since the school had closed for Christmas break. They all sat by the fireplace listening to the radio. William and Lorna were dancing to a song on the radio. It has been a long time since I had seen such happiness in the house. I hope nothing happens to ruin the feelings I have. Lorna almost fell asleep before midnight, but she made it. It was now 1940, and the children went to bed like any other night.

The first day back at school, Amelia ran out to Grace's car and handed her some money. Henry had told Amelia to give Grace some money for picking up the children and taking them to school.

The first day back to school for Amelia, she decided to sit down in the chair and rest from all that had been going on. The next thing she knew was it was afternoon and she had almost slept the day away. Amelia felt guilty so she cleaned something even though it did not need cleaned.

Before Amelia knew it, it was spring. Amelia worked outside on the flower garden and the vegetable garden. The children were getting anxious for school to be over. Henry came home and seemed disturbed by something. Amelia asked him and he told her that there was talking at work about some lay-offs possibly happening. Amelia told Henry not to worry about it till it happens; everything was in God's plan.

The Life Story Of A House

That night after supper, while Henry and Amelia were trying to relax and have the radio on, the man breaks into the music and says that in Natchez, Mississippi a fire at the Rhythm Night Club killed 198. I wonder what a night club is. Henry and Amelia talk about the subject a little until Amelia gets back to reading the Bible.

It is the day the children have been waiting for, the last day of school. The children are especially talkative today from their excitement. When they get home that afternoon, they all tell their Mother that they have been promoted to the next class. I wonder what that means.

The first weekend of summer vacation and Henry has the two boys digging a hole as far back as they can get and not be in the farmer's field. While the boys are digging, Henry is making some kind of a shed or something. After church the next day, the boys work on digging the hole some more. Pretty soon you can't see their heads, it must be deep. Henry is finished with building the shed so he goes over and finishes the digging. When they are done digging, they carry the shed over and put it over the hole in the ground. It is a new outhouse; I should have remembered the first time one was built. The boys laugh because their Father says he is going to use it first. The children come back to the house laughing and tell their Mother.

Henry and Amelia are sitting listening to the radio and Henry tells his wife that he is starting to get a little worried about the war in Europe. I don't know where Europe is. Henry tells Amelia that the President asked Congress for $900 million to pay for 50,000 airplanes to be built per year. The President has also denounced Italy and signed an Act to increase the U.S. Navy's forces by 11%. Henry tells Amelia that there is still talk around work about a layoff happening. Amelia says that we can't control these things, so there is no use to worry about them. Henry says that she is right.

Jacob is going to work this summer, a farmer has agreed to come and get him every day and bring him home each night. Jacob is a little worried but Henry tells the boy he will be just fine, to think about all the work he has done around the house.

The next morning Jacob climbs into a truck and leaves for the day. Jacob has taken a pail with him that his Mother has put food in. That night when Jacob gets home, he is tired, he is not used to the hard work he tells his Mother. When Henry comes home, he tells the boy how proud of him he feels. Jacob does not tell his Father how tired he is. Jacob sleeps well that night, but has to drag himself out of bed the next morning. After a week, Jacob has gotten use to the hard work and is complaining no more.

Before you know it, it is the first of September and school is ready to start. Jacob feels good, having worked all summer. Lorna is excited about going back to school, William is not. Amelia tells William that he will be an adult in no time. William gets his bucket carrying his lunch and goes out to Grace's car and gets in. When the children get home that afternoon, Lorna is still excited and the two boys can take it or leave it. Lorna tells her Mother all about her first day. It sounds like there are a lot of children in one room.

Henry comes home from work and the first thing when he walks in the door Lorna is telling him of her day. Amelia just smiles and Henry listens to the girl until she is finished.

Supper is late because Henry was listening to Lorna when he is usually bathing before supper. Henry is so dirty from working in the coal mine that sometime he is covered with coal dust and he is unrecognizable. After supper as Henry has his cigar and relaxes before bed, the man on the radio talks about the National Guard being activated and ordered to service for one year to a training program in Louisiana. The guard is part of men out of Arizona, Colorado, New Mexico and Oklahoma. Henry says that is a lot of men. The next day, the man on the radio talks about America and Great Britain agreeing to America sending 50 U.S. destroyers needed for escort work in exchange for 99 year leases on

British bases in the North Atlantic, West Indies and Bermuda that the Americans will receive. I have no idea what any of that means, but Henry seems worried.

When Henry comes home the next night, he tells Amelia that the talk of lay-offs at work has stopped because of the war in Europe and the company being afraid that the U.S. will join in. Amelia asks Henry if he thinks the government will join the war. Henry says, "I'm afraid so". Now Amelia is worried, Jacob is 16 and bound to join the Army if we enter the war.

Lorna comes home and tells her Mother that she is supposed to collect as many different bugs and butterflies as she can. Lorna goes outside with a jar and runs around the yard. The first day Lorna catches four bugs and is excited by it. I find it different that for school you would have to go home and catch bugs. When Lorna is finished, she ends up with 11 bugs and gets second prize.

The man on the radio talks every night about the war in Europe, Henry listens and Amelia is tired of the talk. A munitions plant in New Jersey explodes, killing 55 people. Henry wonders if the Germans are involved. The radio says that theory can't be proved. Over the next several weeks Henry listens intently to the news, waiting for the U.S. to get involved. President Roosevelt signed into law The Selective Training and Service Act, creating a draft. I don't know what the draft is, but Henry seems upset by the news. The U.S. imposes a total embargo on Japan, withholding all scrap metal shipments.

This is what Henry was afraid of; the draft registration begins in the U.S., affecting 16 million young men. Then the draft lottery begins. I don't even like the sound of that. Jacob is all this time telling William that if war breaks out, he will join. William tries to talk Jacob out of it, but he has his mind made up.

It is the 5th of November when Henry hears on the radio that President Roosevelt has won the presidential election again over Wendell Wilkie.

The Life Story Of A House

On November 10th, a snow lightly began falling, by morning it was a raging blizzard. Henry and the children stayed home that day. Henry keeps the fireplace going as hot as he can to make the house warm enough. The next day they all stayed home again. That night on the radio the man talked about the blizzard in the Midwest, killing 144 people.

Thanksgiving comes and Howard and Nancy and their four children arrive for dinner. All the men can talk about is the war in Europe. The women try to talk about other things and Jacob is telling all of the children of his plan to join the army if the U.S. enters the war in Europe. Amelia says a special prayer before the meal this Thanksgiving.

Before you know it, it is Christmas already. The children open their presents and then they all get ready to go to Howard and Nancy's house for dinner. They do not come home till late and Amelia thanks Henry for not spending all day talking about the war with Howard.

1941 starts off with the news that most of Europe is snowed in. Amelia prays that the fighting will stop before the United States join in.

Lorna comes home from school and tells her Mother that all they have been talking about in school was the war in Europe. Lorna wonders why all they talk about is the war, but her Mother says that seems to be on everyone's mind. That night while Henry was listening to the radio, some man named Winston Churchill asked the U.S. to send arms to the British, saying, "Give us the tools, and we will finish the job". I hear Henry, but he mumbles that it is only a matter of time before we are involved.

The end of March and all German, Italian and Danish ships anchored in United States waters are taken into "Protective custody". Jacob is secretly doing push-ups and sit-ups; he doesn't want his Father and Mother to know that he is getting ready to join the army.

On April 10th while picking up survivors from a sunken Dutch freighter, the U.S. destroyer Niback drops depth charges on a German U-boat. It seems like every spare minute of Henry's free time is spent listening to the radio. Henry is sure the United States will eventually join the war and starts to talk to Jacob about it. Jacob tells his Father the truth, and they both agree that they should not tell his Mother until it actually happens. I remember what happens in war, people get killed.

It is finally May and the boys are ready for school to end, Lorna is not ready yet. Jacob has lined up the same job that he had the previous year. It will still be another year before William will work through the summer.

On May 20th the first United States freighter the SS Robin Moore is sunk by a German U-boat 950 miles off the coast of Brazil. It seems like the radio is on all of the time now, even Amelia keeps it on during the day.

School gets out in June and Jacob starts working the next day. Lorna stays in her room most days and reads; William has started listening to the radio. Most of the time the radio plays music, but it seems like most days the news breaks in the program to tell of something happening in the war in Europe.

On June 14th the United States froze all the assets of the Germans and Italians. Two days later the German and Italian consulates in the United States are closed and their staff is ordered to leave. I don't know what a consulate is, but they must be angry at the United States to order them closed.

On Saturday Henry decides there has been enough war talk in the household. Henry says they are going to town. The family gets in the car and heads down the path.

When they come up the path and into the house, Lorna is talking a mile a minute. She keeps thanking her Father for taking her to the movie. Jacob and William also thank their Father for not making them go to the movie. It sounds like the boys just messed around town until the movie was over, and then the whole family went out for supper. Lorna finally says the name of the movie, it is a Walt Disney animated movie, "The Reluctant Dragon".

The family can't ignore the war in July. The radio says that one day American forces takeover defense of Iceland from the British. Later in the month the U.S. President orders the seizure of all Japanese assets because of the Japanese taking over the countries of French Indo-China. The end of the month the U.S. gunboat Tutuila is attacked by the Japanese aircraft while the boat is anchored in Chungking. The following day the Japanese apologizes for the incident.

Before long June turns to August and it is about time to go back to school. Jacob wants to quit school and keep his summer job but his parents say he only has one more year.

September comes and Jacob is not to happy to be going to school, Lorna is excited, William doesn't act like he cares or not. When the three come home they are still acting the same as when they left in the morning. When William gets home, he asks his Mother if he can go for a walk, she agrees.   Amelia tells the boy to be home by supper and then William heads down the path and on the road, opposite of the way to town.

William gets home about the same time as his Father, who wants to know where he has been. William says that he has just been walking and thinking. Henry tells the boy that he hopes he has not been thinking too much about the war in Europe. William says that he hasn't as he goes and washes up for supper. After supper Henry takes his usual spot listening to the radio for the news of the day. The first U.S. ship fired upon by a German submarine was the USS Greer, even though the U.S. is neutral.

The Life Story Of A House

William makes it a habit of going for a walk every day. Amelia starts to wonder if there is a girl involved.

Late in September representatives from U.S., Britain and Moscow meet and ask for assistance from Russia. Finally, William tells Jacob that he has been seeing the girl that they ride with to school. Jacob teases William and says that Teresa is awfully young for him (Teresa is in junior high school). William says Teresa is 14 only a year younger than he. Jacob says that Teresa is pretty; he has never looked at her that way. Finally William and Jacob wrestle around like they used too. Jacob is too strong for William and pins him to the floor until he says he gives up, whatever that means. The boys start to laugh when Lorna sticks her head in their room to see what all of the ruckus is. The boys throw a pillow in Lorna's direction. Lorna shuts the door, then opens it and says, "You missed".

On October 17th a destroyer, the USS Kearney is torpedoed and damaged near Iceland, killing 11 sailors. There are all of these words that I have never heard of. At the end of the month the U.S. government gives Russia $1 billion dollars for the use of their lands if the U.S. joins the war. A day later, a German U-boat torpedoes and sinks the U.S. destroyer USS Reuban James, killing more than 100 United States Navy sailors.

The next Saturday, Henry is trying to keep everyone's mind off of the impending war by taking the family to town again. The car goes down the path towards town. When the car comes back, it was like the last time the family had gone to town. Lorna was talking about the movie and the boys said that they were just goofing off in town. It turns out that Lorna was so excited about going to another Walt Disney animated movie, "Dumbo".

What was October turns into November and it is starting to get cold out. William is still walking down to Teresa's house. I guess Grace must not care that her daughter is seeing a boy.

The Life Story Of A House

The middle of the month and two Japanese representatives arrive in the U.S. to negotiate for peace. Henry does not believe them. Three days later the U.S. ambassador to Japan cables Washington a warning that Japan may strike at any time. Henry believes this.

Thanksgiving comes and not too soon for Amelia. She wants to get her mind off of the war, even if it is just for one day. Howard, Nancy and the four children come to dinner. The men talk about the war and the women try to talk about anything else. Amelia says the prayer and she prays to God the war will stop before America gets involved.

America signs an agreement with the French like the one signed with Britain and Russia. On the 27th, all U.S. military forces in Asia and the Pacific are placed on war alert. Henry and Amelia are disappointed at hearing this.

Jacob, William and Lorna come home from school like any other day. Jacob tells his Mother that if America gets into the war, he is going to join and fight. That is what Amelia was afraid of, as she pleads with Jacob not to join. I wonder why people want to kill people.

When Henry gets home, Amelia told him what Jacob had told her. Henry told Amelia that Jacob was 17 and he would be 18 in a few months and they would not have any say in his life then. During summer, Jacob talks to his Father about the war while Amelia just sits there and doesn't say anything. Jacob started listening to the news on the radio with his Father.

On December 6th, President Roosevelt makes a personal appeal to Emperor Hirohito of Japan for peace.

On December 7th, Henry and Jacob listen to the radio after supper like they had been doing. The man on the radio was talking in a more excited voice than usual. Both men were stunned by what they heard on the radio, Amelia cried. The Japanese Navy had launched a surprise attack on the United States naval fleet at Pearl Harbor. Jacob tells his parents that he is going to ride the horse into town tomorrow and join the army. Henry tells Jacob that he must be sure of his decision. Amelia just cries and does not say a word.

The next day Jacob rides into town and Amelia is still crying. William and Lorna go to school like usual, but around the breakfast table all the talk was about the war. Amelia tells Henry that she wants him to stay home with her, but he said that he must go to work to be paid. Amelia is home all alone and lies on the bed and cries herself to sleep.

Jacob comes home about suppertime and says that he has joined the army and he ships out for Biloxi, Mississippi on the 21st. Amelia says, "Four days before Christmas". Jacob says that was as soon as they could take him. It seemed like every young man from town was at the Army office joining up. Henry does not say a word. I wonder if this is part of the war from the first time. That night Henry, Amelia and Jacob listened to the President give a speech and declare war on Japan. Henry and Jacob talk until bedtime about the war, Amelia doesn't say a word until Lorna comes downstairs and says that she is scared. Amelia tries to quiet her daughter but she doesn't sound to convincing. I notice a change in Amelia's voice.

Two days later the radio talk is about American forces repelling a Japanese landing attempt at Wake Island. The man also talks about Germany and Italy declaring war on the United States and the U.S. responding with the same. I have heard of some of these places, but some I have never heard of. The men still talk around the radio about the war, Amelia cries most of the day. Amelia is starting to talk to herself during the day, which I find funny since no one is there.

The next day the radio talks about Hungary and Romania declaring war on the U.S. The man on the radio said preliminary reports out of Pearl Harbor are 9 ships sunk, 21 damaged, 3 repairable. The guess is that there were over 2,400 deaths, 1,282 wounded including 68 civilians, and so much death and for what. It also talks about a French ship, the SS

Normandie being seized by the U.S. William has started joining his Father and brother listening to the radio after supper. Amelia tries to tell William that he is too young to join the army. William tells his Mother that he will be 16 soon, but Amelia insists that William wait as long as Jacob did.

The next day Amelia starts to talk about William joining the army, to herself. I'm not sure, but I don't think talking to yourself is normal.

The day Jacob is supposed to leave; Amelia can't bring herself to ride into town and watch him leave. Amelia hugs and kisses her boy and tells him she will pray for him every day and to be safe. Jacob tells his Mother that he will be in Mississippi for six weeks and he will write as soon as he can. As Henry, Jacob and William drive off down the path and towards town, Amelia is hugging Lorna tightly and they are both crying.

On the 23rd, a second attempt by the Japanese to land on Wake Island is successful. The Americans surrender after a full night and morning of fighting. Henry is starting to notice little changes in Amelia that he asks William about. William hasn't noticed anything different, but they don't know that she talks to herself most of the day.

Amelia doesn't want to go Howard and Nancy's for Christmas dinner but Henry talks her into it, at least for William and Lorna sake. Henry has gone and got the children's presents this year, but William and Lorna do not notice. As the car goes down the path and turns towards town, I worry about Amelia.

I am relieved when the car comes up the path towards the house and everyone gets out of the car.

The radio doesn't have much to say, and the family tries to have a little celebration on New Year's Eve. William even invites Teresa. Henry has been teaching William how to drive and this was the first night that he had driven by himself. Henry felt better knowing there was no snow on the ground. 1942 came, and William took Teresa home a little later.

The next day after the family has awaken, Henry turns on the radio and Amelia yells at him" to leave that damn thing off for one day". William and Lorna have never heard their Mother talk like that, and neither have I. Henry turns the radio off and asks Amelia if she is alright, she just says, "Yes". The rest of the day is quiet as William and Lorna stay in their rooms and Henry goes outside for a while, even though it is freezing out. Amelia sits in the living room alone, talking to herself.

The next day Henry has to go to work but tells William to watch out for his Mother. When Henry comes home that evening, William tells his Father of the odd way he noticed his Mother acting all day. William said that she seemed to dust the same things over and over and she was talking to herself. Henry tells William thank you. William wants to know what his Father is going to do about his Mother. Henry says that they should see how things go and if she starts acting worse he will take her to the Doctor. Henry turns on the radio but keeps it low. Yesterday, United State troops fought the Philippine troops in the Battle of Bataan. New car sales are banned to save steel, the radio also said. Henry sits in his chair smoking his cigar and looking at Amelia.

It seems like every couple of days there is word of the war. I have noticed when Henry turns the radio on after supper, if Amelia is not reading her bible, she is twisting a handkerchief. Amelia has her back to Henry so he thinks she is crocheting, but really she is holding on to the cloth so tight that she almost rips it.

There is actually no war news on the radio for a week. Amelia is not so tense and relaxes a little.

On January 19th, the Japanese forces invade Burma. A week later, Thailand declares war on the U.S. and United Kingdom. The next day, the first American troops land in Northern Ireland. Henry and William are back listening to the radio every night and Amelia is back to being tense.

On February 2nd, Henry is surprised by the news that the President signed an executive order allowing for the internment of Japanese-Americans and the seizure of their property. Henry tries to talk to Amelia about it, but she does not care to hear any of it.

The 8th of February, Jacob calls home that night. Amelia is so happy to hear her son's voice she cries through half of the call. Jacob talks to his Father a while, telling him that he is shipping out for Europe and that he doesn't know if he will have the chance to write. Henry tells his son not to worry about anything but staying alive and to keep his head down. Henry says good-by to his son, maybe for the last time. Henry hands the phone back to Amelia who tells him some useless things, but Jacob listens intently until finally he says that he needs to hang up so another soldier could call home. Jacob tries to tell his Mother not to worry about him, but she tells the boy, that is her job. After the phone call, Amelia starts to cry again, she is repeating everything Jacob had told her, mostly mumbling. Henry is starting to worry about Amelia. Henry tells William what Jacob had said to him. Lorna did not understand why her Mother cried all of the time. Henry tried to tell Lorna that her Mother was just very upset with worry about Jacob's health.

There is a lot of news about the war in the month of February, but calms down in March, April and May. There is still fighting Henry says, but not the big battles that the news likes to report on. Amelia is starting to act better until June, when she can't keep her secret to herself. William and Lorna are home from school for the summer. William is visiting Teresa almost every day. Lorna stays in her room most days, when she comes downstairs for lunch, she finds her Mother dusting and talking to herself. Henry is trying to avoid the situation altogether, he is afraid of the consequences. Henry tells William and Lorna to keep an eye on their Mother that she is not well, and to let him know if she gets worse.

Amelia hits rock bottom June 4th through the 7th, during the Battle of Midway. The radio talks about the battle and the heavy losses, Amelia can't take it anymore. 307 Americans are killed and Amelia doesn't know if Jacob is one of them. Henry tries to tell Amelia that the American Navy defeated the attack of the Japanese Navy. He tried to tell Amelia that the radio had said there were over 3,000 Japanese killed, ten times the American casualties. Nothing mattered, Amelia was mumbling while she dusted. Henry finally told the children that he was going to take their Mother to the hospital in town and they were to stay there and if they had any problems to call Howard. After Henry talked Amelia into getting in the car, Lorna asked William if their Mother was crazy. William said she was having a hard time dealing with Jacob leaving for the war. I was upset that Amelia was crazy, and wondered if I would ever see her again.

Henry admitted Amelia into the hospital for observation. He was told to come back tomorrow evening. When Henry got home he told William and Lorna that they were old enough to watch over themselves during the day, he would be home before dark. Lorna told her Father that she was 13 now and soon would be 14. Henry hugged his daughter and told her he was sorry she had to grow up faster than she was supposed to. Henry told William that instead of being at Teresa's house most of the time, to maybe try to split the time in half between here and her house. William said that he would.

The next day when Henry went to work, he looked apprehensive.

After work Henry went to the hospital to check on Amelia. The doctor told Henry that Amelia needed long term care and that she would have to be put in a sanitarium. Henry was afraid of that. When Henry got home, he told the children what the doctor had said. Henry told them that he went into their Mother's room and she did not even recognize him. Lorna was crying now, and her Father hugged her and told her that she had to be strong for her Mother. He told Lorna that she would have to take over some of the duties of the house. Henry called Howard and

Nancy and told them everything about Amelia and asked if once in a while Nancy could come out and check on Lorna, and Nancy said that she would.

On Saturday, Henry took William and Lorna to see their Mother. He regretted it as soon as he walked through the door. All of the horror stories that Henry had heard about sanitariums were true. Lorna didn't understand why her Mother had to stay in a place like that. Amelia did not recognize anybody. Lorna was still talking about the experience when they came home. I felt bad knowing Amelia had to stay in a place like that. Lorna told her Father that until her Mother was moved to another facility, she would not be visiting her.

William was spending more time with Teresa now that his Mother was no longer at home. They switched between the two houses, but mainly they came to his house where there were no adults half of the time.

There was still no word from Jacob. Henry started to listen to the radio again. Lorna spent most of her time in her room. William spent most of his time with Teresa.

June turned to July then August. In August Henry heard on the radio about a battle in the Solomon Islands called the Guadalcanal. The man on the radio said it was the first American offensive of the war when the USMC attacked and it was still raging on.

It was almost time to go back to school; the house would be empty during the day. Lorna was still keeping house and tending the garden, but she would have less time when school began. Henry had cut his visits to Amelia from every Saturday to every other Saturday; it was just too hard to see her that way. I wonder if she is acting any different than she did here.

School started the first part of September and Lorna was glad to be back at school, she was tired of keeping house. Now she would have homework before she could do any housework. William didn't care much for school anymore; he had told Lorna that he and Teresa were thinking of running away. Lorna asked William if he couldn't hold out till summer, he would be 17 then. William said he would try, but he wasn't promising anything.

On November 12th, 13th and 15th the battle of Guadalcanal continued with a naval battle between the U.S. and Japan and an air battle. The U.S. retained control of Guadalcanal, but the Navy suffered heavy losses.

On Thanksgiving, Howard and Nancy came to the house early in the morning, Nancy was going to cook the meal, but she wanted Lorna to watch. They had just as fine of a dinner, but it seemed sad without Amelia. Howard and Nancy left after they had pie and coffee, the dishes already washed. Lorna cried that night in her room so as to not let anyone see her.

At the end of November, Henry heard on the radio about a night club in Boston, Massachusetts that had a fire killing 491 people. I don't know what a nightclub is, but it sounds dangerous.

Henry came home the first week of December complaining that the government had started rationing gasoline all across the country. Henry was also visiting Amelia less often, she wasn't getting any better and it was too painful for him not to be recognized by his wife.

Soon it was Christmas; Henry had managed finding William and Lorna presents, with a little help from Nancy. The three went to Howard and Nancy's house like they had always done, but this year seemed different without Amelia.

New Year's Eve wasn't a huge occasion anymore. Henry listened to the radio; William was seeing Teresa and Lorna stayed in her room.

It was 1943 and school had just returned too session when William told Lorna that Teresa was pregnant. Lorna shook her head, she had thought William smarter than that, and told him so. Lorna wanted to know what he and Teresa were going to do. William said he did not know, Lorna suggested that he tell their Father. William said he was afraid to, but Lorna said their Father would rather have the truth than have the two run off and not tell him. William thought that Lorna was probably right, he would tell his Father, but he didn't know how to tell Teresa's Father.

That night after supper, William told his Father there was something he needed to talk to him about. Lorna stayed downstairs to give her brother moral support. William told his Father the whole story and asked him what he should do. Henry thanked the boy for having the courage to tell him instead of running off. Henry asked William if Teresa's parents knew, William said that they didn't. Henry said," the first thing you need to do is tell them". William said," what if Teresa's Father kills me". Henry said, "If you want, I will go with you to tell her parents". William said that he would like that. Henry said that they would go to Teresa's house tomorrow when he got off of work and before supper. Henry also said, "Lorna can stay here in case we get shot and aren't home by bedtime, she can call the police". William and Lorna didn't know if their Father was kidding or not.

The next day after Henry got off of work, he stopped the car just long enough to pick-up William. William was not looking forward to facing Teresa's parents. It would help some having his Father there. Lorna had told William good-luck before he left the house. I wonder why Teresa's parents would be mad because she was pregnant. I would think that they would like having a baby around.

Lorna sat downstairs, waiting for William and her Father to get home. When the car finally pulled up the path, Lorna let out a sigh of relief to see two figures coming toward the house. Henry said that he was hungry and was ready for his supper. Lorna had forgotten about supper and told her Father there was probably something she could whip up. Henry said, "Don't bother, I will eat something". Lorna was about to bust because neither her brother nor Father was talking about Teresa. Finally, Lorna said, "What happened at Teresa's". William said, "Teresa and I are going to get married and live with her parents. I will have to get a job somewhere. We decided to finish out the school year and then marry in June. I will be 17 then and Teresa 16". Lorna said, "It is too bad Mother can't come to the wedding". Henry hadn't even thought about that, he told Lorna.

That Saturday, Henry went to visit Amelia in the sanitarium. To Henry's disappointment, Amelia wasn't any better. Henry told Lorna that her Mother would not be well enough to attend William's wedding. Henry told Lorna that Teresa would like her to help with the planning. Lorna was surprised but honored for Teresa to think of her on her special day.

Henry was back to listening to the radio after supper. In February the U.S. government had started shoe rationing. Two nights later, Henry heard on the radio that the United States had finally defeated the Japanese in the Battle of Guadalcanal. It was reported that 7,100 Americans were killed in the battle and the Japanese had 31,000 dead and 1,000 captured, all between August 7th, 1942 and February 9th, 1943. It is hard to imagine 38,000 people dying in one battle.

At the end of February, Henry heard that a mine at Bearcreek, Montana exploded, killing 74 men. I still think mines are too dangerous to work in.

March, April and May seemed to fly by for William, he was telling Lorna that every day. Lorna said, "She did not feel sorry for him, he made his bed, now he had to make it right". I don't know what that means, but when I next see Teresa, her belly is big.

Henry heard on the radio about sea battles, aerial battles and ground battles, with many man getting killed.

The Life Story Of A House

Finally it is June, school is out for the summer and William and Teresa's wedding is this week-end. Lorna tells William that Teresa and she are going to decorate the church.

Saturday comes and William is acting different, Henry says he is nervous. Henry, William and Lorna all dress up in their finest clothes and head out to the car and down the path toward town.

The car comes back up the path in the evening; it only has Henry and Lorna. I guess William and Teresa are married now. Henry tells Lorna that if she gets to lonely, they would get a dog. What is a dog?

Sunday Henry and Lorna get in the car and head toward town. Henry said they were going to visit Amelia and if Lorna felt more comfortable sitting in the car, she could.

That evening when Henry and Lorna got home, Lorna was crying. Henry hugged the girl and said that she should never have seen her Mother that way, he should have known better. They ate a light supper that night. Lorna stayed downstairs that evening although her and her Father hardly talked. Lorna finally went upstairs and went to bed.

The next day as Henry went to work, Lorna asked herself what she was going to do by herself all summer.

When Henry came home that night he had a strange four-legged little animal. Lorna took one look at it and hugged her Father and said, "Thank you for the dog. What is his name?" Henry told her that she could name him anything that she wanted too. Lorna said that she would name him Buster. Henry brought in a sack and told Lorna that she would have to feed and walk Buster. She said that she would. Henry said, "Just remember, do not leave the yard". He also told her that he had fashioned a rope for her to use as a collar so Buster would not run away.

The Life Story Of A House

After supper, Lorna and Buster went upstairs while Henry sits and listens to the radio. The war wasn't getting any better, Henry had told Lorna the next morning. Lorna said that she wished Jacob could at least write. Henry told her that Jacob was probably busy trying not to get shot.

June turned to July and Henry heard on the radio that Americans bombed Hamburg, Germany by day, and the British and Canadians bombed by night. The bombing started on July 24th and was going to last for a while.

William and Teresa visited one evening, having supper with Henry and Lorna. Henry asked William how he was getting along helping on Teresa's Father's farm. William said that he was getting the hang of it. William asked about his Mother and Jacob. Henry said that his Mother was the same and they still hadn't heard from Jacob. Henry asked Teresa if they had picked out a name yet. Teresa said no. I didn't know you could name the baby before it was born. Pretty soon Buster came running downstairs; he had been taking a nap. Lorna said that she almost forgot to tell them that their Father had gotten her a dog to keep her company. William asked Lorna what kind of dog it was, Lorna shrugged her shoulders. Henry told William it was mostly mutt. They all laughed, but I didn't get it. After supper William and Teresa stayed a while and then left, William said that he had to get up early in the morning. William and Teresa thanked them for supper and left. Henry told Lorna that they were probably getting tired of being under the roof of Teresa's parents. What does it matter what roof you have over your head, as long as you have one.

It was the middle of August and Lorna went out and got the mail like usual. She came running in the house, but her Father was at work. She clutched the letter until her Father came home from work that night. Lorna told her Father that it was a letter from the war department. Henry told Lorna that if it were bad news, they would have come in person. Henry opened the letter and read it out loud.

The Life Story Of A House

Henry said, "We are sorry to inform you that your son, Jacob, has had a severe injury. Jacob will be stationed at the hospital in Biloxi, Mississippi while he recuperates. I assure you that as soon as Jacob can come home he will. We will inform you later as to his arrival. We thank Jacob for his service". Sincerely, Franklin D. Roosevelt, President.

Lorna asked her Father what kind of an injury he thought Jacob had. Henry said that he did not know, but he was glad to hear that Jacob was still alive and back in the states. Lorna could not sleep that night from being so excited to hear about Jacob; Henry did not get much sleep either.

The next evening Henry started to listen to less of the man talking on the radio, and more music. I wonder if Henry was listening to the man talk on the radio because he was worried about Jacob. Lorna started to dance to the music with Buster, which made her Father laugh. It was nice to hear laughter in the house once more.

The next evening Henry asked Lorna if she wanted to take a ride and visit William to tell him the news about Jacob. She asked if she could take Buster and he said she could.

When they arrived home that night, Henry and Lorna were talking about going to the sanitarium this Saturday and see if the news of Jacob's return would affect Amelia.

Saturday, Henry, Lorna and Buster got in the car and went down the path and turned toward town. I hope Amelia gets better. When the three get home that night they were quiet until Henry said that maybe Lorna's Mother would respond when Jacob himself visits her.

August turned to September and Lorna was back to school. Lorna tied Buster to the clothes line so he could run back and forth. Grace was still going to give her a ride even though her daughter, Teresa, was out of school. That evening Henry asked Lorna how she liked her new class. Lorna said everything was fine. Her Father said, "Any new boys in your class?" Lorna said that there was one, but he looked like a pip squeak and his name is Fred. They laughed, but Henry said to be kind to Fred because he is probably scared to be in a strange town and a strange school. Lorna said that she hadn't thought of that.

When Henry got home from work one evening in the middle of September, he got a call on the telephone. Henry had said it was something called a party-line. Henry talked on the phone a while and then said thank you for letting me know. Lorna was standing there patiently holding Buster. Henry said, "That was William, Teresa has had her baby. It is a girl, and they named her Emma Elizabeth". Lorna said that was a lovely name, Emma Elizabeth. Henry told Lorna that William and Teresa would bring the baby for a visit this week-end. Lorna started to dance with Buster, singing, "We are going to see the new baby". Henry laughed at the girl's silliness.

Saturday came and Lorna told her Father that she could hardly wait to see Emma Elizabeth. Her Father rubbed Lorna's head and asked her how she and Fred were getting along. Lorna punched her Father in the arm and said, "Very funny". Finally a car pulled in the driveway and came up the path to the house. It is William, Teresa and a bundle of cloth. Lorna runs to open the door and let the family in. Lorna was talking a mile a minute she was so excited. William and Teresa sit on the couch and unbundled their package. It was a tiny baby, the smallest I had ever seen. First Grandpa got to hold Emma and then Lorna. Lorna could hardly wait for her turn. Lorna said how pretty the baby was, it was a good thing she looked like Teresa and not William. They all laughed. William and family had lunch with Henry and Lorna. Lorna had a hard time making them lunch because she kept wanting to look at the baby. Lorna's Father told the girl not to get any ideas about her and Fred having a baby. Lorna said, "Not funny". William said, "Who is Fred?" Henry said it was a new boy in Lorna's class who she is sweet on. Lorna tried to flip her Father with a towel. William told Lorna that she had better wait a few years. Lorna said that she would, if she got lonely she had Buster. After lunch as William and his family are about to leave,

The Life Story Of A House

Lorna says, "If you ever need a baby-sitter, I'm your girl". William said that he would keep that in mind. Lorna is all smiles.

September turned to October and then to November. Henry said he was beginning to worry because he hadn't heard any word from Jacob. It was Thanksgiving and Henry was talking to Howard and William. Howard told Henry that he shouldn't worry about Jacob; at least he was back in the states. William was holding the baby while Nancy, Lorna and Teresa were making dinner. I will never get tired of that smell. There was another car coming up the path toward the house. The car stopped in front of the house and two men got out. One was using a crutch and one was carrying a huge bag. Henry opened the door and hugged the young man and told them both to come in. It was JACOB, and one leg was missing up to the knee. Jacob said, "Are we in time for dinner?" The women were all crying. Jacob introduced his friend as Robert. Jacob asked where his Mother was. Henry told him to sit down and he would tell him the whole story. As Jacob sat down, he said, "By the looks of the baby someone has been busy", and then he smiled at William. Henry told the boy the whole story of his Mother, which made him very sad, but he said that he was glad to be home. During dinner Jacob tried to hide his disappointment about hearing of his Mother. The men all wanted to know where he had been stationed overseas; Jacob told them he had lost his leg at the Aleutian Islands while his troops were trying to invade Attu in an attempted to expel the Japanese forces that were occupying it. He had been shot twice in the same leg but continued to fight until he blacked out and someone had to drag me back behind our lines. Then Jacob said that this really wasn't conversation for the dinner table. Jacob wanted to know about the new baby. He kidded Lorna and asked her if she was hers. She said, "I wish". They all laughed and told her that she had better wait a few years. Henry said, "After all, you have Buster to look after". Jacob said he wondered when we had gotten a dog. Henry said it was to keep Lorna company. They all went into the living room after dinner and the men still wanted to know things about the war. Henry asked Lorna if she would make up his bed for Jacob so he didn't have to go upstairs. Jacob said,' Thanks, he hadn't mastered stairs yet". Jacob asked if it was alright for Robert to sleep a couple of nights on the couch. Henry said, "Of course". After a full day, the visitors all left, happy that the day had been blessed by God. Jacob asked his Father if they could go to bed early, it seems they had driven all night. It will be nice to have Jacob home again.

The next day Henry asked Jacob if he wanted to go visit his Mother. Henry was surprised when Jacob said no. Jacob explained that he was only home for a couple of days and he didn't want to see his Mother until he had his fake leg. He had to go back to Mississippi to have a wooden leg made for him and he would have to have therapy after that. Jacob asked his Father if he could stay there a while after he was done with his therapy. Henry said sure he could. Jacob asked if there would be enough room for Robert. Jacob told him that Robert didn't have any family. Henry said as long as he doesn't mind sleeping on the couch, I think we can find a spare closet for him. Jacob thanked his Father.

Lorna told Buster that Robert was cute. She told Buster that she was 15 now, Robert was only 18. When Lorna came downstairs, she asked Robert how he had slept. The young man said, "It beats sleeping on the hard ground with one eye open for the enemy". Lorna said that must have been terrible. Robert said that he thanked God every day he woke up in the morning; it meant a fresh day trying to stay alive. Lorna said Robert would have to tell her about it sometime. Robert said," they would have plenty of time to talk when Jacob and he came back from Mississippi. Your Father said that it would be alright if when we came back, I could stay here awhile". Lorna tried to hide her smile, but she wasn't doing a very good job of it. Robert asked Lorna if it would be alright with her. She said that would be fine, then she asked the young man if he were going into town and try to find a job when he and Jacob came back. Robert said that he hoped he and Jacob could find work in town; maybe even find a place to rent.

After a couple of days Jacob and Robert prepared to leave. Jacob said he was looking forward to using a cane instead of a crutch. Jacob hugged his Father and Lorna, Robert shook Mr. Johnson's hand and much to Lorna's surprise, he hugged her. Lorna and her Father watched the two young men drive away, and Lorna's Father asked her if Robert and Fred were going to have to fight over her. Lorna punched her Father in the arm and said that she was too young to think of things like that. When Lorna went upstairs, she told Buster that she thought Robert liked her. I wondered how old you had to be to have a relationship.

That night Henry sat and decided to listen to the radio, since he knew Jacob was going to be fine. Henry told Lorna that he hadn't turned on the radio for a while and he thought that he would see if there was any news other than about the war. As soon as Henry turned on the radio, the man said that a battle that started in July was coming to a close. Between the Americans, British and Canadians, some 9,000 tons of bombs were dropped on Hamburg, killing an estimated over 30,000 people and destroying 280,000 buildings. Henry turned the radio off and said it was the same old news.

Lorna asked her Father how long would Jacob need rehabilitation. Henry said that Jacob did not know, and then he asked his daughter if she missed Robert. Lorna said, "Well, he is cute". Henry asked his daughter if she thought that he might be a little too old for her. Lorna said, "Robert is only 18, I'm 15". Henry told his daughter that she should wait until she finished her education before she started looking for a man and anyways he said when you are 18, Robert will only be 21. Lorna called Buster and went upstairs. She told Buster that she did not know if she could wait three years. I wonder what Henry would do if Lorna moved out of the house.

Christmas came and went and it was now New Year's Day. Henry decided since it was not snowing, he and Lorna would take a ride to the sanitarium. It was 1944, Jacob was home safely, William and Teresa had a healthy daughter, Lorna was getting older and maybe, just maybe, Amelia would snap out of the spell she was under. As the car went down the path and turned toward town, I thought everyone was happy except Henry. His family was fine except for Amelia, but knowing she wasn't home, made Henry sad.

I noticed something off towards town that I wasn't sure of, maybe Henry would say something about it.

Henry, Lorna and Buster came home, and Henry was sad because he told Lorna that her Mother wasn't any better. Henry hoped that once Jacob visited Amelia then that would be enough to shake out of it, whatever it was. Henry and Lorna had supper then she said she was going upstairs to relax since she had to go back to school tomorrow. Henry read a magazine while he was sitting downstairs, all alone. Lorna was telling Buster that she hadn't even heard Robert's last name. She didn't even know who she would be after she got married.

Finally, spring came and Lorna only had a month left at school. Lorna had turned 16 and was starting to feel like a woman. She hoped Robert would tell the difference when he and Jacob came home. Lorna was spending a lot of time in her room, standing in front of her mirror saying Mrs. Robert something, and then she would laugh. I was having a hard time understanding what she was laughing at.

It turned to the first of June and Lorna was out of school for the summer. She was planting the garden later than usual this year, her mind was preoccupied but she usually told Buster what she was thinking. A car came up the road from town and turned into the path coming up to the house. It was Jacob and Robert. Lorna was embarrassed because she had been working in the garden all day. She ran up to hug Jacob anyway. After she had a hold of him for a couple of minutes, Robert said, "Save some for me". Lorna was really embarrassed now. The three went into the house. Lorna noticed Jacob was only using a cane. Lorna got the three a glass of lemonade and they sat in the living room. Jacob told Lorna what they had been up too, he also told her he was anxious to see his Mother. Lorna said that maybe tomorrow their Father would take them to town since it was Saturday. Jacob mentioned that the town was expanding toward our house. I wonder what that meant. Jacob told Lorna that he knew they had only been gone six months, but she looked like she had gotten a lot more grown-up. This embarrassed Lorna again. Robert said that some people have growth spurts; Lorna looked up and smiled at Robert. Jacob noticed the way Lorna was looking at his friend.

Robert was bringing in the two men's bags when Henry pulled in the path. He told them he was glad to see them. When they had all settled in, Henry asked Jacob about his recovery. Jacob pulled up his pant legs to show his Father and Lorna his wooden leg. Jacob took it off and showed them his stump, Lorna went into the kitchen then. Jacob said they had taught him at the hospital how to get around almost like he used too. Henry said that tomorrow they would go visit his Mother if he wasn't too tired. Jacob said that he wasn't, he was looking forward to seeing his Mother.

When it got time for bed, Lorna went upstairs and brought down some extra sheets for Robert to sleep on the couch. Lorna was embarrassed again when she came downstairs and Robert had taken his shirt off. He excused himself and said he was sorry, he would have to be more careful. Lorna didn't say a word until she went back upstairs and told Buster how nice Robert's upper half was, plenty of muscles. Lorna was up half the night talking to Buster about Robert. I wonder if Buster understands what people tell him.

Saturday morning came early for Lorna; she was still half asleep when her Father was ready to go to town. She just realized that she would have to set in the back seat with Robert. She ran back upstairs and asked Buster what she should say to Robert, the dog just turned his head to one side and looked at the girl. I thought the first thing that Lorna should do was ask Robert his last name.

Finally Henry coaxed his daughter into going, and they took off towards town. I hope the visit with Amelia will go well.

Later that evening the car came up the path toward the house. They all looked tired and sat down as soon as they got in the house. Henry said that it was amazing that Amelia had recognized Jacob. Jacob said that he was surprised when his Mother looked up and said, "Hello, Jacob". Of course, she didn't say anything else, but that had been the first words that you could understand for a long time. Lorna excused herself; she was going up to her room.

Once Lorna was in the safety of her room, she told Buster that Robert's last name was Talbot. She would be Mrs. Lorna Talbot. Robert had teased her too, Lorna told Buster, she had scrunched against the side of the car when Robert told her that he wasn't going to bite, to move over a little and be comfortable. Lorna looked in the mirror and said, "He wanted me to be comfortable".

Downstairs, Jacob told his Father that as soon as he and Robert could find a job and a place to stay, they would be out of his hair. Henry said to take as long as they needed, unless Robert gets tired of sleeping on the couch. Robert said that he wasn't ever going to complain about sleeping arrangements again, having slept in a fox hole. They all laughed. I wonder what a fox hole is; I wonder what a fox is. Jacob said tomorrow he and Robert would go and visit William, Teresa and Emma Elizabeth. Henry said that they will be glad to see him.

After their visit with William, the two men decided to go back into town and look things over. They told Lorna their plans and wanted to know if she would like to go. Lorna didn't answer right away and Robert said that he promised he was a good driver. Jacob agreed that he was. Lorna said that she would be happy to go.

When the three came back later that evening, Jacob was talking about how big the town was getting. He said, "Pretty soon the houses will be out by ours". I wonder what that meant; the houses will be out by ours.

When Henry came home from work, Jacob told him that he had a couple of places in mind to try and gain employment. Henry asked if Robert were going to look too. Robert said, "He was going to look, he didn't have a family to go home to". Henry said, "You can stay here as long as you like". Robert told the man thank you. Lorna was listening from the kitchen and said, "Yes".

The three men were listening to the radio after supper, when the man said that we had begun an attack on Normandy. The three men discussed how many casualties there would be from taking the island. The man also said that there were over 155,000 allies to land on the beach.

Jacob and Robert decided to take a couple of days off before they went to town and looked for employment. The first day they just sat around the house, listening to the music on the radio. Lorna stayed in her room; she told Buster that she didn't know what to say.

The second day the boys were already getting bored. They asked Lorna if she would like to take a ride up the path opposite of town. She had never been any farther than Williams, so she said yes.

When they arrived home that evening, Lorna told Buster that she had seen four other towns. There must be other towns other than the one down the path. Henry came home that night and told the boys that he had found them jobs if they were interested. Jacob asked, "What king of jobs, doing what". Henry said that the man at the bank told him that he was looking for another clerk if Jacob wanted to apply. The job would mostly be a sit down job, but you would act as a teller if someone had to take a break to use the bathroom or any other reason. Jacob said that he would be interested. Henry said, "Good, go and see the man at the bank tomorrow". Henry then told Robert that there were openings at the mine if he were interested. Robert told the man that he would be interested. Henry asked Robert if he were afraid of tight spaces and Robert said that he wasn't. Henry said, "Until you can find a rental in town, Jacob will have to ride into town with us and sit for an hour until the bank opens. You can always sit at the coffee house". Both men thanked Henry who said," do not thank me until you get the jobs". Lorna went back upstairs and told Buster, "What was she going to do if Robert finds a rental in town. I won't get to see him very much".

Jacob said, "If he got the job then sometimes he could visit his Mother before work". Henry said," that would be a good idea, maybe it would help her".

The next day about 10:00 a.m., the boys went into town to try their luck at getting jobs. They also said that they would look into housing too. Jacob said that he wasn't looking forward to waiting an hour each day for work. Robert said that they had a little money saved up; maybe they could rent something right away if they got the jobs. Lorna did not want to hear that, and after the boys left she asked Buster what she was going to do if the boys moved. I don't know why Lorna keeps asking Buster questions, he never answers.

Lorna paced all day and didn't get any of her work done. Finally the car came up the path to the house. Lorna looked out the window and saw that the two boys were laughing. Lorna said, "That's not a good sign". When the boys entered the house, Lorna was sitting trying to remain calm. The boys did not tell Lorna of their day right away. Jacob was in the kitchen with Robert and told him to let Lorna squirm for a while. Jacob told Robert that Lorna seemed to have a crush on him. Robert said that he thought of Lorna as the little sister that he never had. Jacob said that he would have a talk with the girl and tell her what your feelings are, she will be crushed, but she should not hold out hope for something that will not happen. Robert said that he was sorry, but Jacob told him that it wasn't his fault that he was so damn good looking. Both men laughed until they about split their sides, but I didn't get it.

After supper that evening, Jacob suggested that Robert and his Father take a short ride in the car. Jacob had already told his Father that he needed to talk to Lorna about her feelings toward Robert. Henry agreed, and he and Robert went down the path and toward town.

Jacob asked Lorna if they could have a talk, just the two of them. Lorna said, "Sure". Jacob started by saying he did not know what Lorna was thinking, but it looked as if she had a crush on Robert. Jacob continued to tell the girl about how Robert never had a family of his own, so he saw Lorna as the little sister he had never had. Jacob said that Robert did not want the girl to get hurt and she should be told as soon as possible. Lorna asked Jacob, "How am I supposed to face Robert". Jacob told her that she did not have to act any different and maybe someday you will come to think of Robert as another brother. Lorna said that she did not think that she could ever think of Robert as a brother. She ran up the stairs crying. Henry and Robert came back to the house about half an hour later. Jacob told them what he had told Lorna, but she did not take it well. Robert said, "Maybe I should go". Jacob said, "No, we will look harder for a place in town to rent". Henry agreed that might be the best way.

The next day Lorna did not come downstairs until she saw the three drive off toward town. She asked Buster, "How was she ever going to face Robert again".

When Lorna saw the car come up the path and toward the house, she went upstairs and shut her door. The three men came in the house and noticed Lorna was still upstairs and Robert volunteered to go up and talk to the girl. Henry and Jacob agreed. Robert went upstairs and gently knocked on Lorna's door. She said, "That she didn't want to be bothered". Robert said, "Could I talk to you a minute". Lorna was petrified with fear now; Robert was right outside her bedroom door. She slowly opened the door to let Robert in. Robert said that he would like to have a talk with her and sat on the edge of Lorna's bed. Robert started out by saying that Lorna would make some man a wonderful wife someday, but she needed to concentrate on getting her school work done for the time being. When the time comes, boys will be fighting over you. Robert said that Lorna was mature for her age but she should wait for a couple of more years. Lorna said, "But what if I decide I want you". Robert told the girl that he thought of her as a little sister and that he hoped that she would get over him and find the right boy for her. Robert said he had never felt the love of a family and he so much wanted to be a part of theirs. Lorna started to cry. Robert put his arm around her shoulders and she looked up at him with tears in her eyes. Robert told her that she was a beautiful girl, but they could not be together. Robert gently kissed her on the cheek and brushed her tears away. Robert got up to go when he turned around and said, "Please come downstairs, if you are too uncomfortable with me living here, I will move into town". Lorna got up from the bed and hugged Robert for a long time and then they both went downstairs.

Lorna did not have much to say after her talk with Robert, but she acted if everything was alright. At night, Lorna would talk to Buster and ask him if he thought she should run away. I don't think Lorna should run away.

Jacob had visited his Mother a couple of days each week, she recognized him, but she still mumbled to herself. Robert and Jacob found a house to rent in town, they were going to move this coming week-end, not that they had much to move. Henry had told them that he would buy them two beds to get them started. Lorna was heartbroken; she would not help with the moving.

Saturday came and the boys had borrowed a truck to haul their belongings. After they were done loading the truck, Robert decided that he should go upstairs and tell the girl good-by. Jacob told Robert to tell Lorna that she could visit anytime. Robert went up and knocked on the girl's door. She said that she did not want to be bothered. Robert told her that it was him. Lorna opened the door a crack. Robert told her that they were leaving but she could come to town and visit anytime she wanted to. Lorna opened the door and grabbed Robert in a hug that almost cracked a rib. Lorna looked into his eyes and said, "I don't want you to see me as a little sister," and then she kissed him on the lips. Robert did not pull away although he was telling himself that she was just a young girl. When finally their lips parted, Robert kissed her again. Robert told Lorna that she would make a fine woman, someday. He also told her that she must get her education because someday it would be very helpful. Lorna was still hugging Robert when he started to peel her arms off of him. Robert said, "I have to go, but I will be seeing you when you get older". Robert gave her another peck on the lips and then went downstairs. Jacob asked Robert if she understood now, Robert said that he would tell him later.

Lorna was happy again. She and Buster danced away half of the afternoon, until she heard her Father come home. "I did not even hear him come up the path", Lorna told Buster. Lorna came downstairs and her Father's hand was bandaged. Lorna asked what had happened and Henry told her that he had cut it helping the two move. He already told the people at the mine that he might have to take a week off or two. Lorna said, "At least it was your left hand since you are right-handed". Lorna went to make supper for her Father when he came into the kitchen. He asked Lorna what Robert had said, he looked a little funny when he came downstairs. Lorna was surprised by this; she told her Father that he had tried to explain that he only wanted to be family. She told Buster later that she hadn't lied, if she had her way, they would be family.

That evening when Henry was listening to the radio and smoking his cigar, he thought it was awful quiet now that Jacob and Robert moved to town. The man on the radio said something about a circus fire and more than 100 children died. I wonder what a circus is and how 100 children could die in a fire from it.

Henry continued to go and visit Amelia once a month. Amelia still wasn't the same as Henry told the radio. Henry had started talking to the radio. I wonder if the man in the radio can hear Henry. Lorna started going with her Father and staying at Jacob and Robert's house.

Lorna would always tell Buster all about her visit when they returned home. Lorna told Buster that the house was sparsely furnished; it needed a woman's touch.

It was almost the end of August and for once Lorna was not looking forward to school, she still had Robert on her mind. She found it helped to talk to Buster about her problems. Henry had finally gone back to work. One night after supper he turned on the radio to hear some music and the man broke into the music to say he had a special report. A Japanese unmarked Passenger ship had been sunk by torpedoes launched by a U.S. submarine, killing 1,484 civilians including 767 children. What an awful thing, why can't the war be over, why do so many innocent people have to die?

When school started, Grace continued to give Lorna a ride into town. Lorna was to be a junior this year, she told Buster, only two years to go.

Lorna was having a hard time concentrating at school, she told Buster. She was still in love with Robert and she thought he had feelings for her too. She just didn't think she could make it two more years. She told Buster, that she was not too young.

On October the 8th after supper, Henry turned on the radio and was surprised that there was a show on. The Adventures of Ozzie and Harriet were new and Henry liked it. He would have to remember that it was on.

Thanksgiving dinner was prepared by Nancy, Grace, Teresa and Lorna. Henry had decided this year to invite Grace and her husband, Bill. Jacob and Robert would be there too. Henry thought everyone was together except Amelia. Henry was disappointed that Jacob being home hadn't jarred Amelia out of her walking coma. Well, Henry was going to have a good time anyway. The smell was starting to mix and it was wonderful. I will never get over that smell. During dinner they talked about the war and Roosevelt being elected President for the fourth time. Lorna hoped that she wasn't too obvious looking at Robert every chance that she got.

Teresa noticed but she had news of her own she wanted to let everyone know when the time was right. There was a lull in the conversation when Teresa said, "William and I have some news. I am pregnant again". They all congratulated the couple and patted William on the back. Emma was two and now there would be another baby, I just wished they would visit more often. While the women cleaned up after dinner, the men went into the living room to talk. Everyone wanted to know how Jacob was getting along at the bank and Robert the coal mine. Jacob said he hadn't figured out how to rob the bank yet. The men all laughed. Robert said he was doing fine, as did William. Henry said that he would like to retire from the mine someday before he got too old to enjoy himself.

The women were talking while they cleaned up after dinner. Teresa asked Lorna if there were anything she would like to tell them. She said no, but Teresa said, "I thought I saw you look at Robert, and more than once". Lorna was a little embarrassed. The women all surrounded Lorna and said, "We haven't heard any juicy news in a while". Lorna said that she was fond of Robert. Teresa said it looked more than fond to her. The woman all laughed but Lorna and told her that they would keep her secret, which was a relief to Lorna, as she would later tell Buster.

After everyone had pie and coffee, the people started to go home but not before they were all invited to Howard and Nancy's house for Christmas dinner. William, Teresa and Emma rode with Bill and Grace; they left right after Howard and Nancy. Lorna was in the kitchen cleaning up the rest of the plates when Robert came through the door and asked the girl if she needed any help. Robert got closer to the girl and told her that she looked more grown up every time he saw her. Lorna smiled at that and they snuck in a kiss. They had to be careful not to get caught; she was just a young lady after all. Robert had told Jacob that he had different feelings for Lorna now that she was turning into a woman. Jacob did not care, he thought of Robert as a brother already. So when Jacob cleared his throat loudly, Robert knew that it was a warning that his Father was coming into the kitchen. Robert snuck one more kiss with Lorna before he left the room, meeting Mr. Johnson on the way out.

After Jacob and Robert went home, Henry asked Lorna if there was something she would like to tell him. This caught Lorna off-guard, and she said why. Henry said, "It was nothing really, he thought that she was paying a lot of attention to Robert". Should Lorna tell her Father the truth or should she tell him a fib. She said, "No, I just look at him as another brother". Henry said, "Fine, he just wondered".

When Lorna went upstairs, she told Buster that had been a close one. Several people had noticed her looking at Robert, including her Father.

Henry kept visiting Amelia once a month with Lorna staying at Jacob's. One Saturday Henry left Lorna out at Jacob's, but Henry did not know that Jacob was working that morning. Robert let Lorna in and shut the door. Lorna wanted to know where Jacob was and Robert told her that he was at work. Lorna was suddenly uncomfortable now. Robert tried to get Lorna to sit on the couch, but she hesitated. Robert picked up on this; he kept forgetting that Lorna was still just a girl. Sure she would turn 17 in a couple of months, but he did not want to take advantage of the girl. Lorna told Robert that maybe she should leave. Robert said, "Whatever you feel comfortable with". Lorna said she was sorry, she had dreamt of this moment and now she was scared. Robert told her not to be scared, if she wanted to take it slow it was fine with him. She sat on the couch and Robert sat next to her. They started to kiss and Lorna's fear went away. She felt safe in Robert's arms. Robert said that he wanted Lorna to marry him. That day Lorna went from a girl to a woman and she felt wonderful. It was like everything had changed, she did not want to keep this from her Father any longer. She wanted to show her love for Robert every time she saw him. Robert said that he would talk to Lorna's Father.

Henry asked the girl if something was wrong with her, she looked different. Lorna thought, "I feel different". Lorna asked about her Mother to change the subject. Amelia was the same was all Henry said.

It was time for Christmas dinner and Lorna could hardly wait, she hadn't seen Robert since that wonderful Saturday. She told Buster, "Maybe Robert will take her for a walk since it isn't too cold, then we can be alone". As the two went down the path and toward town, I hope that Lorna knows what she is doing.

When the car turned up the path to the house and the two got out of the car, I could tell that they were upset with each other. Lorna stormed upstairs and slammed her bedroom door. She grabbed a hold of Buster and lay on the bed crying. Henry had caught Robert and Lorna kissing. Robert told Henry that he loved Lorna and wanted to marry her. Henry said that he thought Lorna was too young and that he wanted for her to wait until she got out of school. Henry said that Robert could come to the house for supper and to visit, but he didn't want the two of them to be alone.

Henry gave Lorna some time to calm down and then went to her room to talk to her. Henry tells the girl that she is all he has left and he wants her to grow up a little before she settles down with the first man she cares for. If she still feels the same way when she turns 18, he will be happy for Robert and her to get married. Lorna is still upset and will not even talk or look at her Father.

Robert tells Lorna that they should take it slow, like her Father wants. Lorna gets mad at Robert and tells him that he doesn't really love her or he wouldn't want to wait to get married, either.

The New Year started like the old one ended, Lorna only talking to her Father when spoken to, and not seeing Robert as often. It was 1945 and Lorna would be 17 in a couple of months, in another year she would be 18 and she could do whatever she wished. She knew one thing, she would not have survived going crazy if she hadn't had Buster to talk to.

The Life Story Of A House

Henry was listening to the radio and the man was talking about the first American to be executed by firing squad for desertion. Eddie Slovik was the first man to be executed since the Civil War.

Since he was getting the cold shoulder from Lorna, Henry listened to the radio more often. Most of the news was about the war. Fighting was taking place in Manila, the Bataan Peninsula, Iwo Jima, Okinawa and the continued battles to take Germany. By April, America was starting to hear about the atrocities of the Nazi death camps which held Jews, who were starved to death and in some cases cremated alive.

On April 12th, United States President Franklin Roosevelt passed away in Georgia. Vice-President Harry Truman becomes the President. Henry is sad to hear this news, the radio talks about America mourning the loss.

In May, Germany surrenders unconditionally, which the Allies accept. Henry is happy about this news; he even tries to tell Lorna who really doesn't care.

It becomes the end of May and Lorna can't wait for another year to pass so she can leave this place. Lorna has gotten to talking only to Buster unless William and Teresa visit. Lorna is starting to miss Robert.

In July Japan offers to surrender only if they can keep the Emperor as their leader. President Truman says no. A week later the U.S. test the first atomic bomb. Henry says that he can't imagine the power of the bomb. Five days later President Truman approves the order for the atomic bombs to be used on Japan. Henry cannot believe the country will actually drop the bomb. I think it must be terrible if Henry thinks that it is bad. July 30th, the USS Indianapolis is hit and sunk by a Japanese submarine. 900 men jump into the water and are left floating in the ocean for four days. Almost 600 die before help comes. The Captain is court-martialed and convicted, his name being Captain Charles B. McVay III. Henry was starting to believe the end of the war was about here when this happened.

The Life Story Of A House

On August 6th the United States dropped the atomic bomb on Hiroshima, Japan. Henry cannot believe it. The Japanese still do not surrender. It is estimated that 90,000-166,000 people will die in the first 2-4 months. On August 9th the United States drop another atomic bomb on Nagasaki, Japan. The casualties are 60,000- 80,000 killed. I can't believe all of those people were killed by dropping two bombs. On August 14th the Emperor of Japan announces on the radio of their surrender.

As Lorna is starting her final year of school, the government announces the end to World War II, she could care less. She can only think of one thing, seeing Robert. It has been since Christmas since she has even seen him. Lorna still does not talk to her Father, just Buster. Her Father is sad because his daughter does not talk to him. Henry tries again to talk to his daughter, but she is still not willing to listen. She wished she had made love to Robert and was pregnant just to see what her Father said then.

Nothing much happened the rest of the year; Henry still has Thanksgiving dinner at his house. It seems Henry and Robert have made amends but Lorna is still mad. I don't understand, they should be happy that the war is over.

Henry and Lorna go to Howard and Nancy's house for Christmas dinner. Lorna was not even excited for William and Teresa for having a baby boy. Henry talks William into coming on New Year's so he can see the baby without there being people all around.

William, Teresa, Emma and baby Henry visit on New Year's. Henry tells them that he hopes 1946 is better than 1945. William asks his Father if Lorna is still not talking to him. Henry says yes. The four visit a while and when they leave, Henry goes into town and visits Amelia. For some reason he felt compelled to visit.

On January 9th Howard and Jacob come up the path to the house. Lorna says, "I wonder what they want, maybe my Father got hurt".

The Life Story Of A House

Lorna opened the door and Jacob was crying and she got worried now. Jacob said there was an accident at the mine. Lorna asked how bad and Jacob said 55 men, including Father and Robert. Lorna passed out from the shock and when she awoke, she thought that maybe it had been a nightmare. Howard and Jacob were still there so she knew that it wasn't. The two men took Lorna into town and the workers had already given up digging, they had just lost 55 family and friends. Lorna could not believe it, why didn't she wake up, she had to wake up. The owners of the mine told the rescuers that they wouldn't even try to retrieve the bodies for fear of another cave-in. Lorna told Jacob that she wanted to go home, Jacob tried to protest but she said if he didn't take her then she would walk.

Lorna cried all night, telling Buster what had happened. She told Buster that she would never fall in love again. Lorna was sorry that she never got a chance to tell her Father and Robert she was sorry for the way she had acted. I do not think coal mines are very safe; it is hard to believe Henry and Robert are gone, trapped in a cave-in. I wonder if any of the men survived, even for a while.

There was a service at the mine three days later. Howard came out to the house and got Lorna.

There were a couple of cars that came up the path to the house later in the day. It was Jacob, William, Lorna, Howard, Bill, Nancy and Grace. They were trying to tell Lorna that she could not stay in the house by herself; she would have to move into town with Jacob. Lorna was protesting until finally Jacob and William said that the house would have to be sold. Neither of the boys could afford to keep the house. Lorna ran up to her room crying. Nancy and Grace followed her and tried to talk to the young woman. Lorna said that she had been awful to her Father for the longest time. Nancy said that he knew that you did not mean it, that you were just angry. Then Lorna said, "How do I live knowing Robert is not here waiting for me?" Grace said, "With time it will get easier, I'm not saying you will ever forget Robert, but it will get

The Life Story Of A House

easier". Grace and Nancy finally talked Lorna into coming downstairs to discuss the selling of the house. I will be alone again.

They had not even bothered to tell Amelia that her husband and son were dead. The doctor's said it would be better that way.

It was decided that all of the furniture would be moved to town. Whatever furniture wouldn't fit at Jacob's house would be put in storage until it could be sold. The house would be put up for sale as soon as the furniture was removed. Lorna asked if she could stay at the house until they were ready to move the furniture. The boys asked Nancy if she minded taking Lorna to town until she moved. Nancy agreed. When all the others had left, Lorna and Buster just sat in the living room where Lorna had another cry. I will miss this family.

It came time for moving day and all the men got it accomplished in one day, to Lorna's dismay. William went out front and pounded something in the ground. Lorna and William took one more look around and then they all drove down the path and turned toward town. I have that empty and alone feeling again.

It was starting to warm up finally, the house had been cold for some time when a car turned in the path and came toward the house. It was William and a strange man and woman. William opened the door to the house and told the couple that the house had only been left alone for a couple of months. William told the man and women to look things over; he would be outside when they were done. After the inspection of the house, they told William that they would take it. William said, "Mr. and Mrs. Stone, I think this will make you a fine house". They told William that they had two boys and three girls. I love a big family. William said it would take about a month to do the paper work, but it would be fine with me if you wanted to move in sooner. William asked Mr. Stone what he did for a living and he replied that he was a teacher and that the school had hired him for the following year. William said it would be a new school year before you knew it. Mr. Stone said three months. William told him that his sister, Lorna had just been in the graduating class. Mr. Stone asked if she was going on to do more studies. William said that he did not know, they had recently lost their Father and Lorna's boyfriend in the mine accident. Mr. Stone said he was sorry, he had heard about it. Mr. Stone said they would not move in for a couple of weeks, they should get an idea by then if they were going to get the loan from the bank. William said, "Whenever you want to, you are more that welcome to move in, I hate to see this old house empty". Am I old?

William, Jacob, Howard and Bill helped the Stone's move in. It didn't take them very long at all, as a matter of fact; it only took half of a day. The women made dinner for the whole crew and all the adults introduced themselves and the children too. "Lorna had stayed in town", William said, "She still had not got over the deaths of our Father and Robert Talbot". Mr. Stone is Todd, Mrs. Stone is Diane, and the children are Luke 16, Betsy 14, Lillian 12, Melanie 10 and Mark 8. I like it when a big family moves in.

The Stone's thanked the men and women as they left, it was nice to have friends already. The boys would have their room and girls would have to squeeze three beds in theirs. Todd and Diane would take the downstairs bedroom. The family had a phone and a radio also, and a new cook stove. Todd went out to the pump and was figuring how to run pipes into the house and put the pump in there. He told Diane that he thought he had it figured out. Luke and he would go into town tomorrow and get some supplies. Diane liked the idea of having water in the house.

There was a strange noise when everyone was a sleep. It seemed to be coming from Todd and Diane's room. I cannot figure out the noise though. The next day Diane told Todd that he would have to start sleeping on his side because he was snoring as loud as thunder. Okay, I know where the sound came from, but how does one snore?

The Life Story Of A House

Todd and Luke went in to town after breakfast. When they came home they had a car full of supplies. Todd set up a hand pump in the shoe and coat room. Todd said the floor was wood so all he and Luke had to do was dig down and out to the well. Luke said that it sounded like a lot of work to him. Todd told the boy, "We have all summer".

Mark had toys to play with, as did Melanie and Lillian, but Betsy read in her spare time and Luke liked to go fishing. Luke asked William if there were anywhere close to go fishing. William said that on the farm where he worked there was a pond that was stocked with fish. William told the boy that he could come over whenever he wanted, and gave him directions. William had also told him it was within walking distance because he had done it many times. William and Teresa laughed about that, even though they knew the boy did not understand what was funny. I wonder what to fish is. I don't remember anyone that has lived her who fished.

It took two weeks and a lot of digging, but Todd and Luke were finally able to run water into the house. Diane was very, very happy.

Since there was no war, every time the Stone's listened to the radio there was music. Todd said that he didn't care to hear the news. I wonder if Todd was in the war.

When Luke wasn't helping his Father at doing something, he was messing with what he called a fishing pole. It just looked like a stick with string tied to it with a metal hook on the end. One day, Todd asked Luke if he wanted to go fishing and he said sure. Diane made them a sack lunch and they left in the car away from town. When they came home that evening, they had a whole string full of things, they called fish. Diane said that the boys went fishing and the boys could clean the fish. Todd asked her if she wanted him to cook them to. Diane said she would do that. Todd and Luke went outside and started to hit the fish in the head, I guess to kill them. They sliced the fish open with a knife and cleaned all the guts out, and I am repeating Todd. They cut the heads off and pulled the skins off before cutting off the tail. How barbaric, I wonder if all things eaten are treated like that. It smelled good when they were cooking the fish and they all seemed to enjoy eating the fish, but I bet they don't know how they are cleaned.

Betsy had a lot of books to choose from, Todd was a teacher so he collected them. Betsy was only 14, but she seemed to be very smart. The three younger children liked to play outside, especially tag. The summer seemed to fly by, before you knew it school was ready to start. Todd would take the children to the school with him. He had it set up that if he couldn't work one day, then he would call Grace and ask her to take the children.

With all of the children at school, Diane had plenty of time to clean, do laundry or just read. Diane had worked but when she started having children she stopped working. Diane got in the habit of calling Nancy on the phone once a week. They usually didn't have anything important to say, they just talked to kill time. Since Todd was a teacher, he came home a couple of hours before suppertime. Sometimes they would talk to each other or help the children with their homework. Todd and the children seemed to be settling into the school and Diane at home.

Before they knew it, Thanksgiving was upon them. Howard and Nancy had invited them to dinner. William Johnson and his family were going to join them as was Grace and Bill, Jacob came too. Lorna had moved away, saying it was too painful to stay around there. That left William and Jacob to check in on their Mother once a month.

It seemed different not having Thanksgiving at the house, it felt lonely somehow. There also wasn't the smells of the past years.

When the family got home, they were talking about the wonderful time they had. Todd asked Diane if it was alright to have them all over for Christmas dinner. Diane said that it would be no problem. Todd and Diane talked about how friendly the people were here. They also talked

The Life Story Of A House

about the Johnson family, how they had so much heartbreak in their lives.

It was the first week in December and Todd decided to turn the radio onto a news station for a change. He turned it back to music because the man on the radio talked of a fire at a hotel in Atlanta, Georgia that had killed 119 people. That was the kind of news he told Diane that he didn't want to hear.

It was Christmas break and Todd and the children had a week and a half off of school. Todd decided to take them all to a movie called "It's a Wonderful Life" with Jimmy Stewart and Donna Reed. When they got home, they were all talking about the movie, even when the children went upstairs to bed.

Christmas day came and it seemed different with Diane cooking the dinner, although the smells were still the same. They all seemed to have a good time. Emma Elizabeth was three now and in to everything. Mark tried playing with the girl but she wouldn't hold still long enough. When the adults were setting around the table and saying the prayer, Todd added that he was thankful to have so many friends so soon. After dinner the radio was turned on low, they were playing Christmas music while the adults talked. Teresa had to keep an eye on little Henry and Emma, but William and the men were talking about all sorts of things. Diane and the women were off to themselves talking also. The children had gone upstairs to play with the new toys they had gotten that morning; Betsy was looking at her new books. Teresa took Emma upstairs and asked Betsy if she would play with the little girl long enough so she could talk for a while. Betsy said she would even though she had two littler sisters', she wasn't comfortable around a girl so young. Betsy shared the room with Lillian and Melanie so she was trying to think of something all four of them could play. They decided on hide and seek; only they would stay upstairs, and they would pester the boys.

When everyone was about worn out, they said their good-byes and left. Todd and Diane sat down in the living room; it had been a long day.

New Year's Eve came next, and Todd had gotten something he called fireworks to shoot off at midnight. Todd made the children stand back as he lit a match and some of them went into the sky and exploded into pretty colors. Some Todd just lit and threw them on the ground and they made a large bang. The children seemed to be quite excited. Finally, Todd said that he had no more fireworks, but then he pulled out a big one and said only this one. Todd lit it with a match and it flew high in the night sky and exploded in the most beautiful colors. The children all screamed and yelled and danced around their Father saying he was the greatest Father in the world. When Todd and Diane got the children calmed down enough, she took them upstairs to bed, but the children had a hard time going to sleep. Todd and Diane went right to sleep when their heads hit their pillows.

It was time for school to begin again only Melanie was sick. Todd told Diane that he would stop at the doctor's office before school and send him out to the house. When the doctor arrived, he told Diane that the girl had the mumps and that they were contagious. I don't know what contagious means or mumps. Diane set a little bed up in the living room for Melanie to sleep on. Contagious must mean that Melanie can spread the disease to the other children. When Todd and the other children got home and Diane told them what the doctor had said, the children all kept as far away from Melanie as they could. Melanie had to put up with sleeping downstairs for a week, and then Betsy got them.

The second week of the New Year, 1947, the man on the radio said that there had been a brutal murder in Los Angeles of an actress, Elizabeth Short. She would be nicknamed the "Black Dahlia". Isn't there enough people accidently killed without someone taking someone's life on purpose. Some people must be really cruel. Todd said that is why he doesn't like to turn on the news, it is all bad.

The Life Story Of A House

It is finally getting warmer and Diane tells Todd that she will wait a couple of more weeks before she plants the garden. Diane starts to listen to the radio when she cleans, mostly music, but sometimes they break in with a news story. On March 25th the radio broke into the music to let people know that a coal mine had exploded in Centralia, Illinois, killing 111 miners. I don't know when people are going to quit mining because there are so many killed. Now it seems like every week there is a disaster. April 9th, tornadoes hit Kansas, Oklahoma and Texas, killing 181 people and injuring 970. On April 16th, an ammonium cargo on the USS Grandcamp explodes in Texas, killing 552, injuring 3,000, causing 200 lost and destroying 20 city blocks. So many people hurt or killed.

School finally gets out for the summer and all the children have their own plans to spend the time. The littler ones will play, Betsy will read and when Luke isn't helping his Father, he plans on doing more fishing this summer than last. Todd says that he is going to take it easy.

Todd and Diane have to laugh every time someone on the radio talks about U.F.O.'s. I don't know what that means but the radio is starting to talk more about it. Supposedly two are seen in Washington, and one crashed in the desert of New Mexico. Todd tells the children about the stories and that they should keep their eyes towards the sky, Diane says that Todd shouldn't scare the children. Luke and Betsy said that they didn't believe it unless they saw it.

The children are trying to talk their Father into buying a television, but he is resisting. Todd says that maybe next year. The way it is explained, it sounds as if it is magic. A picture in a square box and sound to go with it, it is hard to imagine it.

Todd doesn't have any big jobs this summer, so he does some little ones and takes most of the summer sitting around. Before he knew it, the school year had snuck up on him. Not sure what that means, snuck up on him how.

The Life Story Of A House

This is Luke's last year in school and he is excited to get it over. Luke doesn't know what he is going to do with the rest of his life, but he figures he has a year to decide. Betsy is 16 now but she is still into reading. Todd thinks he is getting old, little Mark is 10.

Thanksgiving, Christmas and New Year's leads up to the end of the school year. It has gone faster than Luke had expected he hadn't decided what he wanted to do yet and 1948 was almost half over. Todd tells Luke that he needs to decide what to do; it is time for him to grow up and fend for himself. I hope he doesn't choose a job at the mine.

This is how Luke tells his Father how his day went. I go into town and ask Jacob Johnson if he has heard of anyone wanting to hire. Jacob tells me that the glass factory might be hiring. I thank him and go to the glass factory and talk to the owners. They tell me that they can always use another man, so I get hired and start this Monday. I go back and tell Jacob and he tells me that I could rent half of his house if I wanted. I told him I wouldn't get a check for a while. Jacob said that didn't matter, he would know where I live. We both laughed and I told him that I would move this week-end if it was alright with him. Jacob told me that he would arrange for a couple of trucks to come to my house on Saturday. Todd tells his son that he has accomplished a lot for one day and congratulates him. Diane looks sad, but she knew this day would come as she tells the two men. That night after supper, Todd was sitting in his chair when he decided to turn the radio on. He was just in time to hear about an airplane that crashed in Pennsylvania that killed all 43 people on board. Todd changed the channel to some music.

On Thursday Luke and his Father go fishing and they come home with a bucket full. Todd and Luke set about cleaning them and Luke tells his Mother that they could have fish tonight. She scrunches her nose up but she has to admit that she likes to eat them.

Saturday morning comes and a couple of trucks come up the road and turn onto the path that comes up to the house. It is William and Jacob

Johnson, and Howard and Bill were with them in the other truck. They
load the trucks in no time with six men doing the work. Luke tries to tell
his Mother that this way his Father didn't have to haul him to town in
the summer. Luke says that he can walk to work, also. Luke and his
Father follow the other trucks to town as Diane stands at the door and
cries.

When Todd gets home, he tells Diane that the boy is only in town and
they could visit him anytime. This cheers up Diane a little, but she tells
her husband that once the children start to leave the house, it won't be
long until they are all gone. Todd hugs his wife and tells her that her
Mother had to watch her leave; just as Mother's all through the ages
had to watch their children walk through the door, some to never come
back. Todd tells Diane that at least Luke is in town. Diane said that she
hadn't thought of it that way and was in a better mood from then on.
The next week-end the family goes into town and visits Luke. When
they get home Todd tells Diane that he told her Luke would be just fine.
Luke has adapted to living in town and he likes his new job.

As quickly as the school year ended, it was September already and
school was to begin. It was hard for Todd to think of his little Betsy as
being 16. Maybe Diane was right about the children grow up to fast,
and he told Diane as much.

School goes well, Betsy has joined the school chorus, and Lillian,
Melanie and Mark are all making their grades.

Before Todd knows it, it is Thanksgiving weekend and they are invited
to Bill and Grace's for dinner. Diane said that she enjoyed Thanksgiving
and Christmas as there were so many people together.

The family comes home and Todd said that if he had to eat that much
every day, he would be fat. He lifted up his shirt and chased the
children around the house with his stomach pushed out to make himself
look fat. It will never get old to hear laughter.

The Life Story Of A House

It is getting close to Christmas and the school is having a show where all of the grades get up on stage and sing a couple of songs. The children are all nervous about being on stage. Betsy has been practicing all school year, but the other three children have only been practicing a month. When they get home the children are excited by the thrill of being on stage. Todd and Diane are telling them how good they were, but Diane took Betsy aside and told her that she did especially well. The children sing for the next few days and it sounds wonderful.

Christmas day arrives and Diane is busy making dinner for the family and the group of people they have invited, but she is especially looking forward to seeing Luke. Since Luke moved into town the family has seen less and less of him. People start to arrive, first Bill and Grace, then Howard and Nancy. William, Teresa and family come, and then Jacob and Luke show up last. The house is full of happy sounds and grand smells; I think if every day was like this I would be in the Heaven that Diane talks about.

The children are happy that their Father has gotten fireworks to shoot of on New Year's Eve, even though it does not seem the same without Luke. Luke was invited, but he said some of the men had invited him to a party.

Soon it becomes 1949. The year goes like most years at the school. The only news of importance to Todd was between January 4th and February 22nd, Nebraska, Wyoming, South Dakota, Utah, Colorado and Nevada have a series of winter storms that killed tens of thousands cattle and sheep. The storms produced up to 72 mph winds. On August 28th, the last 6 surviving veterans of the American Civil War meet in Indiana. On September 5th Howard Unruh killed 13 neighbors in New Jersey with a souvenir Luger. Unruh was a World War II veteran and his was the first single-episode mass murder. Thanksgiving, Christmas and New Year's all go the same as previous years, only this year, Luke brings a girlfriend with him, Olivia Griffin.

The Life Story Of A House

1950 starts with an armored car robbery on January 17th. Eleven thieves stole more than $2 million in Boston, Massachusetts. Todd and his children get through another school year. Todd doesn't have any plans for the summer other than taking the family to see the newest Disney movie, "Cinderella". The children rave that the movie is the best they have ever seen. Todd teases them saying it is the best until the next movie they see.

There is trouble starting June 25th when North Korean troops cross the 38th parallel into South Korea. Todd is worried that Luke might be drafted. On the 27th of June President Harry Truman orders American military to aid in the defense of South Korea. On the 28th, North Korean forces capture Seoul.

Luke hasn't heard any news yet from the military but tells his Father that he expects too. The men decide to keep the information from Diane until it happens.

September begins as Betsy starts her last year of high school. Todd is excited for her but is still worried about Luke. I wonder if this war is part of the last war.

Todd starts to listen to the news on the radio every night to hear what is going on in the war. On September 15th the allied troops commanded by Douglas MacArthur begin a U.N. counteroffensive by landing in Inchon which is occupied by North Korea.

On September 30th Luke receives his draft papers from the military. He calls his Father to tell him to let the rest of the family know. Luke says he will come to the house on Saturday. Luke tells his Father that he is to leave for Biloxi, Mississippi the following day for six weeks of training. Diane is very upset to hear the news about Luke. Todd tries to tell Diane that there is nothing that can be done but pray.

Luke doesn't even get to come home after his military training in the middle of November; he is to ship out to where the fighting is. Olivia wanted to marry Luke before he went, but Luke told her that it would be the first thing he did when he got home. When Diane heard this she sobbed even more.

Thanksgiving is a little less festive as years before. The Stone family still goes to Bill and Nancy's house, but return sooner than usual. Todd turns on the radio as soon as he gets home. The big news is that a huge winter storm has ravaged the northeastern part of America, bringing 30 to 50 inches of snow and below zero temperatures, killing 323 people. I am glad we don't live there.

The next day there is word of Chinese forces joining North Korea to battle South Korea and American forces. The newscaster says that this action dashes any hope of a quick ending to the conflict. Three days later, the North Koreans and Chinese forces force a retreat of the United Nation forces. The next day MacArthur threatens to use nuclear weapons in Korea.

The children are trying to practice for the Christmas musical; Betsy has a solo this year. There still has been no word from Luke.

President Harry Truman sends U.S. military advisors to Vietnam to aid French troops.

The Christmas musical goes off with no problem and Betsy singing is the talk of the school. The family is all raving about it when they arrive home, although Todd and Diane are still thinking of Luke.

Christmas dinner is a little quieter than usual; Jacob brings Luke's girlfriend, Olivia to be part of the family. The radio is on all day, even if it is barely heard.

The family agrees to skip this year's fireworks, so 1951 enters quietly. The Stone's receive a letter from Luke. It says:

Dear family,

I hope the family is all well. We are in battles about half the time. The Generals say that there is more at stake now that the Chinese are involved. I guess that the U.S. being involved doesn't matter. I hope this conflict is short because I am ready to come to see everyone. Tell everyone I said hello and please pray for me.

Love,

Luke

Diane cries, but she is happy to hear that her son is still alive. On the same day they receive the letter; the news on the radio says that the North Koreans and Chinese troops have captured Seoul. Ten days later the U.S. drop a 1-kiloton nuclear bomb in Nevada, the government says it is a test. I can't believe people can't get along; it has not been that long since the world war.

Todd listens to the radio every night, sometimes even ignoring the rest of the family. Diane talks to Todd about it, he says he will try and do better. On February 6th a Pennsylvania Railroad passenger train derails in New Jersey, killing 85 people and injuring over 500. Todd has a talk with Betsy and asks her what she is going to do when school gets out. Betsy asks her Father if there is enough money for her to go to college. Todd asks the young lady what she is going to study, and she says, "I want to be a teacher, just like you".

The Korean Conflict continues with battles March 7th, March 14th, and President Truman relieving General Douglas MacArthur of his command on April 11th. The U.S. continues to test thermonuclear weapons in the Marshall Islands.

Another school year ends and Betsy graduates, finishing her high school years. Todd throws a get together, with all their friends present. Betsy decides to attend college in town so she can live at home. Todd said he would give her his car and buy himself a newer one. Todd is happy that Betsy is going to stay at home. He doesn't think Diane is ready for another child to leave the house.

On July 10th the United Nations and North Koreans begin peace talk. Betsy has already signed up for college and been accepted. She has a couple of weeks to decide what courses she is to take.

Todd decides that everyone has been thinking of the war too much, so he takes them all to the movies. They see Walt Disney's animated film, "Alice in Wonderland". Todd was right; the movie took everyone's mind off of the war, at least for a couple of days. I still wonder what a movie is.

In the middle of August, Todd has Betsy go into town with him. Two cars come up the path to the house. Todd is in one and Betsy is in the family car. Betsy is happy that her Father has taken care of her. She has been practicing driving up and down the road. It is hard to believe Betsy is 18, Lillian is 17, Melanie is 15 and Mark is 13. Todd spent part of the summer with Mark, fishing.

Betsy starts college a few days before Todd starts high school. The first couple of night's Betsy is excited, she has found out what classes she needs to take in the four years of college to become a teacher.

Todd tells Diane that he thinks the summers are getting shorter. Diane kisses her husband good-bye, as well as the three children. It is just me and Diane again. She turns on the radio while she is doing her chores in case there is the littlest bit of news from the war that Luke is in.

In the blink of an eye, it was Thanksgiving already. The family all rode together to Bill and Nancy's house for dinner. When they came home, they were still in a festive mood. Diane asked Todd not to turn on the radio for one night, Todd agreed.

Two days later, Todd loaded everyone in the car under the premise of just taking a ride. A couple of hours later the car turned up the path toward the house. The children were all excited and talking about the movie they had just seen. The family had went and seen "A Christmas Carol" with Alastair Sim starring. Todd was thinking of ways to keep their minds off of the danger that Luke must surely be in.

Like usual, Christmas dinner is held at the Stone's house. The talk was more relaxed this year, they had still remembered about Luke, but were trying not to confine their conversation to just that subject. They all asked Betsy how she was doing in college. Betsy told them that it was a little harder than high school but she thought that she could handle it. William and Teresa's daughter, Emma was 8 now, time was flying by. For some reason William and Teresa only had the two children, Emma and Henry. William is still worked on the farm for his in-laws. Olivia is still waiting for Luke to come home, although Jacob and she are spending more time together.

Two days later a letter arrives from Luke. Todd reads it to the family.

Dear family,

I hope this finds you all well. I have gotten a month to rest before I have to go back to the line of fighting. We are holding our own, for now. I hope this will be over soon. I bet my brother and sisters are growing like weeds. Has Betsy started college yet? Tell her to study hard. I hope to be home before Mark is old enough to be drafted. Tell everyone hello and that I love them.

Love,

Luke

Diane started to cry knowing that her boy was safe for the time being. The children were excited to get the letter from their older brother.

The family had a little party amongst themselves on New Year's. Soon they would turn the calendar over to 1952 and go back to school.

On March 21st the radio broke into its programming to announce that tornadoes had ravaged the lower Mississippi Valley, killing 208 people. It is still cold where the Stone's live.

William calls Todd after he gets home from work to tell him that his brother, Jacob and Olivia are going to get married. William wants to know whether Todd thinks it wise for Olivia to write Luke to tell him. Todd tells William to tell Olivia not to write Luke, if he comes home then she can tell him. William says he is sorry, but Todd tells him that it is not his fault. William tells Todd that he hopes it won't end their friendship. Todd tells him it will not. After Todd gets off the phone and tells Diane, she says that she was afraid of that. Diane says that this would be one more thing for Luke to worry about. Todd told Diane that he told William not to write Luke, Diane was glad. Poor Luke, he didn't even have a chance with Olivia.

The school year ended on the first of June. Betsy was already to start her second year, she had gotten straight A's in school and thought school was easy. Lillian would be a senior in high school the following fall but she already has a boyfriend, Terry Sawyer. Diane knows about the boy, but tells Lillian she should finish her final year of high school before she gets in a serious relationship. Lillian says that she will try. There hasn't been much word on the radio about the war. Todd tells Diane that it is good news not to have heard anything.

One Saturday a truck came up the path to the house and Todd went out to greet them. It was Bill and Howard. The men unloaded a pole off the truck and then they connected the pole and hooked it to the side of the house. They put a wire contraption on the top of the pole and ran wires from the contraption on top of the pole to inside the house. The men then carried a box into the house, the children were all happy and so was Diane. The men hooked the wires to the back of the box and pulled a knob on the front of the box. Slowly a picture appeared on the box, it must be magic. The men call the box a television. The children spend the rest of the summer watching the box; Diane sneaks a peek, too. The children say there are different shows on the television. Diane is interested in something called soap operas. The picture is black and white on the television, while everything in the house is in color. I wonder why the boxes pictures are not in color.

Before they knew it, it was time for Betsy to go back to college and Todd and the children back to high school. It is hard for Diane to get her work done with the soap operas on in the daytime on the television.

On November 1st the United States detonates the first hydrogen bomb in the Marshall Islands. The bomb has a yield of 10.4 megatons. Todd tells Diane the bomb is a lot bigger than the one used in Japan. Why would anyone build such a thing? Since Todd got the television, they show scenes of the destruction in Japan. It is worse than I could ever imagine. Three days later, Dwight D. Eisenhower wins the presidential election; Harry Truman had decided not to run.

I think the news is more awful now that you can see pictures instead of just hearing about it. The television shows Dwight Eisenhower visiting Korea, trying to find out what he can do to end the conflict.

The family goes to Howard and Nancy's house for Thanksgiving dinner. When they return, Diane is talking about Jacob and his new wife, Olivia being there. Todd tries to calm his wife down, but to no good. Diane says that we are not going to invite them for Christmas dinner. Todd tells her to remember her Bible, forgive and be forgiven or something like that.

Todd is ready for the Christmas break, for some reason, he is tired. The school puts on the Christmas Musical and Melanie and Mark participate, but Lillian does not.

Five days before Christmas the news on television shows an Air Force jet crash in Washington that kills 86 servicemen. I do not think I like this television, I do not like seeing pictures of the destruction. There are other shows, but Todd watches the news most nights.

Christmas comes and Todd has talked Diane into inviting Jacob and Olivia, for William's sake. Olivia and Jacob do not say much.

On December 31st the U.S. government says there are nearly 58,000 cases of polio, with 3,145 dying and 21,269 are left with mild to disabling paralysis. Todd says that he prays to God each night that nobody in his family get the disease. Instead of watching the fireworks outside, the family stays in the house and watch television. 1953 comes in quietly.

Two days later, there is a letter from Luke.

Dear family,

I hope that this year will be when the fighting ends. I am more than ready to come home. I should be thankful that I have not been killed. Some of the friends that I have made over here have been killed. Please tell Olivia that I think of her every day, and also my family. I hope Betsy is doing well in college and Lillian has not gotten married yet. I had the idea that Lillian would not be furthering her education. Tell Melanie and Mark hello, I bet they are getting big. Please pray for this awful war to end.

Love,

Luke

Diane says that Luke is going to be broken hearted when he comes home and finds Olivia has married Jacob Johnson. Todd tells his wife not to worry about it until Luke walks through our door.

Five days later, outgoing President Truman announces that the U.S. has developed a hydrogen bomb. Todd tells Diane that the world will soon be coming to an end. First we will make the bombs, then some other country will and pretty soon, half of the world will have them pointed at each other. Todd says that he prays that he and his family do not live to see it happen. I don't want to either.

On January 19th Todd and Diane watch the episode of the comedy "I Love Lucy" which Lucy gives birth.

It is a cold and snowy winter this year, but one weekend in February has good enough weather for Todd to take the family to see the movie, "Peter Pan". The children love it, even if they are getting older. Todd knows that the children will grow up someday, but he hopes that it is not too soon.

On March 17th the first nuclear test is conducted in Nevada in front of 1,620 spectators. I guess the people wanted to see the awesome power of the bomb.

Lillian tells her sister, Melanie that she has a secret that she wants to keep from their Mother and Father, she is pregnant. Melanie asks Lillian what she is going to do. Lillian says," Terry will ask Father for us to get married as soon as I graduate from high school. Hopefully, I won't be showing by then". Melanie says that she wishes them luck and wants to know where they are going to live and where is Terry going to work. Lillian says that hopefully Terry will get a job at the glass factory, but he has been helping out at the car garage. We hope to get a little house in town.

On May 11th Diane has her soap-operas interrupted by the news of a F5 tornado going through the middle of the downtown district of Waco, Texas killing 114 people. It takes a while, but the news crew arrives to show the destruction.

Terry Sawyer finally talks to Todd and Diane about Lillian and him marrying. Lillian is not showing yet so her Father doesn't suspect anything. Diane has a feeling about Lillian, but she isn't talking. Todd recommends a fall wedding, but Terry is insistent on getting married after school is out. Todd finally says that they can get married after Terry gets a job better than working at the garage. Todd tells Terry there is no way he can support a family on his current salary. Lillian is looking worried when Terry agrees. Terry tells Todd as soon as school is out, he will start looking for a better paying job.

It finally is June 1ˢᵗ, and school is out. Todd is glad for the rest, Terry immediately starts to look for work and Lillian hopes Terry finds a job soon because she is starting to put on weight. Diane notices her daughter getting a little bigger and takes her a side and asks her if she is with-child. Lillian starts to cry and says that she is. Diane says that she will let Lillian's clothes out just a little so no one will know. Lillian thanks her Mother and tells her that she hopes Terry finds a better job quickly. I wonder what Todd would do if he knew?

On June 8ᵗʰ there was a tornado outbreak in the area around Flint, Michigan, killing 115 people. The next day a tornado hit Worchester, Massachusetts, killing 94 people. It is from the same system that had hit Flint, Michigan the day before. I am glad we don't live in those two areas.

After the fourth of July, Terry gets a job at the glass factory and says that he wants to marry Lillian the following week-end. Todd asks the boy if he doesn't think he should see if he can handle the job or not. Terry says no, he doesn't want to be apart from Lillian anymore. Todd is suspicious, but agrees. Diane had done wonders with Lillian's clothes.

Betsy comes home from college for the summer so she can see her sister get married. They all wish that Luke could be there. The wedding is only a small ceremony with both sets of families and Howard, Nancy, Bill and Grace. The wedding will be at the church, but they will come back to the Stone's for the reception. Before they leave for the church, Todd and Diane tell Lillian how lovely she looks.

It looked like a half a dozen cars coming up the path to the house. Everything was so festive; it was almost like Thanksgiving or Christmas. Diane had made a huge cake and there was a huge bowl of what they called punch. I thought that was to hit someone, but I guess it means both things. It was way past dark before the non-family members started to leave. Howard and Nancy had said that they had a spare bedroom and Terry and Lillian were going to stay there, at least for the night. Before they all left, Diane was crying, hugging her daughter, Todd was shaking Terry's hand and welcomed him to the family. I wonder if Todd would welcome Terry to the family if he knew about his daughter, Lillian.

Todd didn't have any plans for updates on the house, so he and Mark went fishing a lot. Terry and Lillian had gotten a small house in town. Betsy already wanted to go back to college. Melanie and Betsy helped their Mother, if only to watch the soaps when Todd and Mark were gone fishing.

On July 27th the United States, China, North Korea and South Korea signed an agreement ending the war. Todd and Diane were so happy they were dancing around the house with the two girls and Mark, although Mark said he was too old for such things. Todd and Diane would be looking for a call from Luke telling them when he was coming home. The call never came in the first couple of days and Todd was beginning to worry.

On August 5th Diane just happened to be walking past the television when it was on and she let out a scream. Todd came running in from the garden and Diane was sitting in a chair in front of the television. Todd asked her what is wrong. At first she didn't say a thing, and then she slowly said, "The U.S. and North Koreans were exchanging prisoners of war and I thought I saw Luke". Diane said, "Oh Todd, it looked like the prisoners from our side had all been starved. You could see their ribs sticking out from the starvation". Todd put his arms around Diane and said, "Let's pray for all of those men even if it wasn't Luke that you saw". But it was, I saw him on the television, and he looked terrible.

Todd and Diane still never received a call from Luke. Todd told Diane that if Luke had been starved, the army would make sure he was back to normal before they released him from service.

The Life Story Of A House

Betsy was crying as she left for college this year. She was worried about her brother Luke. Diane told her that they would call her as soon as they had heard anything. Shortly Todd and his youngest two children would have to go back to school too.

It was the middle of September when a strange car turned up the path towards the house. Diane didn't see it at first; the car had something strange on top of it. Luke got out of the car and then stuck his head back in the window. Luke looked almost like a skeleton that you would see on television. I am glad he is safely at home. Diane heard the car but she was in the back room that they use for a pantry. When she came into the kitchen, there was Luke. She ran over to him and started hugging and kissing him, crying the whole time. Then she noticed his appearance and she was shocked by his condition. Luke asked to sit down and Diane helped him into the living room. Diane had a million questions, but Luke said that he would rather answer them to his Father and her together. Diane asked Luke if he wanted a sandwich since it was almost noon. Luke said, "Yes please". Diane made him a ham sandwich and got him a glass of lemonade. While Luke ate slowly, Diane told him of his siblings. "Betsy was in her third year of college, Lillian had gotten married to Terry Sawyer but your Father was not supposed to know she was with-child, but she couldn't fool me". Luke laughed a little. "Melanie is 17 now and Mark is 15". Diane had almost run out of small talk when Luke asked if he could lie down. Diane took him to her and Todd's bedroom and told Luke he could lie there a while. When Diane went into the kitchen, she started to cry thinking of all the terrible things her son had to endure. Diane never called Todd at school unless it was an extreme emergency, she called him today. When Todd got to the phone, Diane started telling Todd, "Luke had arrived by cab and that he looked just awful. He had to lie down and I put him in our room. Luke says that he will tell us what happened when we are together, so please come home now". Diane said, "Good" and then hung up the phone. I wonder what the difference between a car and a cab is.

Todd pulled up the path to the house; he had Melanie and Mark with him. Todd ran in the house but Luke was still lying down. The four of them sat in the living room quietly while they waited for Luke to get up. Diane did take the time to go in the kitchen and call Lillian and Betsy. Betsy was upset, Diane would say later, she could not come home until Christmas break.

Finally Luke got up and came into the living room. His Father got up and hugged his son; Mark shook his hand but then hugged him. Melanie couldn't help herself, she was crying as she gave Luke a long hug. Luke mentioned how much Melanie and Mark had grown. Luke sat down and started to talk. He said that he and five others had been captured about six months after they had gotten to Korea. He was in a prisoner camp the rest of the time. He said," by the way I look, you can imagine how they treated us and I will not go into detail. We were not told the war was over until the day we were released, three of us didn't make it". "I kept thinking about my family and how you all and Olivia would be waiting for me". Diane started to cry again. Luke said, "The army says that I should take things slowly for a while, and I was hoping I could stay here for a while". Todd said, "Of course you can stay as long as you want to". Luke said, "Thank you, I hope that I am well enough by spring to marry Olivia". Diane could not hold it any longer, she ran up the stairs crying and laid on Melanie's bed. Luke said," I did not wish to upset Mother or anyone, but I had no place to recuperate other than here". Todd told his son not to worry about anything; it would just take his Mother a little time to adjust to him being home. Luke said that he would sleep on the couch, but when Todd said that he could sleep in Mark's room, Luke said that he could not walk up the stairs yet. Todd said that they would figure something out; Luke would not have to sleep on the couch. Mark and Melanie both volunteered to stay at Lillian's and Terry's in town. Todd said, "We'll see. Lillian told your Mother that she and Terry would come out once Terry got home from work, we'll ask them then". Luke asked if it was alright for him to lie down again, and his Father said, "Of course".

Todd told Melanie and Mark to go into Mark's room when he found Diane in Melanie's room. Todd talked quietly to Diane so Luke would not hear. Todd told her," they would wait until tomorrow to tell Luke about Olivia, unless he wants to call her. Then we will have to tell the boy".

That evening, Lillian and Terry came to the house. Lillian looked like she had a ripe watermelon in her stomach. Todd figured out she was with-child when they were married. After Lillian visited Luke for a while, Melanie got her things together so she could stay with Lillian and Terry. Melanie and Lillian hugged Luke good-bye; Luke wondered why Olivia had not at least called. Luke guessed he would call her tomorrow. Todd and Diane moved some of their things to Melanie's room so Luke could have theirs downstairs.

The next morning Todd told Mark that they were staying home and Mark didn't argue with his Father. When Luke got up, the three of them sit at the kitchen table, Mark had breakfast and was told to stay in his room until further notice. After Luke had a piece and a half of toast and some coffee Todd told him he had something to talk to him about. Diane started to cry and Luke thought that maybe Olivia died. Todd told his son that he had bad news, Olivia had gotten married. It was our fault that she didn't write you, we thought you had enough to worry about. Poor Luke just hung his head. Luke wanted to know if he knew who the man was. Todd said, "Jacob Johnson. Luke said, "She is part of the reason I kept myself alive". Todd hugged his son and said, "He knew, that is why it was best not to tell you until you came home". Luke said, "I thank you for that. I need to lie down now". Luke got up and slowly walked to the bedroom, hanging his head the whole time. Diane was still crying and Todd was trying to comfort her. Mark came downstairs to get a sandwich and went back upstairs when he saw his Mother still crying.

The next day Todd and Mark went to school, Luke sat on the couch in front of the television looking at it, but not really watching it. He told his Mother that he needed to lie down. Luke got a glass of water before he lay down.

Todd and Mark arrived home and Luke still wasn't up. Todd told Diane that Luke probably had a lot of sleep to catch up on. After supper Todd began to wonder, and when it was bedtime he told Mark to go to bed and for Diane to stay in the living room. Todd walked into Luke's bedroom and saw that Luke was still asleep. Luke looked white as a sheet though. Todd cried as he felt for a pulse on his son, he had been dead for some time. Todd covered Luke's body completely up and went out to tell Diane. Diane could tell that her husband had been crying and she knew the worst had happened. Diane started to cry and ran into Todd's arms. Mark came downstairs and his Mother told him that Luke was dead. Mark was stunned; his Father told him that Luke's heart was probably too weak to take the strain of rejection. Todd was trying to decide whether to call the girls or not, but Diane said that he should.

Todd called Lillian's house and Terry answered the phone since it was so late. Todd told Terry to tell Lillian and Melanie that Luke had died that day and we just now found him. Terry was shocked, but he said that he would handle it and that they would see him tomorrow. Todd then made the call that he didn't want to make. One of the girls answered the phone and said that they would go and get Betsy. As soon as Betsy heard her Father on the other end of the phone, she knew it was bad news. Todd told her about Luke and after Betsy cried for a couple minutes, she told her Father that she would be home for the services. Todd told Diane everything that Betsy and Terry had said. Now Todd had to call the undertaker. Todd told the man that he could wait until the morning and the man agreed since he was already for bed. Todd told Mark to try and get some sleep; he and Diane would be up pretty soon to go to bed also. Diane and Todd set on the couch and just held each other. Diane said, "Luke couldn't take the news about Olivia". Todd told her she was probably right. "Luke had been in so much pain that he couldn't stand the strain of Olivia getting married to someone else; she was the one reason for him to stay alive", Todd said.

Todd and Diane went upstairs to bed, although they knew they would not be able to sleep.

The next morning the undertaker showed up to take Luke's body away. Luckily he had a helper with him; Todd did not think he could help carry his son's body. The undertaker wanted to know when the family wanted to have the service. Todd said, "As soon as my daughter, Betsy gets home from college". Lillian, Terry and Melanie came out to the house, just missing the undertaker. Lillian and Melanie held their Mother for a while, then they asked why they thought Luke had died. Todd told the girls that they had told Luke about Olivia and they thought that his heart couldn't take the strain; he was so weak and worn down.

Betsy arrived by cab that evening and the family had one big cry.

The day of the service was clear, but a little cold. Some people came back to the house afterwards, but not Olivia and Jacob. Diane was surprised Olivia had the nerve to show her face at the funeral.

On November 13th Lillian had a baby boy. Terry and Lillian decided to call him Luke.

The family didn't go anywhere for Thanksgiving or Christmas. They had a meal at home that included turkey and all of the fixins. On New Year's Eve, there was no celebration. Betsy came home for the holidays and left after New Year's Day. No one was in a festive mood.

On January 20th and 21st, Todd, Melanie and Mark stayed home from school, it was 70 below zero. Even I felt that they were having trouble keeping the house warm.

Ever since Luke had died, Diane seemed to be just going through the paces. During the winter most of her day was spent watching television.

As soon as June arrived, Melanie graduated high school and she turned 18 years old. Melanie's Father asked her if she were going to continue her education like Betsy. Todd was surprised by her answer. Melanie said, "Why bother, you never know when you are going to drop dead, I will look for a job in town, maybe I can stay with Lillian until I can afford to rent a room". Even Betsy tried to talk her into going to college but Melanie wanted no part of it. Lillian had already told Melanie that she could stay at her house for a while. Mark was 16, Todd expected him to move out when he turned 18, but not Melanie. Diane didn't have an opinion one way or the other.

Todd could not believe it; Melanie had gotten herself a job at a bar. She was to serve drinks and get the men to continue to buy them. I don't know what Melanie is going to be doing, Diane doesn't seem to care about anything anymore and Todd doesn't have anyone to talk too.

By the end of June, Melanie had packed her things and moved to town with Lillian.

Todd tried to take Mark fishing most days during the summer, Diane was still acting strange and Todd was hearing disturbing things about Melanie. Diane had not even planted a garden this year. I wonder if Diane is going to act like Amelia.

One night in August, Lillian calls her Father to tell him that he should check on Melanie. Todd tells Lillian that he has been hearing disturbing things about Melanie. Todd said that he would come in town tomorrow to check Melanie out for himself. Lillian finally told her Father that Melanie had moved out and she was living above the tavern in one room.

The next day, Todd drives into town; he takes Mark with him since he is 16. Todd tells Diane that he is going to visit Lillian and little Luke. Todd repeats his story to Diane, even though she does not act like she cares. Todd said that he went to the bar where Melanie lived and she was already downstairs working. She was wearing a skimpy dress that went above her knees; she was showing off her breasts too. Melanie was surprised to see her Father. Todd could tell she had been drunk most of the time. Todd was also worried that she had a room just to take men. Todd finally said, "What possibly made you want to work here, it wasn't the way you were brought up". Melanie said, "Luke dying". Todd asked Melanie to come home with him, but she refused, and said," I like to drink and I like men too". Todd just shook his head and went and found Mark. They went home without Melanie and Todd knew what kind of girl she had become. Telling this to Diane didn't seem to faze her. Todd guessed that Diane wasn't dealing with the death of Luke to well, either.

September couldn't come soon enough for Todd. Diane still wasn't talking much and Mark had told his Father that as soon as he got the last two years of school out of the way, he was going to move to another town. It was nothing against his Father; he just couldn't take it anymore. Todd told his son that he understood.

One day when Diane was home alone, a car came up the path to the house. A man got out that I did not know. When he knocked on the door, Diane asked what his business was there. He told her that he was a door to door salesman. Diane told him to come in the house and she made him some lemonade. He introduced himself as Luke Prescott and he was selling silverware and other kitchen items. Diane thought that this man named Luke must be a sign from God. Diane listened to the man's presentation and then asked the man if he would take her with him. The man was shocked. Diane told him that her son had just died and that she needed to get away, to many bad memories. The man was hesitant, but Diane was persuasive when she had to be. The man finally told her he was going to another town up the road and Diane said that it wouldn't take long to pack what she needed. The man sat on the couch waiting for this strange woman, but he did get lonely on the road. Diane came out about ten minutes later and told the man that she was ready to go. The man and Diane left and she did not even look back.

When Todd got home, he found the house empty. He walked around the inside and the outside of the house, no Diane. He walked into the bedroom and noticed a few things missing and he figured Diane must have left. Todd drove into town with Mark but there was no sign of Diane. The two had to go home empty handed.

Todd and Mark finally went back to school. While at home Todd quizzed Mark as to what their next move should be. Mark said that there wasn't any use of having a big house like this, they might as well move into town next summer. Todd agreed, to many bad memories. I must be cursed.

For Thanksgiving and Christmas, Lillian and Betsy came home and made dinner for Todd, Mark and themselves. Melanie did not come. Todd told the girls that Mark and he were going to move to town in the summer. Todd and Mark stayed home by themselves on New Year's Eve.

There was one day that the weather was so bad Todd and Mark had to stay home from school. Todd had pretty much given up on Melanie. He couldn't understand how a sweet, smart girl would end up in that kind of life. Lillian was with-child again. Betsy would be home from college in May for good. She would have her teacher's license and she already lined up a job two towns over. Todd told Mark that he was happy that Betsy could stay close to home.

One evening the phone rang and Todd answered it and said that he hadn't talked to him in some time. Todd said, "Yes this Saturday would be fine. Good, I'll see you then". Todd told Mark, "William Johnson wanted to make an offer on the house. I told him he could come Saturday". I was excited that I might get back into the hands of the Johnson family.

William and Teresa came to the house Saturday afternoon and they had five children with them. I couldn't believe it, Emma Elizabeth was 12 years old. The men talked business and Todd accepted William's offer. Todd told William that he could take possession of the house the second week of June. The two men shook on it and William and his family left. I will be sorry to see Todd and Mark leave but I am excited to see William's family moving in.

It was April when Todd and Mark came into the house talking about finding a house in town to rent. Todd had decided that with Mark only having one more year of school he should get a smaller place. They would move as soon as school was out for the year.

Before you knew it, June was here and Howard, Bill and William were helping Todd move out. Todd, Mark, Betsy and Lillian walked through the house one last time. I am glad I got to see them all except for Melanie.

The day after moving out the Stone's, Todd and Mark helped William, Bill and Howard move William in. They got it done in one day, but they almost had to work until dark. William told Todd, "My Mother is still in the sanitarium".

William still worked for Teresa's parents, but he could drive to work now. Teresa had her hands full with five children although Emma and Henry could almost take care of themselves. The first Saturday in their new/old home, William took his family to see the movie by Walt Disney, "Lady and the Tramp". When they returned home that was all the children could talk about, although it was hard to tell if four year old Richard understood the movie, but it was animated.

It was late in the season, but Teresa planted a garden anyway.

The Johnson's had two cars, a newer one for Teresa to go to town in and an older one so William could get to work. It was time for school to start; it just seemed like yesterday when Todd and Mark came home for the last time from school. Teresa had to take all the children to town even though Emma, Henry and Amelia were the only ones going to school.

The Life Story Of A House

When Teresa came home she turned the television on for the children to watch some kiddie show. At lunch Teresa sat down to watch the news. The destruction of the northeastern U.S. was being shown, although the storm had struck in August. Hurricane Diane hit the area, killing 200 and causing $1 billion in damage.

William was excited because a new western show was going to debut on television September 10th. William ended up watching "Gunsmoke" with Henry; Teresa said she was busy and told Emma that she just didn't want to watch a western. The younger children would be excited when "The Mickey Mouse Club" started on October 3rd.

Thanksgiving came and Jacob and his family and Bill, Grace, Howard and Nancy came for dinner. No one had heard from Lorna and Amelia still could not get out of the hospital for a visit. It was still nice to hear the laughter and smell the smells.

Christmas was held at Bill and Grace's house. The children would get presents at Bill's and at home. William and Teresa thanked the Lord for their health, the roof over their head and food on the table.

The Johnson's had a quiet Near Year's Evening by themselves. They had invited Jacob and his family but he was going to stay home too. The clock turned over to 1956 and William carried Emma to bed and then came down for Henry.

Time was flying by. In April, Teresa watched the first episode of "As the World Turns" and gets hooked on it and watches it every weekday.

Summer comes and Teresa has put in her garden, she can still do her chores and watch her soap, the children can play outside during this time. Emma is to watch and make sure Howard and Richard do not stray. On June 30th the news breaks into Teresa's soaps to say that two planes had collided in the air over the Grand Canyon in Arizona, killing all 128 people. Teresa prays for the people lost, but why did they have to interrupt her soaps. I wonder what the Grand Canyon is. I must be getting hardened to accidents and people killing people with bombs and such. Nothing seems to shock me anymore.

It is September and time for Teresa to go back and forth to town twice. Emma says that she has Mr. Stone this year.

William can watch the "Huntley-Brinkley Report" starting at the end of October. William starts getting all of his news from there.

Thanksgiving comes and the Johnson's have the same guests as they had the year before. They have Christmas at Bill and Nancy's house again.

1957 comes in as quiet as last year, but the only one William has to carry upstairs this year is Henry, Emma stays awake.

Henry starts to watch the news with his Father but William has to explain about half of the stories. Henry asks his Father why men in white sheets made a man jump off a bridge and the man drowned. William tells his son that the men in the white sheets think they are superior to anyone who isn't white. There are really people like that; they think they are better than anyone else.

William and Henry are watching the news on February 17th when they tell of a fire at a home for the elderly in Missouri that killed 72 people. William has to explain why the firemen couldn't get some of the people out. Henry says that maybe they did not try hard enough and are just not telling us. William tells Henry to remind him to go visit Grandmother on Saturday.

Saturday came too soon for William, he only had two days off of work but he had told Henry they would visit his grandmother and Henry did not forget. William decided to take Emma and Henry with him. They hadn't seen his Mother for a long time. The two youngsters were excited, maybe Grandmother was better. Teresa was going to stay home with the three youngest. William would tell her all about it when he got home, although, she thought, it's the same thing every time. When William and the children get there, William tells them not to get their hopes up. When they go inside, William notices his Mother has lost a lot of weight, but he hasn't seen her for a while. Emma and Henry run up to their Grandmother who is sitting down. They both say who they are. William hugs and kisses his Mother. Amelia looks up at him and gets the kind of expression like she is trying to remember who he is. William tells her," it is William and I have brought two of my children". Amelia tries to mouth William but her mouth is to dry. It is the first time in years that his Mother has made any recognition of him or Jacob. William gets her a drink of water and Amelia says, "William". William starts to cry, he wishes Jacob was here to see this. Amelia then says, "Please take me home, William". William tells her that he will the next time he visits, he has to get a place ready for her. Amelia doesn't say anything else, just looks at the children like she is trying to recognize them. When he is going past Jacob's house, he stops to tell him about his visit with their Mother. William also asks Jacob if he would go with him next Saturday to see if she knows who you are. Jacob starts to say that he doesn't want his family in that place. Although William doesn't agree with his brother he is glad he has agreed to go for a visit.

The next Saturday William goes into town to get Jacob. Jacob was hoping his brother would forget.

William and Jacob get to the sanitarium and walk in to find Amelia sitting by the door. The two boys sit on chairs beside her. Amelia asks if they are going to take her home now. She looks at Jacob and thinks for a minute, Amelia says, "Where have you been Jacob?" Jacob doesn't know what to say. William seeing this tells his Mother that the doctors have to release her first. Amelia starts to talk but William says that we haven't made a place for you to stay yet. Amelia looks at Jacob and says, "What about with him?" Jacob says that he has a wife and two small children at home. Amelia asks where Lorna is, but William lies and says she is at work. Lorna wanted to come but couldn't get off. William excuses himself; he says he is going to talk to the resident doctor on duty. Jacob was uncomfortable alone with his Mother. He thought it was silly to feel that way though. William finds the man he is looking for and asks about his Mother. The doctor said, "You're Mother is lucid most of the time, she has made tremendous strides in the last few months, but in my opinion Amelia needs more therapy because she is not at full strength, in body and mind". William thanked the doctor and slowly walked back to Jacob and their Mother. William was amazed by the fact that his Mother and Jacob were having a conversation as if there was nothing wrong with her. Jacob asked William what the doctor told him. Amelia lowered her head and said, "The doctor said I wasn't ready to go home yet". William just nodded and said," The doctor said you were a lot better, but you weren't quite there yet". William and Jacob both said that they would visit more often. Amelia said, "I hope so, and see if you can get Lorna to come visit, it seems like ages since I have seen her". The boys kissed their Mother good-bye after talking for a while, then left. William said to Jacob, "What did I tell you". Jacob admitted that he was surprised. William asked Jacob how they were going to find Lorna and Jacob just said, "I don't know".

After William let Jacob off at home, he went home just a little happier. William told Teresa every detail of the visit with his Mother. William told Teresa that there was one problem though, Mother wants to see Lorna. Teresa asked William how he was going to find her and William said, "I don't have a clue". Since Lorna moved away no one has heard from her.

William had made friends from other towns as a farmer as had Jacob as a teller in the bank. The brothers had told everyone they had ever met from other towns to look for a woman named Lorna Johnson. Jacob did not think Lorna would look for another man since Robert Talbot had died.

June came and school was out, William still had to work but Teresa was home to watch the children. Howard would start school next school year, and then Teresa would only have Richard home. Teresa still watched her soaps while the children played. Emma was talking in the mirror like Lorna used too. Emma was 14, caught between a girl and a woman. That is what Emma told her mirror, but she had not found the right boy to share her feelings with. Emma had been told about her Aunt Lorna and Emma thought her story was romantic and tragic. She wondered if they would ever find Lorna.

William and Jacob visited their Mother twice a month; the boys thought that she was getting better. Amelia was almost 55 years old and the boys had decided that their Mother should stay where she was. The doctor told the boys again that their Mother shouldn't leave the hospital. William had asked the doctor if his Mother could come home for Thanksgiving and Christmas. The doctor thought that this would only confuse Amelia. The brothers were not having any luck finding Lorna either.

At the end of June William was watching the world news and they were talking on television about hurricane Audrey smashing into Louisiana, killing 400 people. I really do dislike seeing pictures of the destruction.

Emma had gotten a little transistor radio and she would dance to the music of Elvis Presley. In August "American Bandstand" aired on television so that is where you would find Emma every Saturday, at least for a while. Emma thought that she was turning into a woman even though she was only 14. That is younger than Lorna had been when she changed. I hope Emma doesn't have the tragedy in her life that Lorna did.

School started on the first week of September and Teresa was ready. Teresa still had one child at home, but only one. The three months in the summer seemed to wear her out although she was only 31 years old. I wonder if I am really cursed.

One day in the end of September William came home and Jacob called him. Jacob had talked to someone in the bank that lived three towns over. The man had told him that there was a woman working in one of the bars named Lorna. Jacob wanted to know if William wanted to go for a ride on Saturday. William said, "Sure". William told Teresa what Jacob had said, William was excited that it might be his sister.

Saturday came and William was walking out the door when Teresa suggested he take Emma and Henry with him. William said that a bar was no place for children. She insisted. William took the two to town and left them at Jacob's to watch his two youngsters' as their Mother was in bed sick.

William told Teresa all about his and Jacob's trip when he got home. "They had gone to the town the man at the bank told them to. There were three bars, but in the third one they saw a woman sitting at the bar drinking a cup of coffee, talking to the bartender. She did not notice us walk in. We stood behind her and Jacob said in a low voice, "Lorna Johnson". The woman turned around, she looked a lot more ragged, but it was Lorna. Lorna hugged us and we went to a table and talked for hours. Lorna said that she had made it to this town when she ran out of money. The only job she could get was in this bar. She was surprised that I was living in the old house. She acted happy when she heard that she had seven nephews and nieces. She thought that our Mother would never come out of her funk and was surprised that she had asked for her. She said she had never gotten married. She thought about it for a while, but eventually agreed for us to come and give her a ride to visit our Mother. We hugged before we left, and told her please to not run away from our lives again. She promised that when we came next Saturday she would be there. We hugged again and told her how happy we were to finally find her".

The next Saturday, William took Emma and Henry into Jacob's to watch his children as Olivia was still in bed sick. Emma wanted to know if they could take the children for a walk, Jacob agreed. When they got to the town three towns away, William and Jacob walked into the bar and the bartender said that Lorna was gone. She had left the day after the boys and she talked. All Lorna said was to tell her brothers that she was sorry. The bartender said he had asked Lorna where she was going and she said it was better that he didn't know. William thanked the man and they left. The two didn't have much to say on the way home. Emma wasn't expecting the two men back so soon, they hadn't even had time to take the children for a walk. Jacob told her maybe next time. William and Jacob said good-bye and William and his two children went home where he told Teresa everything that happened. I thought poor Lorna; she must be still messed up in the head.

It was the end of October when William came home to a note from Teresa. She told him that she wanted a divorce and that he could have the children. William was shocked and just stood there staring at Teresa's note for a long time. Teresa was 16 when she had started wanting to hang around him. William called Teresa's parents and they said that they had not heard from their daughter and they couldn't believe she would run-off without her children. William got off the phone and sat down on the couch and held his head in his hands. William thinks that he will have to find another job; it would be just too awkward to work for Teresa's Father.

Emma came downstairs and sat by her Father on the couch. Finally she asked where her Mother was. William said that she was gone. Emma said, "Gone for a visit?" William said that she was gone for good. Emma looked at her Father like she didn't understand. I am beginning to think that I am cursed. Emma put her arms around her Father and tried to tell him it would be alright. Emma said, "You will find another job and we will make it fine, Richard has started school and if we find a ride to and from school I can baby-sit when we get home". William hugged his daughter for a long time and asked her when she had grown up?

William called Jacob to tell him about Teresa and Jacob could not believe it. William said that if we go and visit our Mother that Emma would have to watch all of the children. Jacob asked if Emma was ready for that much responsibility, all William could say was that she was almost 15.

William took the children to school and looked for a job until they were excused at the end of the day. Emma had taken over the role of a Mother figure, she cooked and cleaned and made sure the others were clean before they went to bed. After a while, Emma decided that being a Mother took a lot of work and she had a new respect for her Mother, although she was still mad at her for leaving them. William had told Emma that her Mother made it plain that she did not want anything to do with her children.

William told Emma that if he didn't find a job soon, they would lose the house. William had begun talking to Emma like she was the woman of the house.

William got a job at the coal mine and found a lady that agreed to take the children back and forth from school for a small amount of money. I don't like William working in a coal mine.

Jacob invited William to his house for Thanksgiving dinner if Emma was willing to make the turkey, Olivia couldn't seem to get rid of the bug that she was carrying. Emma agreed, she decided the other children deserved a nice meal after what their Mother had put them through. Thanksgiving came and William took the children into town to Jacob's house.

They decided to have Christmas dinner at Uncle Jacob's, since Thanksgiving dinner had gone so well.

The New Year of 1958 started with William still working in the coal mine and Emma taking care of the household chores, although, it was getting harder for Emma to do her school studies and the housework too.

The Life Story Of A House

Before I knew it, snow and cold invaded the area. Finally the snow starts to melt and it gets a little warmer.

One day a car pulls in the path that comes up to the house. It is Jacob and some woman. As they come in the house I can hear what the two are talking about. Jacob says, "If you come home, Lorna, and take care of the children, Emma can go back to just worrying about school work. I can't believe it is Lorna. Jacob tells Lorna that Richard; the youngest will turn 8 soon so you would have housing for at least 10 years. "You and the children can put in a garden and I know you can handle the children, they are well behaved. Lorna said that she would give it a try but she wasn't promising anything. "If the children give me any trouble at all, I'm ought of here". Jacob hugged his sister and said, "Maybe we can work on you to try and visit Mother". Lorna said, "Yeah, we can work on it".

It was June the 1st when Lorna moved in, William wasn't sure it would work but he was willing to give this a try. Lorna had the three youngest children help her clean up the garden to plant a late one. Henry talks Lorna into going fishing, she tells him he can go, but be careful around the water. "Henry is 14 now and he should be a responsible young man", Lorna tells Emma. Emma agrees.

Henry comes home with five good size fish. He holds them up to his Aunt Lorna and asks her if she wants to clean them. Lorna said, "Yuck, get them nasty things out of my face". She starts to chase him around the house pretending like she is going to whip him. They are all laughing. Henry cleans the fish and Lorna fries them for supper. William is surprised Henry is going fishing by himself.

It didn't take long before Lorna started to tuck the little ones in bed. Lorna would try with Henry, but he said he was too old to be tucked in. Lorna would usually hit him with a pillow or throw one at him. They would all laugh, it is good to have Lorna home and back to her old self. Lorna asked Emma if she would stay up a little later than usual, William had asked her to have a talk with Emma and he went to bed early. William thought that another woman should handle that little task. Lorna tried as best as she could to tell Emma the facts of life. Before Emma went upstairs, she stopped, turned around and said, "Thank you, Aunt Lorna". Lorna said, "Quite alright".

Lorna decided she wanted to have Thanksgiving here this year. Lorna asked Emma if she would help her with the dinner and Emma readily agreed. Lorna figured it would help the girl to show her she was able to handle the big dinner. Jacob and his two children came out for dinner, Olivia was still sick. The children all had a good time. Jacob asked Emma when she was going to talk her Aunt Lorna into seeing her Mother. Emma smiled and said," Sometimes a person is better off not seeing their Mother". Jacob regretted asking, he had forgotten that Teresa had abandoned the children. Jacob said that he was sorry, but Emma said," her Mother had made her choice and when her Mother got old Emma would make a choice also, not to see her". Jacob said something to Lorna about their Mother, but again she said she did not want to visit her. No more was said of Amelia. Emma seemed like she had a generally good time, Lorna wished it would last longer. Lorna did ask Jacob if he wanted to have Christmas dinner there also. He agreed, Jacob said that he liked having most of the family together.

Emma even watched "The Wizard of Oz" with the other children when it was on television on December 13th. Emma told Henry that their Mother was the wicked witch of the west. Henry and Emma laughed.

The family had as good a Christmas as they had on Thanksgiving. Lorna told Jacob that they should make both holidays an annual event out at the house, he agreed. He told Lorna," He did not know what was wrong with Olivia, but he was worried". William was letting Lorna be in charge of the family and it seemed to be working out.

1959 quietly turned into 1960 as the family stayed home and watched television.

The Life Story Of A House

It was March the 3rd the same day that Elvis Presley had returned from Germany after being gone for two years that Amelia died in the sanatorium. Amelia never got to come home and Lorna never went and visited her. William took the children to the services but Lorna did not go in.

Henry was starting to watch the news more since the U.S. had just sent 3,500 soldiers to Vietnam. Henry was 15 and it wouldn't be long before he was draft age. Henry and Emma talk about his concerns. Emma tells Henry not to worry about getting drafted until the time came.

Lorna was made to be a Mother, although she had no children of her own. She managed the children like a Mother would; even William was getting used to having his sister around.

June came and Lorna asked Emma what she was going to do after one more year. All Emma would say is, "I'm not sure".

The summer went like usual, children out playing and Henry going fishing. Lorna was busy trying to show Emma how to sew and knit.

There was bad news in August, Olivia died. Jacob had thought for a long time that the stress of having twins was just too much for her. What mattered was his kids would not have their mother.

September started along with the school year. Emma was excited that it was her last year.

The family had Thanksgiving and Christmas dinner with Jacob and his two children. Jacob told Emma that there may be an opening at the bank by June, if she was interested. Emma said that she would be.

1960 turned into 1961, Lorna said that it seemed like time was going faster since she was getting older. I wonder if time can go faster.

The Life Story Of A House

On January 20th John F. Kennedy became the 35th President of the United States. He must be an important man; Henry had to write a report about him.

Something called the Bay of Pigs happened on April 17th and failed two days later. I have no idea what that means. It is something that was said on the television.

June is about to arrive and Lorna is trying to talk Emma into maybe going to college. Emma says that she would rather work for a while.

Emma went into town and got the job in the bank as a teller. It was decided that Emma would stay with her Uncle Jacob during the week and come home on week-ends. Emma told Henry she would be able to save some money this way because she wouldn't have the expenses of owning a car.

I started noticing something; the town seemed to be getting closer to me. Lorna said that the way the town was expanding; it would be at our backdoor in ten years or so. I wonder what Lorna means when she says at our backdoor.

Jacob would call Lorna and tell her that Emma was working out fine at the bank. She was even coming home at the end of the day and making supper. Lorna was going into town on Saturdays to get Emma and taking her back on Sunday night, unless it was during the school year, then Lorna took her to town along with the children to go to school.

Right before Thanksgiving, Henry saw something on the television that he didn't like. President Kennedy sent 18,000 military advisors to South Vietnam. Henry still had a year and a half before he graduated, but he did not want to go to college or the army.

The two families had Thanksgiving dinner but before Christmas Henry heard some news that really spooked him. On December 11th the Vietnam War started as American helicopters flew into Saigon with 400

U.S. personnel. I didn't know what spooked was, or a helicopter until I saw one on television. When Emma came home that week-end she tried to get Henry not to worry until the time came. He told her that all the other boys couldn't wait to go over to Vietnam and fight. Henry was afraid to tell his Father that he didn't want to fight in the war. Henry was afraid he would shame his Father.

Christmas came and went and before anyone knew it, it was 1962. Emma told Henry that she was able to save more money than she expected, maybe he could go to Canada; she had heard there were some men going over there.

Henry does not like what he is hearing on the television, he has started to watch it every night now. First the U.S. embargo against Cuban and then all U.S. related imports and exports are banned from Cuban. I don't know what an embargo or an import or export is.

June comes and with it comes the end of the school year, Henry has one more. Lorna has planted the garden and the children are getting too old to run around and play. The youngest, Richard is 11 now. Howard and Richard still play catch with a baseball, but they have included fishing with Henry as part of their routine. Amelia is 15 now and Lorna is trying to teach her the ways of taking care of a household. Emma still comes home every week-end.

Emma told Amelia that there was a man that came in the bank every Friday that was quite handsome. The man always flirted with her, but she didn't know how to flirt. Emma asked Amelia if she should ask Aunt Lorna. Amelia told Emma that who better to ask than Aunt Lorna. So Emma did, and Lorna was extremely pleased that Emma had shown an interest in a man. Lorna and Emma talked for a couple of hours on Saturday and again on Sunday. Before Emma got out of the car, Lorna told Emma not to be afraid to let her emotions go.

Henry didn't know what he was going to do if the war continued. Henry started to talk to Howard and Richard about him going to Canada.

The Life Story Of A House

Howard tried to tell Henry that there was still a year before he graduated, maybe the war would be over by then.

Before Henry knew it, school had started, his senior year. Lorna was proud that the children were well learned and also proud that she had turned her life around.

Emma was a little scared when Friday morning came. Jacob picked up on this fact and asked Emma what was wrong. Emma decided to trust her Uncle Jacob since he had been so kind to her. Jacob laughed and said the man was over 30 years old. Emma asked Jacob if age mattered. Jacob told the girl, not really if you have affection for each other. The man came in the bank and Emma decided that she just couldn't flirt with the man. He asked Emma if she would like to have supper some night. Emma looked up from counting the man's money and said, "I would love to". The man said, "How about tonight"? Emma said, "That would be fine". The man told Emma that he would pick her up at 6:30, just tell him where". Emma asked him if he knew where Jacob Johnson lived and he said that he did. The man said, "Good, I'll see you then". He turned and walked out of the bank. Jacob asked Emma if she knew who the man was. She said, "Mark Stone". Jacob told Emma that his mother had run off, some say with a traveling salesman. Emma said, "It's the same Stone's that we bought the house from?" Jacob said, "Yes". The rest of the day, Emma tried to figure out what to talk about at supper.

Mark was at Jacob's house right at 6:30. Jacob and Mark talked while Emma was deciding what to wear. When she finally came out, she almost took Mark's breath away she was so lovely. Jacob told the two to have fun as they left.

Mark took Emma to a nice restaurant and the conversation was kind of slow, but soon they were talking about their families. Mark broke the ice, telling Emma that his Father had died young, his sister, Betsy lived a couple of towns over and that she was a teacher but hadn't found a man yet. His sister Lillian was married to Terry Sawyer; they lived in town and had five children. My sister Melanie is kind of the lost soul of the family, she works at the tavern here in town and I live here in town by myself. Then he said, "My mother run off and we don't know where she is". Mark said, "Now it's your turn". Emma started by saying," her Mother had abandoned them when she was a young girl. My Father works in the coal mine, we hardly see him anymore, and my brother Henry will graduate high school at the end of the school year. My sister Amelia is 15 and my brothers Howard and Richard are 13 and 11. My Aunt Lorna Johnson had a hard life, but when my Mother left us Lorna came to live with us and she has done a great job of bringing us up. I live with my Uncle Jacob during the week and I go home every week-end". They didn't talk much as soon as their food was brought out. After the meal Mark had coffee, Emma sat there and they talked about what they saw themselves doing in the future. Mark said that he was a salesman for the glass factory and planned on continue to work there; he said he made pretty good money. Emma said that she would stay at the bank right now but she had no long term plans. Emma said that she was saving most of her salary and hoped that if Henry needed it, it would be enough for him to live on for a while. When they got to Jacob's door, Mark said, "I hope we can do this again sometime". Emma said, "Thank you for a lovely evening". Mark said, "I would like to take you to supper again." Emma said, "I hoped you would say that".

Emma told Jacob part of the story, but when she got home she told Lorna every detail that had happened. I thought it odd that Emma would run into Mark Stone.

Henry was worried even more by the Cuban Missile Crisis; the Soviets were trying to build a base with nukes a part of it on Cuba. Kennedy had told the Soviets that the U.S. would not permit such an action. The U.S. put a quarantine around Cuba. Five days later Nikita Krushchev, leader of the Soviet Union announced the withdrawal of all Soviet nuclear bases in Cuba. The U.S. agreed to end the quarantine after the Russians agree to remove their missiles. Henry was sure the U.S. and

Soviet Union were going to blow each other up. Henry was so worried that he did not even talk to Emma about going to Canada.

Thanksgiving was a little worrisome in 1962; between the Vietnam War and the Cuban Missile Crisis everyone seemed tense. Emma had told Lorna that she had seen Mark one more time; she didn't know what to do. Lorna told Emma," to just follow your heart. If he is the one, you will know it. If you can't stand to be apart and it is easy to talk to each other, if he makes you laugh and if you can imagine spending the rest of your life together, he is the one". Emma thanks Lorna for her advice. Emma will talk to Henry after the first of the year, why spoil Christmas.

By Christmas, Emma and Mark have had two more dates.

After the Christmas dinner when Lorna, Emma and Amelia are cleaning up the dishes, Emma talks to Lorna about Henry. If Henry feels he has to go to Canada, then that will be his decision. Lorna said that it took her years to figure this out. Good advice.

Henry is watching the news with his Father like he does every day, and the man says on December 30th, that it snowed five feet in Maine. I don't know where Maine is or what five feet is, but the man sounds like it is a lot. Two days later it was 1963. Henry had five months of school left. He should have thought of this before, he could have flunked his classes. Henry figured it was too late now. Henry asked Howard what he would do. Howard said, "You want advice from a 13 year old?" Howard says just do what you feel is best, but try not to worry about it for five months because it doesn't help to worry about it.

Emma told Lorna that her and Mark were seeing each other every other Friday. Emma said she was worried about something. Lorna asked her what it was. Emma said, "What if Mark wants to have sex with me and I freeze". Lorna asks if Mark has tried anything and Emma says that he has not. Lorna said, "Maybe he respects you enough not to pressure you into doing something you are not ready for". Lorna says, "And just maybe he is sensitive enough to wait until you get married".

Sounds like good advice to me. Emma thanks her Aunt for all of her advice; Emma tells her how much she has meant to not just her, but to all of the children. Lorna starts to cry and Emma puts her arm around Lorna and says that she has made a difference.

Emma goes in to Henry's room and asks the other two boys if they could have some privacy. Howard and Richard go downstairs to watch television. Emma says, "I don't know what you are planning, but I have saved a year's worth of expense money if you still choose to go to Canada". Henry says, "He does not know what to do. He is afraid to mention it to their Father for fear of shaming him".

When Emma gets back to town, she asks Jacob if he would have a talk with Henry. Emma tells Jacob Henry's story and says that he is still undecided as to what to do after he graduates. Jacob said that he would and Emma feels better getting it off her chest, as she would tell Lorna later.

Jacob goes out to William's house and asks Henry if he can have a talk with him. Henry walks outside; it is abnormally warm for February. Jacob tells the boy that he always can ask him about anything. Henry says that he doesn't know what to do after he graduates, he is not sure that he wants to be drafted into the army. Jacob said that everyman who has ever been in war is afraid. Henry asks Jacob if he was and Jacob says every day. Jacob says, "I have a piece of advice that I wish was told to me". Henry asks Jacob what it is. Jacob said, "Join the Navy". Henry looks at Jacob funny and Jacob says, "If you join the Navy you will not have to go inland, you'll be in enemy waters but your chances of survival are a lot greater, there are hardly any Naval casualties". Jacob tells Henry that he has three months to think about it but anytime that he wants to talk to him about anything; all you have to do is ask. Henry thanks his Uncle Jacob. Jacob sticks his head in the door and says good-bye. Henry feels better now that he had this talk with Jacob. Henry knew his Uncle Jacob would not tell his Father. I hope Jacob is right I will worry less about Henry.

The Life Story Of A House

In April Henry signed up for a two year hitch in the Navy. After high school he is to report to the Naval Academy in Chicago, Illinois the second week of June. Henry decided for sure he didn't want submarine duty as he heard about the U.S. nuclear submarine Thresher sank and killed all 129 crewmen. I don't know what a submarine is, but I heard Henry tell Richard that it was a giant tube shape contraption that sailed under the water.

Emma was seeing Mark every Friday evening now. Sometimes they would go to a movie and Emma always told the other children about it. In May they watched a James Bond movie,"Dr. No". Emma told the other children that it was very exciting.

The end of May arrived and after Henry's graduation, he was just a little nervous about joining the Navy. Jacob told the young man that it was the right decision to make. Henry would be able to see some of the world that he might not get to see otherwise. William was proud of his son even if Henry didn't tell him. Henry found out that after six weeks in Chicago he would spend a month in Hawaii. I don't know where any of those places are, but Jacob told Henry that he would love Hawaii.

It was a Saturday when Henry was to leave. There was a small get together for him. Jacob and his two children came, as did Mark Stone. Henry was to take a train to Chicago from town; Emma and Mark were going to take him. What's a train? When it came time to leave, Lorna and Amelia were crying and Henry was trying not to. William just hugged his boy and told him to do his best. Jacob and his two children went home as soon as Henry left. I found it to be a sad day.

Mark brought Emma home after they had let Henry out at the train station; Emma was still crying a little. Mark gently pulled her close to him, cupped her face in his hands and gave her a passionate kiss. Emma responded like this was the only thing she wanted in the whole world at that very moment. Mark said good-night and Emma went in and told Lorna all about her first real kiss. It was everything that she had wished it to be. Lorna hugged Emma and said you are a beautiful young lady and you should be kissed like that every day of the rest of your life. I wonder what passionate means.

It was the end of July when Henry called on the telephone to tell Lorna that he had survived basic training and he was going to ship out to Hawaii tomorrow. Henry told Lorna to give his love to his family and to tell Uncle Jacob that he was right. Lorna repeated the whole conversation to William and the children.

September came and Amelia, Howard and Richard had to go back to school. Amelia was 16 and starting to feel like a woman, she started noticing boys at school this year. Howard was caught in the middle at 14 and Howard at 12 thought that girls were still yucky. Jacob's two children were getting older to. The twins Keith and Robin were 10. It seems to me time is flying by and Lorna said the town was getting closer and I agree, I can almost see the windows.

Lorna was watching television on November 22nd. She got to see President Kennedy get shot and killed in Dallas, Texas. Lorna started to cry as they showed the man that allegedly did the awful deed, Lee Harvey Oswald. Vice-president Lyndon Johnson was sworn in to the Presidency aboard Air Force One. For the next three days that is all that was on television. Lorna didn't watch all the time, but the television was never off. No one seemed to notice the little news story the next day of a nursing home in Ohio that burned and killed 63 elderly people.

The children stayed home from school Monday so they could watch the services. On the 24th, Lee Harvey Oswald was being brought out of the courthouse when Jack Ruby shot Oswald dead on national television. On the 25th schools were closed so that everyone could watch President Kennedy's funeral.

The family still celebrates Thanksgiving, but is not as festive because they are still in mourning for the dead president. Emma and Mark were going to announce their engagement but decided to wait until

Christmas, but Emma tells Amelia if she promises not to tell. Amelia doesn't think she can keep it secret for a month.

On Christmas Day Jacob, his two children and Mark Stone attend dinner. Emma is looking especially happy, Amelia has kept her secret. After dinner, Emma says that she and Mark have something to say. Emma says," You have all been a big part of my life and Mark and I would like you to spend the day of our wedding together as well as be part of our lives. We are going to have a spring wedding; I just wish Henry could be here as he has been a big part of my life too. I hope you all will welcome Mark into the family". Jacob is the first one to shake hands with Mark, then Lorna hugs him, William doesn't say a word but congratulates the couple; all the other children are surrounding Emma to congratulate her. Then they turn to Mark and he sees first-hand the love in the house. It will be odd to have Emma become Mrs. Mark Stone, odd indeed. Emma and Mark said to celebrate; they are all invited to the movies tomorrow, their treat. The children give out a yell when Emma tells them there is a Walt Disney movie out, "The Sword and the Stone". Emma insists that Jacob, Keith and Robin come too.

The next day, the children all come home excited and talking about the movie, even Amelia has forgotten boys and enjoyed the movie. William decided not to go. When all the children have quieted down, Amelia turns on the radio and hears something like she never has. There is an English group called The Beatles and she goes crazy when she hears "I Want to Hold Your Hand" and "I Saw Her Standing There". Amelia starts dancing around the room like a crazy person, good beat though.

1963 turns to 1964 with the hope that the country can heal from the loss of their President.

The winter has been mild and Emma and Mark decide to get married the first part of April. They are going to have the wedding at the house; this will be a first for me. William is going to give Emma away, whatever that means. Mark invites Betsy, Lillian, and Melanie to attend. Emma has Lorna be her maid-of-honor. Mark asks Jacob to be his best-man. They decorate the living room and there is a cake in the kitchen. Lillian, Terry and their five children come in with Betsy, Melanie doesn't attend. Mark hoped that she would, he had went down to the bar where she worked and invited her in person. Melanie didn't look like the sister he remembered, she looked as if she had a very hard life. Mark couldn't believe that Melanie was only two years older than he was. He couldn't help but think Melanie could have been anything that she wanted to. Mark wished Melanie would have come, but he wasn't going to let it ruin Emma and his day. Emma is telling Lorna that she wishes Henry were here, about that time the telephone rang. The family was going to ignore it, but finally Lorna answered it. Lorna laughed and called Emma. Emma said who is it into the telephone and starts to laugh and dance around. She talks about five minutes and then hangs up. She announced to everyone that Henry was on the phone and wished us a happy life together. Henry said that he was in the sea somewhere around Vietnam, but doing well. Now Emma could truly be happy. All the women cried during the service, some even after, but it was a very happy occasion. I thought that it was a better time even more than Thanksgiving and Christmas.

After the ceremony all congratulated the couple. People mingled and the children played. Betsy was still a teacher, Lillian and her family had to get a bigger house, but both sisters wished that Melanie would have come, just for Mark's sake. Lillian told Betsy that it had been almost a year since she had seen Melanie. I guess Melanie is a lost cause.

Right before night fall, the newly wedded couple was getting ready to leave. Emma was going to throw her bouquet of flowers over her head. How strange. It looked like Betsy let Amelia catch them. Everyone applauded the couple and then the couple left. Betsy told Lillian that she would spend the night at her house. Jacob and his two children were the last to go. Jacob kept hugging his sister, Lorna and told her, "I am proud of the way you changed your life and came through for William's children". Lorna started to cry again. Jacob left and Lorna

The Life Story Of A House

went into the house and saw that Amelia and the two boys were dancing to a Beatle's song. Lorna had a good laugh and went into the kitchen to clean up a little. William kicked off his shoes and sat on the couch to watch some television.

Emma and Mark didn't go on a honeymoon; Emma took a week off from the bank as did Mark from the glass factory. Emma drove Mark's car out to visit Lorna. After telling Amelia, Howard and Richard hello, Emma got Lorna alone. Emma said, "I won't tell you all of the details, but it was like you said. It was wonderful; Mark was so gentle with me, it was all I could have wished for", and then she hugged Lorna for a long time. Then the two women talked about women things. I wonder what was so wonderful that Mark did.

One day during the first part of August Lorna was walking by the television and it being on and the news talking about Vietnam, she stopped to listen. The U.S. destroyers USS Maddox and the USS C. Turner Joy was attacked in the Gulf of Tonkin. The USS Ticonderoga supplied air support and sunk one Vietnamese gunboat and scared away two more. A day later U.S. aircraft carriers USS Ticonderoga and USS Constellation bomb North Vietnam in retaliation for the strikes the day before. Lorna knows that Henry is on the USS Constellation, so he is seeing some action. Lorna still worries about Henry though. I thought being in the Navy was safer.

School is about to start and Lorna asks Amelia what she is going to do next June when she graduates. Amelia says, "If I don't find a man to marry, I guess I'll have to get a job". Lorna laughs, but I think Amelia is serious.

During September Amelia finds a new television show to watch, "Shindig", which has musical groups from the 1960's. A night later the whole family sit down to watch "Bewitched" starring Elizabeth Montgomery as a witch who is married to a mortal. The whole family sits every week and watches this show.

The Life Story Of A House

Emma and Mark come to the house once in a while as does Jacob. The town seems to be getting closer to me every year.

Thanksgiving comes and Jacob, Keith, Robin, Lillian, Terry and their five children all are invited to dinner. Betsy even comes, it seems she had a wonderful time at the wedding and wanted to enjoy her family more. And of course, Emma and Mark, the surprise guest was Henry; he has a two week leave before he has to return to the USS Constellation. Everyone is trying to ask Henry questions all at once before and after dinner. This is the happiest I think I have ever seen the family, I can feel the love flowing so freely. No one wants to leave at nightfall, but realize that they have to leave sometime. After Mark shakes Henry's hand Emma hugs him for a long time. William tells his son he is proud of him, Henry just smiles.

Henry asks Howard and Richard if there is enough room for him to stay in their room. The boys say, "Of course there is". Henry tells Amelia that it looks like she has grown up a lot since he last saw her. Henry said, 'I know who the next one to get married will be". He even told Lorna that it looked like she was getting younger. Lorna blushed and flipped a towel at him.

The two weeks seemed like they flew by and it was time for Henry to leave. He told the boys that next time he hoped it was warmer so they could go fishing. Henry told Amelia that she would probably be married the next time he saw her. She smiled sheepishly. He hugged Lorna and told her that he loved her for taking care of them. Lorna was crying before but now it was like the flood gates opened. I don't know where I heard that from. William hugs his son when Emma and Mark pulled up the path to the house. Henry put his things in the car and they all waved good-bye. Mark and Emma were going to take Henry to the train station.

It did not take long for Christmas to arrive. Everyone came who had come for Thanksgiving except for Henry. They had fun anyway. Betsy tried to talk Amelia into going to college.   Mark still wished Melanie would come, me too.

   1964 turned to 1965 and hopefully 65 would be as happy as 64 had been.

   On Palm Sunday April 11th, an estimated 51 tornadoes hit 6 Midwestern states, killing between 256 and 271 people and injuring 1,500 more. It was extremely stormy that day, it was a good thing Lorna and the three children didn't get caught out in it in the car. Some of my shingles blew off and the outhouse blew away. Terry came out the next day to rebuild the outhouse. Jacob hired some men to fix my roof.

   June came and Amelia graduated from high school. At the small celebration Emma told Lorna that she was pregnant. Emma didn't want to ruin Amelia's day. Emma and Mark had been talking in the house and decided that they could afford it if Emma quit her job at the bank. They would tell Amelia there was an opening at the bank. Emma took Amelia off to the corner of the room to tell her about the job. Amelia didn't look too enthused, but thanked Emma and said she would go in and talk to the bank president Monday. Emma told Amelia that Jacob would probably agree to let her stay at his house during the week and coming home on the week-ends.

   Monday Amelia took Lorna's car into town and went to the bank. When Amelia came home she told Lorna that she had gotten the job as a teller. Lorna congratulated the girl but she still didn't look too happy about it. Amelia talked to Jacob while she was at the bank and he said it was fine for them to have the same situation as with Emma. Amelia was to start at the bank the following Monday.

   Amelia told Howard that she was none too happy to have to work at the bank, she thought that she would be engaged by now but there were no prospects at school. Howard told Amelia, "At least you do not have to worry about being drafted into the army.

July came and Amelia didn't like working at the bank, as a matter of fact, Jacob had to have a talk with the girl more than once. Amelia told Howard that working at the bank was boring; she needed some excitement in her life. Howard told her that the President just ordered the number of U.S. troops in Vietnam from 75,000 to 125,000 and to double the number of men drafted a month from 17,000 to 35,000. Howard said, "The next time you get bored at your job, think about the boys that have to die for their country even if they do not believe in the cause. Think about Henry being on that ship so he wouldn't have to go inland. If the war is still going on when I graduate, I to will join the Navy". After Amelia left the room, Howard asked Richard how Amelia had gotten so spoiled.

When school started in September, Howard was a junior and Richard a freshman. When Howard and Richard got home, they tell Lorna that all the older boys are talking about the war. Some are going to college, some to Canada and some are just going to join. Lorna tells Howard not to worry about it for another two years; a lot can happen between now and then. Howard took Lorna's advice. He told Richard that he wasn't going to worry about it until he graduated.

Amelia came home on the week-end and didn't lift a finger to help out Lorna. Lorna didn't say a word, but you could tell she was upset. Amelia is watching American Bandstand but they break in to talk about hurricane Betsy. It hit the shore near New Orleans, Louisiana, causing 76 deaths and over a billion dollars damage. The storm had winds of over 145 miles per hour. Amelia was bored so she took a chair outside to get some sun. Amelia told Howard that was all the rage, getting sun tanned. Lorna asked Amelia if she would set the table for lunch and she said that she was busy. Lorna told her that just because she had a job during the week didn't mean she didn't have to do anything on the week-ends. Amelia got mad but set the table. Amelia told Howard and Richard that when Lorna took her to Jacob's house on Sunday night she wasn't coming home anymore. If Jacob wouldn't let her stay there on week-ends she would find someplace else, maybe she would ask Emma.

The Life Story Of A House

Sunday night came and Lorna wanted to ask Amelia why she had a bag of clothes with her. Before Lorna could ask, Amelia said, "I want to keep some things at Jacob's house". No other words were said. Amelia got out of the car and didn't even say good-by. When Lorna got home she asked Howard what was wrong with Amelia. Howard said that he didn't think Amelia was coming back. At first Lorna thought she had pushed the girl to hard, but after some talking to her she decided that Amelia was spoiled and would have to learn the hard way.

Friday night came and Lorna did not even go into town to get Amelia. This shocked Amelia, she had been practicing all week as to what to say. Howard asked Lorna if she were going into town to see if Amelia changed her mind. Lorna said, "If she wants a ride, then she can call". Jacob called later to tell Lorna that the girl was there. He also said Lorna would have to tell him sometime what had happened.

November was a weird month. The television told about a man setting himself on fire in protest of the war on November 2nd. Another man set himself on fire to protest the war on November 9th. You have to be crazy to set yourself on fire. The Pentagon told the President that if planned major operations against the Viet Cong were to succeed, the number of American troops in Vietnam would have to increase from 120,000 men to 400,000. Crazy!

Thanksgiving was held at William's with every one coming that had come last year except for Amelia. Jacob told Lorna that Amelia was too embarrassed to show her face. Lorna told Jacob that she would fix a plate for Amelia for him to take home to her. Now Melanie and Amelia were not coming. Emma was looking like she had a basketball in her stomach. Even with the absence of the two women, the rest of the family had a good time. Just like she said she would, Lorna sent a plate of food home when Jacob left. Lorna told Emma that she hoped to see her on Christmas.

The Life Story Of A House

On December 9th Howard, Richard and Lorna watched "A Charlie Brown Christmas" on the television for the first time.

Christmas was the same as Thanksgiving, no Amelia and Melanie. Emma said that she still had two months before she would deliver her baby. William seemed to let Lorna run the household while he hardly talked to the children, it was like they had grown apart.

1965 turned to 1966 and the war protesters were gathering in strength. On January 18th, 8,000 more U.S. troops arrive in Vietnam bringing the total so far to 190,000. On March 8th, the U.S. says it will increase the number of troops in Vietnam. By the end of April there are 250,000 U.S. troops in Vietnam. By May 15th tens of thousands of anti-war protesters picket the White House.

Emma has her baby on February 27th. The baby is a girl and Emma and Mark name her Lorna Elizabeth. Lorna starts to cry because they have named the baby after her. Lorna tells William and the boys.

The first of June arrives and Howard and Richard are out of school for the summer. Howard tells Lorna that since this will be his last summer at home he and Richard are going to fish a lot. Lorna tells him that is a good idea. He should enjoy his last summer at home. Howard and Lorna have come to realize that it would take a miracle for the war in Vietnam to be over in a year.

On June 8th we have a big storm at the house that blows the outhouse away again. This storm blows a tree down. The television says that a massive tornado has struck Topeka, Kansas killing 16 people and injuring 100's more. The storm caused thousands of homes to be damaged or destroyed. Terry and Mark come and build the outhouse again and chop up the tree, they figure it can be used for firewood.

Every other day, Howard and Richard bring home fish to clean and fry. The boys catch so many that Terry comes out to the house and takes some fish home and drops some off to Jacob and Mark.

Emma is surprised by the fact that Amelia is still working at the bank, she tells Lorna on the telephone. Lorna says that maybe Amelia is having trouble finding the right man to marry. Emma agrees. Emma feels a little sorry for her younger sister.

Henry calls home when he has docked; he is glad that Emma's baby is alright. He is sorry to hear Amelia is having such a hard time. Before he gets off the telephone with Lorna he asks to talk to Howard. After Howard hangs up he tells Lorna that Henry told him to join the Navy.

The start of August and Howard is watching the news and hears that a man named Charles Whitman has killed his wife and mother, then gets atop of a building at the University of Texas and shoots and kills 13 people and wounds 31. People are crazy.

Howard starts his senior year of high school in September. On the 8th a new science fiction television show premieres named "Star Trek". Howard and Richard watch it every week.

Lorna is starting to tell Emma on the telephone that once Howard graduates Richard only has two years more before she has to find another place to live. William would not need a housekeeper/babysitter anymore. Emma tells her not to worry about it, it is three years away.

The first of November Jacob calls Lorna and tells her that Amelia did not come to work that day and when he got home she and her belongings were gone. Jacob was just calling there to see if she had come home. Lorna says that she has not and is quite upset that the girl has run off just like she had done. Jacob says he has already called Emma and she is upset also. Jacob says that he is going down to the bar and asks Melanie if she has seen the girl. Jacob finds Melanie about half drunk. She looks to be 50 when she is really 30. Melanie says that she has not seen the girl and tells Jacob to leave her alone. Jacob calls Lorna back and tells her what Melanie said.

Thanksgiving comes and although Amelia hasn't attended for a while they are all sad because she has run off.

On the 18th of December Howard and Richard watch "How the Grinch Stole Christmas" on television. They laugh until Lorna comes in to join them and all three laugh.

Christmas arrives and all the usual people attend at the house. No one has heard from Amelia. Henry calls to talk a couple of minutes, just to wish everyone a Merry Christmas. He is really upset to hear about Amelia, Henry says that he wishes he was home to go and look for his sister.

1966 turns to 1967 and still no word from Amelia. Howard and Richard take Lorna's car on the weekend and search other towns for Amelia to no avail. Howard would like to know where Amelia is before he has to go away to the service. William seems to not be worried about his daughter; he figures she has run off with a boy.

March 4th, Betsy calls Mark and tells him of a murder of a young lady. The police described the body but have not been able to identify her. Mark calls William and asks if he is up for a ride. William says that he is and Mark and Emma drive out to the house to get him. Lorna tells them to call her as soon as they learn anything. I hope it is not Amelia.

When they return, it is way past dark. They all come in the house and they are all crying but Mark. William just keeps saying that he can't believe Amelia was murdered. Emma says, "Amelia was only 20 years old". Lorna breaks down when she hears about Amelia. Mark calls the newest branch of the Navy to have them tell Henry to call because his little sister has been murdered. They all stay at the house that night; Lorna Elizabeth is staying with Lillian and Terry. In the morning, Henry calls and talks to Mark. Mark says that Amelia was strangled and raped. The police haven't a clue as to who did it. Henry says he has already talked to his C.O. and told him he needs to go home for a death in the family. Henry says that he will be there as soon as he can make it.

Emma woke thinking it was an awful nightmare she had, but then she remembered and started to cry again. Mark asks Emma if they should call their Mother and tell her. Emma said, "She didn't want to raise us, so why should she want to bury us, besides we still don't know where she is."

Henry gets home in three days, so the funeral is planned for the day after. Emma picked out the best dress that Amelia had left in the house.

The family went to the services at the church and then returned to the house. Every woman was crying and all the men huddled together to talk. There was a small meal served but all the family members were not hungry. Betsy lived the farthest away, so she left first. She hugged Emma like she had known her all of her life. Betsy told Mark that if she heard anything, she would call. Slowly they all began to leave. Emma didn't want to, but she knew she had a baby to tend to. Emma hugged her Father and brothers before she left and kept saying, "I just can't believe she is gone".

Henry stayed another day, but he had to get back to his ship. Henry told his Father and Lorna that he had re-upped for two more years. Howard and Richard were still stunned. Howard would have to leave to in 3 more months, and he thought about poor Richard being by himself.

Howard hated to do it, but after graduation he had to leave his little brother Richard alone with his Father and Lorna his only company. Howard was to report the first week of June to the Naval Academy in Chicago, just like his brother Henry, but instead of going to Hawaii like Henry, he was to go to San Diego, California for more training. Howard and Richard hugged each other like they would never see each other again. Mark and Emma came out from town to give Howard a ride into the train station.

Richard was depressed all summer and part of the new school year. Richard was a junior now and all of a sudden he started noticing girls. It seemed like the girls were noticing him also. Richard didn't want to talk to his Father, so he started asking Lorna all sorts of questions. Lorna was glad that the boy was taking his mind off of his sister's death. Lorna started to let Richard borrow the car so he could go and visit a girl or two. Lorna told Richard at his age he shouldn't tie himself down to one girl unless he knew she was the one that he wanted to spend the rest of his life with.

Time seems to fly by, it is Thanksgiving already. The family gets together like usual only plus one. Richard has brought a date. Her name is Cathy Knight and she is in the same grade as Richard. She is shy to begin with but with all of the different characters at the house, they won't let her be shy all day. They all have a toast for Amelia and the safety of Henry and Howard, then they all have a good time, at least they act like it. Betsy tells Mark that the police still have not figured out who murdered Amelia. Mark, Betsy and Lillian had given up on Melanie. Mark asks the girls if they had ever thought that Melanie would end up that way. The girls said, "No". The men were hanging around poor Cathy trying to embarrass her until Lorna finally saved the girl from their tormenting. By the end of the night, Cathy was starting to open up and was having a good time also. They all hated for the day to be over, but they all said that they would see each other at Christmas. Richard took Cathy home once she had thanked her hostess. Before they all left, Lorna said that she had heard from Howard and he was assigned to the ship USS Pueblo. She had almost forgotten to tell them.

Richard was seeing Cathy every weekend and talking to her on the phone every night. Lorna was starting to feel alone. William basically ignored her now that the children were almost all grown up, but she guessed she had better get used to it; Richard only had a year and a half of school left. Lorna had not even thought about when the children were out of the house, what would happen to her. Lorna guessed she would worry about it when the time came. She thought, "Maybe William is just upset about Amelia".

Christmas Evening had seen six inches of snow and Lorna wondered to Richard if he thought the gang would come this year? Richard said that they would. They had too much of a good time to miss even one year, anyway, he said, "It's only six inches".

Richard was right, everyone came. He had to go get Cathy, but Jacob and his two children rode with Mark, Lillian, Betsy and little Lorna. After the meal and before anyone could get up from the table, Emma says that she and Mark had an announcement. Emma said that she was pregnant again and expecting the baby in July 1968. Everyone applauded and started to get up when Richard said he had an announcement too. Cathy and he were going to get married, Cathy was pregnant. Everyone was quiet for a minute and then they all applauded them and got up to congratulate both couples. Everyone wanted to know when Richard and Cathy were going to get married, when the baby was due. They wanted to know if Mark and Emma's house was big enough for another child. Emma laughed and said, "As long as it is another girl", and winked at Mark. Lorna got Richard off to the side of the room and said, "I thought I brought you up better than that" and then laughed and hugged the boy. Richard and Cathy told everyone there that they were invited to the wedding on January 30th. Richard said that he would have to stay in school to avoid the draft, but if the war was not over by then, he would have to join. After him and Cathy were to get married, they were going to live with her parents in town until he graduated and saw if he had to join the service or not. Lorna was happy for the couple but she couldn't help but wonder what was to happen to her. Jacob took Lorna a side and told her not to worry, when Richard moved out, she could live with him if she wanted to. Lorna said that would be fine but asked if he had enough room? Jacob said, "If you don't mind sharing a room with a 12 year old girl". Lorna laughed and said, "Are you sure the 12 year old girl wants to share a room with a 40 year old woman?" Jacob laughed then and he said," it didn't matter, the way things are going in today's world, she will probably only live with me for 4 or 5 years". They both laughed then. Things were surely changing, it sounds like I will be alone again at the end of January. Lorna wondered what William would do in the big house by himself.

1967 turns the calendar over to 1968, and it promises to be a lonely year.

On January 23rd a week before Richard and Cathy were to be married, the family was shocked to hear that the USS Pueblo had been seized by the North Koreans because they claimed the ship violated its waters while spying. The shock to the family was that Howard was aboard the USS Pueblo.

Richard and Cathy went ahead and got married on the 30th. The family was all there along with Cathy's family, but William, Richard and Emma were worried about Howard.

The next day Richard got most of his things from his room. He thanked Lorna for stepping in and raising them and gave her a hug and a kiss and then he said, "My own Mother could not have done a better job". Lorna was crying now, the two hugged one more time and Richard said, "Anyway, we are going to need a baby-sitter". The two laughed and then Richard left. Lorna was all alone. She didn't count on William for much conversation. It had been years since she had been alone and now she was used to someone being there.

Lorna couldn't sleep that night, to quiet. Mark came out in a truck and he still had to make two loads of Lorna's things. Lorna was surprised when William told her, "There will be an auction in the spring to sell the contents and to see if anyone wants this old house". Before she left, Lorna patted me and said, "It has been a good old house".

William moves into town so he can be closer to work and his family. He doesn't need such a big house anymore.

Here I am all alone and cold again. I guess I'll never find out if Howard will be alright or whether Lillian and Cathy's babies are boys or girls.

The Life Story Of A House

It has been a long lonely winter. One day when it is getting warmer, a man in a truck pulls in the path and stops and walks out front by the road and hammers something into the ground. He then comes in the house and looks in every room, writing things down. Then he gets in his truck and leaves.

At least it is warming up. One day William, Mark and Richard come out to the house and lots of other cars and trucks arrive. The man that pounded the sign in the front yard was there also. Some of the men were talking about some man by the name of Martin Luther King, JR being shot dead at a motel in Tennessee. The men said there were riots for several days afterward. They never said anything about Howard's ship. Pretty soon the one man started calling out numbers so fast you almost couldn't understand him. People were raising their hands and when they were done raising their hands; the man would point to someone and say, sold. Then the man would start all over until he said sold again, this lasted all day. Whenever the man said sold for something, someone would pick up the piece of furniture. It took all day to clear me out so I was totally empty. Then the man tried to auction the house, me. No one wanted me, I went unsold. William, Richard and Mark told the other man to put a for sale sign in the front yard, which he did. I wonder how long I will have to stay empty.

A couple of days after the auction I seen the man that farmed behind me. He looked the grounds over and went away. Maybe he is going to buy me. The next day the auction man and the farmer pulled into the path that came up to me. They were standing by me so I heard them talking. The farmer asked if he could buy the land that came up to the path behind me. They talked price and then the farmer and auction man shook hands. They drove away without even talking about me.

Sometime later the farmer came on my property and started to tear the outbuildings apart. Outhouse, shed, barn, all are gone. Then the famer worked the ground up to my path and planted some crops. The town seemed to be getting closer too.

The Life Story Of A House

At least it is summer, maybe someone will buy me before it gets cold.

After a while the man's crops are ready to harvest and he takes them out. It looks like another cold and lonely winter.

Spring comes and I see the man working the dirt again. One night five cars came up the path towards the back. They turned all their lights off and a bunch of high school kids got out to talk. They left their car doors open, I guess to listen to music. They are all drinking something out of bottles; maybe they work at the glass factory. Sometimes they come to the side of me and take what they call a leak. It does look like they are leaking. Most of the time when the bottles are empty, they throw them at me. Sometimes it breaks out my windows; sometimes it busts the bottles on my side. The kids start to come out almost every night once they had gotten started. Most times it was boys and girls and sometimes they stayed in their cars with the glass fogged. They even came in the winter unless there was too much snow on the ground. These kids are the only people I see other than the farmer every once in a while. The farmer comes over and takes a leak too.

After a while all of my windows have been broken and the boys have kicked my doors open. Sometimes they come in and try to scare the girls by telling tales about murders and ghosts, usually the girls scream and run out, the boys just laugh. The boys go around front and kick the for sale sign down. Every spring when the grass starts growing it gets really tall until the first snow knocks it down.

It seems like years of the same thing. Since the doors are open, animals are entering and leaving me as they please. Since the windows are broken the birds make their nests inside and live with the animals. The birds are messy things, even worse than the animals. The kids don't come as often now, I guess the animals spooked them.

The years keep going by and not even a visit from one of the family members. I really am disappointed at their absence. The houses are getting close enough for me to see their windows, but not close enough to stop the kids from making a mess. I don't know how tall the pile of broken bottles is and they have even ripped some of my siding off. Years of storms have started tearing my shingles off. During one storm, a tree fell through a front window.

I wonder whatever happened to the families that lived here. I think eight or nine families lived here. I miss the joy, happiness, love and the smells, now it does not smell too good, urine, mold and things I do not want to think about.

Since it has been years and all my windows are knocked out, siding pulled off as far as the boys can reach, the inside tore up, now there are holes in my roof. I have come to the realization that no one is ever going to want me again. If there really is a God above that all of the families prayed to, I pray that I do not have to suffer too much longer.

The farmer must have sold part of his land, because houses are being built behind me. Once the houses are finished and the families move in, the kids won't come around here any longer. I can't believe that when I was new I could not see the town and now it is right behind me.

I wonder how long I have been empty.

I am so sad, it won't be long now, and a big piece of equipment has been unloaded off of a truck in my path. I pray to God that being torn down does not hurt. I hope I have been a good house, I have tried my best.

The next day a car pulls into the path that comes behind me. They have trouble getting around the machine. Two ladies get out of the car. One is old and being helped by a young girl. I do not recognize them. They are actually coming in as if the mess doesn't make a difference. The two ladies are quiet until the younger one says, "This is where you were raised Grandma?" The old woman said," I was and had some wonderful memories. I just wish someone had kept it up so it wouldn't have to be torn down to make room for a new house". So I am to be torn down and replaced with a new one, I hope it is quick and it doesn't hurt. The girl asks her Grandmother if she had a room upstairs. The old woman said, "Yes, and it was very cold in the winter, I would go upstairs if I could". The girl said, "Great-grandfather Adam was a bank teller then wasn't he?" The old woman said, "Yes, I was just a girl when we lived here". Please say your name; I know you were a Wilson, but which one. The young girl asks, "How old do you think the house is?" The old lady says, "Well, its 1996 now, I guess over a hundred years". I have been empty since 1968 and now it is 1996, I have been empty for a very long time. The young girl says something; all I hear is "Grandma Kendra". It is Kendra Jean Wilson, Kendra took time to come and say good-bye. It makes me so happy to know that Kendra loved me and came out to show her granddaughter where she was raised. A man in a truck comes up the path and sees that there is a car there. The man comes up to the door and tells the two women that they need to leave he has orders to tear this house down today. Kendra tells the man that she was a little girl in this house. The man does not seem interested. Before the women go through the door to the outside, Kendra rubs the doorway and cries. I wish I could cry. I am so glad that Kendra came out to see me one last time. Although I will never know what happened to the other families, at least I know Kendra lived to be an old lady.

Some historical facts were taken from:

Wikipedia, the free encyclopedia

August 2012

Made in the USA
Charleston, SC
20 December 2013